I0725560

AWAY FROM KEYBOARD COLLECTION

BRAVING HIS PAST

PATRICIA D. EDDY

Copyright © 2021 by Patricia D. Eddy

All rights reserved.

No part of this book may be reproduced in any form or by any electronic or mechanical means, including information storage and retrieval systems, without written permission from the author, except for the use of brief quotations in a book review.

This is a work of fiction. Names, characters, places, and incidents are either the product of the author's imagination or used fictitiously. Any similarities to real persons or events are purely coincidental.

Cover Design: Deranged Doctor Design

Cover Photography: Paul Henry Serres

If you love sexy romantic suspense, I'd love to send you a short story set in Dublin, Ireland. Castles & Kings isn't available anywhere except for readers who sign up for my mailing list! Sign up for my newsletter on my website and tell me where to send your free book!
http://patriciadeddy.com.

CHAPTER ONE

Eight Years Ago

Graham

Draining my second bottle of beer, I glance around the crowded bar. I don't know why I let Oskar and Simon talk me into this. But it's New Year's Eve, and in two days, we'll be headed to Alaska. My bunkmates wanted to party, and they dragged me along—probably because they know I'll get them back to the cutter on time.

Assuming I can find them. The music is loud enough, I feel it in my gut. This isn't my scene. All night I've had to fend off drunk advances from chicks who just want a night with a guy in uniform.

One of them—she couldn't have been more than nineteen —was so aggressive, I finally had to tell her I bat for the other team. She spent a full five minutes cursing me out for "leading her on." The fuck? I ignored her for an hour. Didn't tell her my name. Just a polite, "Sorry, I'm not interested." Over and over again.

It takes more than ten minutes of fighting through drunk revelers to find Oskar. "Dude, we need to head back."

"It's almost midnight, Peck. Live a little." His words slur, his arm draped around a tall, willowy woman with jet black hair.

"Yeah," his companion says. "Have a little fun. Want to come join us in the back?"

Oh, hell no. Holding up my hands, I shake my head. "Not my thing. But you two have fun." Before I start looking for Simon, I lean in so I can shout in Oskar's ear. "I'll be outside in fifteen minutes. You're not there in twenty, you can find your own way back to the cutter."

He toasts me with his beer bottle seconds before he and his "date" start sucking face.

Simon, Oskar, and I aren't close. Then again, I'm not tight with anyone on board. It's easier that way. No need to make up a story about the girl back home or brag about past conquests that never happened.

I'm not sure why I agreed to come out with them tonight—except we're shipping out in forty-eight hours, and this is my last chance to see the inside of a civilian bar for at least two months.

Simon's nowhere to be found, so I make my way to the door just as the DJ announces it's one minute until midnight.

Spilling out onto the sidewalk with the rest of the overflow, I shove my hands into the pockets of my jacket and breathe in the foggy San Francisco air. Everyone else is cheering, hugging, and kissing, but I find a spot against the wall and try to ignore the party happening all around me.

A big, burly guy—probably the bouncer—gives me the side eye, and I shrug. "No one to kiss at midnight."

He scoffs. "Coast Guard? You're not looking hard enough, man. Plenty of ladies in there who'd be all over you."

I glance around, then lean in. Between the look in his eyes and the slight bulge in his tight black pants that I *know* wasn't there a second ago, he's sending signals like a fucking beacon. "*Ladies* don't do it for me."

As the whole bar shouts, "Three, two, one," the bouncer fists my jacket and pulls me in for one quick, hard kiss. It's nothing but heat and the pressure of his lips crushing mine, and for all of three seconds, I lose myself to it. To him.

Until I realize where I am. In public. In uniform. With two of my bunkmates inside.

My shoulders hike up, and I press my palms to the bouncer's massive chest. "Sorry...bad idea," I manage, then add, "Happy New Year."

His cheeks, already flushed from the cold, turn beet red, and he steps back. "Thought I caught a vibe, man."

"You did. But...you know. Doesn't change anything." I can't muster much of a smile as I peer back inside, hoping Oskar and Simon aren't *right* there. "If you see two guys dressed like me stumbling out of here in the next few minutes, send them south. I'm heading for the light rail station."

"Sure."

I haven't kissed anyone on New Year's Eve in years. Five steps down the street, I turn. "Bad idea or not...that was hot as fuck."

He flashes me a killer smile before focusing his attention on a couple of drunks starting to get loud behind him. Not more than two blocks later, the fog so thick I can only see a foot in front of me, the punch comes out of nowhere.

"Get his hands!"

I can't see anything but white as I'm thrown to the ground. Someone jerks my arms behind my back, and the distinct sound of a belt buckle flaps seconds before the leather's wrapped around my wrists.

My cheek lands in a pile of dog shit, and the sound it makes squishing into my ear when a boot presses to my temple is one I know I'll never forget.

"Let's give this piece of fairy garbage what he deserves," another angry male voice says from above me.

"Let me go, assholes," I manage and kick, trying to catch one of them—any of them—somewhere vital.

"You're not going anywhere, pretty boy. Except into the dumpster when we're done with you."

The boot to my side steals my breath, and the distinct crack of bone and lance of pain reminds me of the time I fell out of a tree when I was eight. At least one rib. Maybe two.

Then they're all around me. Punching. Shoving. Ripping my pants and yanking them down to my ankles. Exposing my ass. There are too many of them. Time stops as they take turns doing their worst. I don't know what they use. Don't want to know. *Things* mostly. Bottles. A pipe, maybe. Until the end. Until everything's dark and red with pain.

And then someone shouts. I know that voice. The bouncer.

"Hey. Get the fuck off of him!"

There's a punch. A groan. Scuffling. Swears. And then it's almost quiet and a big hand touches my shoulder. "They're gone. I'm calling 911."

"No..." I manage, but I can't lift my head. Or see. One of my eyes is swollen shut and the other...there's too much blood.

"You're torn up, man. Sorry. You don't get a choice." The bouncer doesn't let go of me as I start to shake, shock and fear mixing together until I hear sirens and give in to my body's uncontrollable urge to retreat somewhere dark and warm where nothing else can hurt me.

THE CALL to the staff duty NCO is one of the hardest I've ever had to make. Because he asks why I'm in the hospital. Details about my injuries. Whether I'm fit to return to duty. And why the assholes targeted me in the first place.

It doesn't matter that I'm allowed to serve. That the Coast Guard makes a big, official deal about accepting everyone these days. There are still too many guys ready and willing to protest. Guys who would love to hassle me. To make my life a living hell.

I could lie, but the bouncer filed a police report. Mike—I only found out his name hours later when the police came to question me—was doing his job. Hell, he probably saved my life, and if I thought I could handle seeing him, I'd track him down and thank him. But that report...that public record? It's the end of my career.

❦

Thirty-Six Months Ago

Quinton

Water pours down the windows in sheets. February in Dallas is always a crapshoot, and today, it's like a monsoon. The *Dallas Bystander*—a little alternative weekly newspaper —has its offices on the tenth floor of one of the city's older buildings, and the glass rattles in the frames as the wind picks up.

But from the owner's desk, where I'm currently sitting while troubleshooting his crappy internet speeds, I can see half the city.

Not a bad place to be.

"Any luck?" Frank asks as he picks up his briefcase.

"Your system's all kinds of jacked up," I reply before catching myself. "Sorry, Mr. Smythe. I just mean—"

He chuckles. "Relax, Quinton. I'd be more concerned if it worked perfectly for you. Take your time. I have a meeting downtown. I won't be back for at least a couple of hours."

With a mock salute, he grabs his rain coat and heads for the door, leaving me to do my job in peace.

I've only worked for the *Bystander* for two months. It's a good job, though the salary isn't great. I could make more with one of the large tech firms in the area. But last year, the stress of being on call 24x7 caught up with me, and the breakdown it caused? Epic. I'll take the pay cut to work in an environment where no one needs me to fix their entire network at 2:00 a.m. Plus, this job gives me enough spare time to pursue my passion —an anti-anxiety phone app I think could really help people.

Little by little, I chip away at the truly amazing amount of random electronic *crap* Frank has on his laptop. The anti-virus basically laughed at me when I asked it to run the first time.

"Well, that's got to go," I mutter as I find yet another folder *full* of temporary files that are taking up more than ten percent of his hard drive. I've rarely seen one person screw up their computer this badly.

Leaning back in his chair, I let the anti-virus have another run at the system while I watch the rain. I wanted to go out tonight. Check out the new bar on Sixth. It's supposed to be quiet. A good place to meet another guy and actually *talk* rather than just grind away on the dance floor or hook up for anonymous sex. I don't do well in crowds, and though I've met a few guys I liked enough to see multiple times over the past few years, none of them were long-term relationship material.

Midway through my thirties, the idea of a one-night stand doesn't do it for me like it used to. I want more. Something *real*.

The program errors out with a beep, and I dig through the logs to find out why. "Huh? What the hell...?"

Buried four levels deep, there's a folder named *_Recycle Bin.* It's the underscore that catches my eye. And the size. Whatever's in there is consuming a quarter of his hard drive space.

"Fuck. Fuck, fuck, fuck."

The second I open it, I wish I hadn't. Kids. Pictures of kids.

Thousands of them. And they're...not good pictures. Not legal ones. Photos no one should have ever taken.

My stomach cramps. I slam the lid down on Frank's laptop and race for the bathroom, barely making it into the stall before I throw up.

What am I supposed to do now? I can't just ignore what I saw. Those are someone's kids. A lot of someone's kids.

Fifteen minutes pass before I'm no longer retching, and I stagger to the sink to rinse out my mouth. Thank God the office is quiet today. Only two of the reporters are at their desks. Everyone else is either out covering a story or working from home.

Back in Frank's office, I take out my tablet, open a program to mask my identity, and then Google "what to do if you find child pornography on your boss's computer."

Every link tells me to call the police. I know it's the right thing to do. I couldn't live with myself if I didn't. And I'll never be able to look Frank in the eyes again.

I don't touch his laptop. Leaving it closed, I head for one of the little privacy booths we have set up around the office for employees who need to make phone calls they don't want overheard.

I hate being in these things. Claustrophobia, coupled with my already raging panic, makes my chest tight, and I can't take a steady breath. After I pop one of the fast-acting anti-anxiety pills I always have on me, I close my eyes and rest my head against the back wall.

You can do this. Focus. In. Out. In. Out.

When I no longer feel like I'm about to pass out, I look up the number for the Dallas PD.

I'm going to ruin a man's life. But those kids? Their lives are more important.

"This is the Dallas Police Department, how may I direct

your call?" the bored sounding man on the other end of the line says.

"Um, I need to report someone for possession of child pornography."

~

Six weeks later

NO ONE SAYS GOODBYE. With my small box of personal effects tucked under my arm, I leave the *Bystander* for the last time.

I know I wasn't here long, but I liked my coworkers. I thought they liked me too. But apparently getting our boss put away on more than five hundred separate counts of possession of child pornography didn't endear me to them. No one at the paper believed me. I've heard variations of "There's no way Frank would ever..." a dozen times.

Along with being called a snitch, a rat, a piece of shit, and a cocksucker. That last one...I do enjoy sucking cock—assuming it belongs to someone I'm dating—but I doubt it was meant as a compliment. Especially since the guy who said it punched me in the face a half-second later.

At least there won't be a trial. My panic attacks have been bad enough just dealing with the police, the FBI, and my own lawyer. Frank, for all his faults, owned up to what he did and asked for psychological counseling. He even helped the FBI find the assholes who took those pictures in the first place. Two dozen kids are a hell of a lot safer now because of it.

He's still going to jail for fifteen years, but supposedly, his deal got him assigned to a better facility where he won't be confined to a cell for twenty-two hours a day.

At the elevator, I pause and look around the office one last time. No one meets my gaze. Especially not the new Editor-in-Chief. Frank was his mentor, and when Will *suggested* I find another job? I didn't argue. He can't make me leave—we both know it. But why would I stay where I'm not wanted?

The doors ding, and I meet a pair of curious gray eyes. The man smiles as he asks me for my floor, then runs a hand through his shaggy blond hair. He's cute. Mid-forties.

"Lobby," I say quietly, then stare down at the box in my hands.

"Last day?" the guy asks. His voice is gentle, almost sympathetic. "I work upstairs at Anderson Investments. I've seen you around before."

"Y-yeah. Time to try something new," I mumble. I don't want to talk about the hell of the last six weeks or how the only job I could find on such short notice was at a call center out in Plano. Hiring a lawyer—which my older brother, Connor, insisted I do—decimated my savings, and I'm still at least six months away from having an app prototype I can shop around to investors. Or release all on my own.

The rest of the ride passes in silence, and when we reach the lobby, I try for a quick escape, but instead, a gentle hand touches my arm. "I've never been very good at this," the guy says. "Every time I've seen you in the elevator, I've wanted to say something, but...y'know. What if I were wrong?" He waggles his eyebrows hopefully, and I know what he means.

It's not like I wear my sexuality on my sleeve or have some bright flashing light over my head that says, "I'm gay and available."

When I don't respond or pull away, he smiles again. "I'm Alec. Maybe you'd like to get a drink with me sometime?"

"Quinton." I don't think before I reply. But now, I don't know what else to say. *"Thanks, but I just got fired."* Or maybe, *"You sure about that? According to my former coworkers, I'm a piece of shit."*

"Quinton. I like it. Do you ever go by Quint?" He doesn't wait for me to answer. "So...what about it? I know a place.

Quiet. Intimate. Drinks that are only *moderately* overpriced. What do you say?"

With a little shake of my head, I take a step back. "I can't, Alec. I'm sorry. I'm not in a good headspace right now."

Stupid, Q. He's hot, he seems nice, and you haven't had a real date in six months.

Alec's smile fades. He pulls out a business card, leans forward, and tucks it into my pocket. "Well, if you change your mind...give me a call. I'll miss seeing you in the elevator." He backs away, watching me the whole time until he reaches the building's front doors. "Always did enjoy the view."

~

"ALEC, I NEED TO WORK TONIGHT."

I try to infuse what I hope is some finality into my tone as he plops down beside me.

We've been dating for a month, and I've barely touched my app at all. Between the drive to Plano and back for that soul-sucking call center job and all the texting, video chats, and "hey, just come over for an hour" visits that turn into all-nighters, Alec has become a constant presence in my life, and I don't have space to think, let alone get any work done.

"Aww, come on, Quint. It's been a hell of a day. I need to relax with you. Besides, I rented that documentary on Mars we talked about the other day and we only have twenty-four hours to watch it." He slides his hand down my arm and links our fingers. "We can order Thai, then after the movie, we can try those new cuffs I picked up the other day. And maybe the blindfold too."

My dick juts painfully against my khakis, even though my anxiety flares at the same time. But Alec keeps saying this—bondage—will be good for me. For my panic attacks, claustrophobia, and social anxiety. A way to find some peace. And fuck, do I need that.

"I guess I can take one more night off." I press a firm hand to his chest and look him I the eye. "But tomorrow, I'm going straight home after work."

Alec tugs me closer and grabs my ass. "If you're going to leave me all alone on a Friday night, Quint, you'd better make it up to me over the weekend." There's an edge to his voice that gives me chills—and not the good kind—but before I can process why, he kisses me, and I forget what I was worried about in the first place.

A FIVE-CAR PILEUP on the way home means my solitary Friday night is a hell of a lot shorter than I planned. It's well after seven by the time I unlock my apartment door, only to find my brother and Alec sitting on the couch, heads bent towards one another.

I know my brother isn't gay, so the alarm bells ringing in my head have nothing to do with their proximity.

Connor jumps up when I shut the door. "Quinton. Finally. We were worried."

He offers me a quick, one-armed hug, but my stare is glued to Alec. "I told you I had to work on my app tonight. And that key was for emergencies only."

"*See?*" Alec mouths to Connor, and I take a step away from my brother. "This *is* an emergency. We're worried about you, Quint. All you do is work and obsess over that damn app. You're going to make yourself sick. Or end up having a breakdown."

This again. It's been an ongoing theme since I started my new job. *The breakdown.* But it's not like I have a choice. I have to work. No matter how stressful it is.

"Look, I know the Plano commute isn't ideal, but it's what I have right now. And I don't 'obsess' over the app. It only feels that way because you want to hang out every single night and that doesn't leave me any time to work on it." Turning to my brother, I arch my brows. "Why are you even here? It's not Christmas or my birthday."

Connor and I aren't close. Never have been. He's twelve years older than I am, and while he's a stand-up guy, he joined the army when I was six. He's out now—some government job he doesn't talk about—and other than special occasions and family dinners every six months or so, I haven't seen him in years.

"Alec called me. You look like you haven't slept in a month. And your place..." Connor sweeps his hand around the room. "I've never known you not to be a neat freak."

The apartment is a mess. Clean clothes strewn over one half of the sofa because I'm never home long enough to fold and put them away, a fine layer of dust everywhere...and I don't want to look in my fridge. I was planning on ordering pizza tonight. Alec only lives ten minutes away, and he's always insisting I come to *his* place rather than hang out at mine.

"He-lll-*oo*?" I draw out every syllable, as if that's suddenly going to make my argument more logical. "That's why I told Alec I needed a night to myself. So I could clean up a little, do some coding, and go to bed early."

"You love the time we spend together, Quint. You don't need a night alone to relax." Alec's overly patient tone grates. For once—just once—why can't he listen to me?

"Yes, I do!" I'm almost in tears now from the frustration of having this fight over and over again, and shit. I haven't cried in so long...not since Dad's funeral.

Sidling up next to me, Alec drapes his arm around my shoulder and pulls me close. "Don't shut me out, Quint. Please. I can help you through this."

"Through what?" I'm afraid to ask. The look in Connor's

eyes? The pity? The concern? I've never seen him like that before. Never felt so...out of control and uncomfortable in my own skin.

Alec's lips brush mine, and all the harsh words, the personality so big it feels like it takes up the entire room, they melt away, and it's just the two of us. Me, the guy who can't get his life together and the man who night after night, orders our meals, rubs my back, and never fails to make sure I'm satisfied in bed.

Which is why his response hurts more now than it ever has before.

"Through this darkness," he whispers. "You're going to end up hurting yourself, and I—we—love you too much to let that happen."

"I'm not—"

Connor's flinch silences my protest. Maybe I have been too rigid. Too focused. Too...everything Alec says I am. He's been right about so much. He convinced me I feel steadier when I drink decaf coffee. That I like cider better than beer. That popsicles are a healthier choice than ice cream. Maybe he's right about this too.

Alec smells like every fantasy I've ever had, and we spend so much time together, I haven't seen any of my other friends in months. We said "I love you" after a week, and ever since, it's been hard to figure out where he ends and I begin.

Maybe it's because my place is with him. Or maybe I don't have a place at all.

CHAPTER TWO

Quinton

I HAVEN'T BEEN able to relax all day. Oh, who am I kidding? I haven't relaxed in months.

You're not having a breakdown. You're not having a breakdown. You're not having a breakdown.

My newest mantra. Ever since the last big fight I had with Alec.

"I just told you I had to call Jessie to come get the gun out of my apartment! And you don't even react? You're so fucked in the head, you don't care?" he asks in the middle of dinner at a crowded restaurant.

I stare at him, mouth agape, spoon poised over the soup bowl. Who does that? Just casually admits to suicidal thoughts—or a hell of a lot more than thoughts—like they're saying they like apples with peanut butter?

"Well? You're still not going to say a word?" he hisses. "God. You're so close to a breakdown it'd be almost comical if I weren't so worried about you."

"I'm not..." I protest quietly. I know I'm not. Or, I hope I'm not.

Thankfully, the server intrudes. "How is everything?" she asks with a bright smile.

"Um, great. Thanks," I mumble, then stare into the soup I didn't want to order in the first place. Alec chose it. Like he chooses everything. The restaurants we go to. The movies we watch. When we have sex. And how.

"Quint, I love you. And I thought you loved me too," he says, now solicitous as he reaches across the table and rests his fingers on my arm.

I want to tell him how much I hate that nickname. How much I hate tofu. And spicy food. And the blindfolds, the cuffs, the way he just expects me to be submissive in the bedroom. But I don't say a word. Instead, I meet his gaze, and those gray eyes are so desperate for love and acceptance, I force a smile. "I do, Alec. Really. I'm just... shocked. I need to process a minute. Let's...get out of here, okay? Go back to your place where we can really talk about everything."

The dark cloud over him lifts, a hint of a smile touching his lips as he signals for the server. "Can we have the check?"

That was a month ago. The last night I trusted him. The last night I didn't see right through him. Because the next day, I quit going to the therapist *he'd* suggested and found a new one.

One who listened to me empty my soul for fifty minutes, then took out a notebook and wrote down the title of a book. "Read this," she said. "At least the first two chapters before your next appointment. Then we'll talk."

I stayed up all night plowing through the book with Alec sleeping next to me. Every time he rolled over, I panicked and switched over to a card game app, holding my breath, ready to lie and claim insomnia.

The book, all about how to tell if you're in a relationship with a psychopath or a narcissist, so closely mirrored the past six months of my life, I briefly wondered if the author had been spying on me.

I left for work before Alec woke up, called him from the car, and told him I needed some time alone. To think. He still texted me twenty times a day. Still tried to call. To FaceTime. And more than once, I answered, even though I knew it was a mistake.

But now...? I know what I need to do. Cut him out of my life completely. He's dangerous. A narcissist and a sociopath, possibly with antisocial personality disorder. And I'm his mark. According to the literature, this is what people like him do. They fixate on one person, changing them, molding them into the perfect partner, and often pushing them to the brink of sanity.

Why didn't I see it until now?

Alec's mood swings, his constant, yet subtle put downs, the way he twists the truth to make me look like the unstable one... He's cut me off from everyone I know. Become my entire life. And when I started to question, to push back, to see the truth, he only tried harder.

I don't know why he picked me. Or what his end game is. But if I don't get away from him soon, he'll use me up and leave me with nothing but the broken pieces of my life.

And there are enough of those already.

The GPS leads me to Highland Park, one of my favorite neighborhoods in Dallas. It was warm today, but now that it's well after six, the temperature's falling rapidly. I should have grabbed a heavier jacket. And gloves.

I'm five minutes early, but to Alec, that's ten minutes late, so I hustle around the corner until he comes into view.

Dammit. Why does he have to look so fucking good every time I see him? I *know* he's bad for me. I *know* I need to end it. I know if I don't do it now, I'll lose my nerve. But then he pulls me in for a hug, and I take a deep breath, inhaling his cologne. Old Spice. I've always had a weakness for that scent.

"I've missed you," he purrs in my ear, and when he kisses

me, his mouth is velvet heat, firm, yet still soft. He captures my lip gently, then tugs, just once as his fingers thread through my hair. "I don't want to fight, Quint. Ever. Just tell me what you want from me and I'll give it to you. Anything at all."

He's so earnest, I want to believe him.

And I have. More than once. Hell, I even have screenshots of his text messages. He promised me a hundred times to stop talking about my impending "breakdown." To give me however many nights a week I need to work on my app. To go to whatever therapist I want—together.

Most narcissists are experts at becoming someone else. They'll promise you the world. Then take it away in the next instant.

"Alec, I—"

I fumble for my phone where I have a dozen of these warnings and affirmations saved in my notes app just in case.

"Wait. I want to show you something first," he says. "And you're freezing out here." Wrapping his hand around my arm, he swipes a keycard over a secured door to a four-story condo complex. It's brand new construction, and only a couple of the units have lights on.

Despite being about to tell him what I needed—and having him cut me off and ignore me like he always does—I let him lead me up three flights of stairs where he presses a key into my hand. "Open the door."

"What is this?" He doesn't live here. His apartment is ten miles away.

"Just open the door." Now he's impatient, and my shoulders tense, sending a headache curling up from my neck all the way to my forehead. It's easier to do what he says than argue, and I need to take a deep breath—or three—before I can tell him I'm breaking up with him.

As soon as I walk into the condo, I understand his game. This is exactly the kind of place I've always wanted. Floor to ceiling windows that look out over the city. Sleek, modern lines, stainless steel appliances, marble countertops. All open space.

It's largely empty. A couch along one wall. Flat screen mounted over a fireplace. And a bottle of wine and two glasses next to the sink.

"Alec? What did you do?" I ask, turning to find him only inches from me. Instinctively, I take a step back, but he follows, tugs off my jacket, and reaches for me. "Stop. Tell me what's going on right now."

"This place could be ours. I have an option on it for the next forty-eight hours. It comes furnished. There's a bed, and I packed us an overnight bag..."

"No!" The word escapes harsher than I'd normally risk, but this is too much. The exact *opposite* of what I wanted to happen tonight. "You promised to give me space. I have it in writing." I pull out my phone and try to scroll through the thousands and thousands of messages he's sent me over the past few months. "You said...you said we could take things slow."

Frantic, knowing I'm going to lose this battle if I don't take a stand right the fuck now, I keep scrolling until Alec snatches the device from my hand and shoves it into *his* pocket.

"I need my phone," I say, my voice trembling.

He surges forward, his hands cupping my head as he crushes his lips to mine. I stumble, and my back hits the kitchen counter. I don't want this. When he bites down and I taste blood, I jerk my head away.

"What the fuck?" The stinging in my lower lip distracts me, and I don't notice him undoing my belt until he's already slid the zipper on my pants down. "Alec, please. We're not...I can't do this."

Shock steals my next words as he spins me around and bends me forward over the counter, his fingers digging into my ass. His favorite position. A way for him to top me without having to see my face.

That icy ball I've carried around all day long? It's taken over my entire body. I don't even fight him. I *know* I should, but I can't.

"You want this, Quint. You know you do. We're so good together."

Tell him no. Tell him to stop.

But I'm frozen until he spits on his hand. There is no way I'm letting him fuck his way out of this. If he does...I'll stay. I know I will.

"Get away from me." I buck and kick, but with my pants around my ankles, I only catch him in the shin. He swears under his breath and stumbles back, and when I face him again, the rage in his eyes... Shit. I never thought he'd physically hurt me. Not beyond rough sex.

But right now? He's scaring me.

"I'm leaving," I say, forcing as much bravado as I can into my words. "I never want to see you again, Alec. Don't call. Don't text. Don't come to my apartment. Or my work. Leave me alone. We're done."

I'm shaking so badly, it's hard to pull my pants up, grab my coat, and edge around the counter to the door, but I don't want to turn my back on him. Screw my cell phone. I can get a new one.

Alec stalks towards me, his hands clenched into fists at his sides. "You need help, Quint. You're having a breakdown. Right now, in fact. I don't know why *you* can't see it, but I can. Everyone can. I thought this place could be a fresh start for us. Somewhere you could heal. With my help."

"Fuck you." Over the threshold, I can breathe again, but he's still advancing on me. "Get back."

"Quint—" He lunges for my arm, and my foot misses the top step.

For a moment—one very long, terrifying moment—it's like I'm in some sort of suspended animation. My arms flail, grabbing for the railing, for anything to hold on to, but all I see is Alec's face. And the lack of emotion in his eyes.

Impact. Pain. Then nothing.

Quinton

"Traumatic brain injury"

"You probably won't walk again."

"I'll take care of you, Quint."

My dreams are as fragmented as my memories. And my thoughts. I can't seem to hold one for more than a few minutes. The morning sun slices across the end of the bed, and I stare at it for a good ten minutes before Alec breezes into the room, a wide smile on his face.

"Time to get up, baby. Can't sleep the day away. Breakfast is ready." He slides his arms under me, lifts me out of bed, and sets me in my wheelchair.

My stomach rumbles slightly, but I'm not truly hungry. I don't remember the last time I wanted to eat. At least two months ago. Before I fell down a flight of metal stairs, fracturing three vertebrae in my back, cracking my skull in two places, and breaking my femur.

"He was lucky, but the nerve damage? It'll be with him for the rest of his life," Alec says to someone I can't see. Machines beep all around me, but no matter how hard I try, I can't open my eyes.

When I finally did, Alec was there. Explaining everything. Two days in a medically induced coma. Two surgeries before I woke up. Three more in the weeks following.

He's been at my side the whole time. The stairs that took my ability to walk—or even stand for more than a few minutes— are just outside our condo door, and every single day, he tells me he's so sorry we have to live here. But my old apartment building isn't accessible, and he'd already given up the lease on his former place.

At least with the open floor plan, I can get around. Though, there's no elevator in the building, so my entire world has been reduced to these four walls and what I can see from the windows.

I have enough mobility and strength to take care of my morning needs, but that's about it. My legs are shaking by the time I'm back in the wheelchair, and I'm a little dizzy.

Rolling myself out to the main room leaves my arms feeling like limp noodles. Every day, the trip is harder than the day before. Shouldn't I be getting stronger by now? I need to ask Alec to check the wheel locks again.

"Pancakes," he says as he sets a plate in front of me, then leans down and kisses me. No matter how many times we fight, this is one thing we do well. The man can kiss like it's an Olympic sport and he's going for the gold medal. Even if I do hate pancakes. They get soggy. "Here are your meds."

Four pills tumble into my palm, and Alec nudges the glass of juice on the right side of the plate.

Oxycontin for the nerve pain. Prozac for the anxiety I can't seem to shake. A multi-vitamin, and...something else. Why can't I remember what the last one is? "Alec? What is this one?" I ask, holding up a little white pill.

"You ask me that every morning, love," he says as he sits next to me. "It's a mix of homeopathic herbs for pain and mental clarity. Don't you remember Dr. Trax coming a few weeks ago?" Pulling out his phone, he taps the screen a few times and shows me smiling next to an older man with a kindly face and hair as white as his doctor's coat.

"No. I mean...maybe?" The memories are fuzzy. All of my memories are fuzzy. Trax's hands were cold. He tested my range of motion. Said I needed more medication.

The accident destroyed my back. Stole my ability to walk.

But that's not all. My mind will never be what it was. A tear burns my eye, and Alec cups the back of my neck and wipes it away. "It's okay, Quint. I'm here, and I'll never leave you. I love you."

He loves me. That's the one thing I haven't lost. I still matter to him. So why does it feel like he's holding something back? That behind his earnest blue eyes and encouraging smile, there's something he's not telling me?

"IT'S FUCKED." My voice cracks as I slam the lid down on my laptop. "I can't remember how to do anything, Alec. It's *right there!*" I slap my palm against my forehead like I can shake all my former skills loose if I just hit myself hard enough. "I was so close...*before*. I think I was just a couple of days away from a prototype."

"You had an idea. Some buggy code," Alec says. "Nothing workable yet. Why don't you take a break? We can check out that new Netflix special on social media."

Alec starts to massage my shoulders, his strong fingers stroking the sides of my neck where the muscles feel like rubber bands about to snap. "You've been at this all day, love. It's not good for you to hunch over your laptop for hours on end."

He presses a thin, filmy square behind my ear, and in seconds, the world turns soft and a little fuzzy. The pain patches keep me from dissolving into tears every six hours, but I hate how they make me feel—like nothing matters anymore.

And then I'm moving. Alec wheels me into the living room, scoops me into his arms, and settles me on the couch with him. I don't protest. Just let him do what he wants. Pick what we watch on TV. Decide when to pause Netflix and start to fool around—as much as I can without being able to walk.

And when the show's over, I can't remember what it was about, because all I want to do is sleep.

CHAPTER THREE

Quinton

"Pancakes," Alec announces as he sets the plate in front of me. "And your pills. Drink up, love."

Every day, it's the same dance. Pancakes. Pills. Alec's overconfident smile. My sullen obedience. I hate this. Hate my life. Hate being trapped in this chair, in this condo, in this relationship.

What am I saying? Alec loves me. He takes care of me.

Get it together, Q. You need Alec. How the hell would you survive on your own?

Staring at the pills, I can't remember what they're all for, but I know I don't want to take them. Alec nudges me again, and I pick up the glass of juice. A fine, white powder dusts a part of the rim. This...isn't right. None of this is right.

"If he works hard at his physical therapy, there's a chance he can regain most of his strength and muscle control."

I can't place the voice in my head. Is this a memory or just wishful thinking?

"He's not ready to leave the hospital yet, Mr. Harrow. If you check him out now, the damage could be irreversible."

"He's coming home with me today," Alec says. *"I'm the only one who can take care of him."*

I swallow the Oxycontin with a sip of juice. My back is throbbing, and the pain zinging down my legs feels like that one time I stuck my finger in the light socket when I was six. Within a few minutes, the voices in my head: the doctors, Alec, someone else… my brother, I think…start to fade into nothingness. Replaced by a pounding that can only be a migraine starting. I never used to get them, but since the accident, they happen every couple of days.

"Who the fuck is that?" Alec mutters as he pushes back from the table, and I pinch the bridge of my nose.

There's someone here? This isn't all in my head?

Alec's voice carries from the door. "Go away. He doesn't want to see you."

Huh? Who's he talking to? Though the Oxy is starting to make me a little light headed, I back my chair up, spin it around, and wheel myself towards the door.

"Quinton!"

"Connor?" My brother shoves his shoulder against the sleek, black wood and Alec stumbles back a couple of steps. He's a big guy. Strong enough to lift me out of bed every morning, carry me to the couch at night, help me bathe…all the things I can't do for myself. But he's not as big as Connor. My brother has at least fifty pounds of muscle on Alec, and from the look in his eyes, he's pissed as hell.

Connor sidesteps my boyfriend and drops down to one knee next to my wheelchair. "Quinton, you look awful."

My eyes burn, and I reach out to hug him. "I've sent you a hundred messages," I say quietly, barely able to control the emotion in my voice. "Where have you been?"

I don't understand the shadow that passes over his face, but he stands and puts himself between me and Alec. "If you know what's good for you, you'll stay the fuck out of my way. Quinton is coming with me, and you're never going to contact him again."

"What?" I ask. "Connor, Alec has been doing everything for me. I...need him." Even as I say the words, something about them makes my stomach turn. I'm nauseous, my head hurts, and I don't understand why the two of them are staring one another down like they're about to kill each other.

"Everything?" Connor snorts. "The doctor wanted you in physical therapy five days a week. You haven't been once!" He scans the living room, spies my laptop, and grabs it, along with the power cord, then shoves them into my lap. "Your chances of walking again? They were upwards of eighty percent when this asshole checked you out of the hospital. How many steps have you taken since then?"

"I...don't know."

Alec springs for my brother and lands a punch, but Connor doesn't go down. Blood stains his lips, and he swears and wipes it away. "Is that the best you got?"

"Stop it! Both of you!" My words feel slow and unwieldy, and it's like I'm seeing Connor through ten feet of water as he rounds my chair and starts pushing me out the door.

"Come at me again, and you'll be the one in a wheelchair, asshole. You fucked with the wrong family."

Everything's happening too fast. Nothing makes sense. But the door slams and then...we're in an elevator.

"This building doesn't have an elevator," I slur, and Connor crouches down once the doors slide shut.

"Q, this building has always had an elevator. I didn't believe you before the accident. Hell, I was on Alec's side. He said all the right things, and I was positive you were having a breakdown. But I picked up a box of your shit from your old landlord last week, and..."

The doors slide open, and we're moving again. Outside. Fuck. I can't be outside.

"It's dangerous out there, Quint. Up here, you're safe."

My breath saws in and out of my chest as Connor wheels me to a black car, opens the door, and lifts me into the front seat.

"Connor...please." I can't breathe. "Back...inside."

"No." After he fastens my seatbelt, he puts his hands on my shoulders. "In and out, Quinton. Listen to my voice. You're safe. In. Out. In...out."

Once I no longer feel like I'm about to pass out, he shuts the door, leaving my wheelchair on the curb.

"But...I need that..." I say when he takes his place behind the wheel.

"You don't need a fucking thing from that asshole. I'm sorry it took me so long to come for you. But you're going to be okay now." Connor guns the engine and after we've made three turns and I have no clue where we are, he stops at a red light and glances over at me. "I found your journal, Q. Your landlord called me. When Alec packed up your apartment, he left a bunch of shit behind. Dad's old pocket watch, that ceramic Christmas tree with the glass lights, and this." Pulling a small leather notebook from his pocket, he sets it in my lap.

I have to squint to read it, but the handwriting is most definitely mine.

Alec is a classic narcissist. It's possible he also has Antisocial Personality Disorder. He doesn't feel emotions like normal people, but he's great at faking them. He's using you, and when he's done with you, he'll find another victim and leave you with nothing. You have to break it off with him. Tonight.

"Look at the date," Connor says quietly.

My brain hasn't worked right since my accident, but the date it happened? I'll never forget it. And on that page, it's staring back at me.

"Fuck." I let my head fall against the seat, panic wrapping a chain around my chest and twisting until I'm not sure my heart's still beating. "How...?"

"Quinton? Calm down." My brother reaches across the center console and presses his hand to my heart. "We're going somewhere Alec won't ever find you. You're going to walk again, and we're going to make sure that fucker goes to jail for a very, *very* long time."

THAT SOMEWHERE TURNED out to be an emergency room in Fort Worth where Connor demanded the doctors run every test under the sun to find out exactly what Alec was giving me.

Eight hours later, he wheels me into an accessible suite at a five-star hotel. I'm exhausted, and I still can't think straight, but right now, I suspect that's more from hunger than anything else.

Connor drops down into the chair at the polished wood desk and flips through a binder. "What do you want to eat?"

"Huh?" The question confuses me, even though I know it shouldn't. But for more than eight months, Alec made all the decisions.

"Quinton?" Connor holds my gaze, the seriousness in his dark blue eyes helping me focus. "You have to be hungry. What do you want for dinner?"

"I..." Panic sets in again. Most of what the doctor told us before they discharged me didn't make any sense, and I can barely feel my legs after the cortisone shot they gave me. "I don't..."

"Breathe. Count backwards from ten. Right now."

My brother was in the army for more than a decade. He knows how to get people to listen to him, and the command in his tone? It snaps me back to reality.

By the time I reach one, my hands have stopped shaking. "S-sorry," I whisper.

"Don't apologize." Connor squeezes my shoulder gently. "Just tell me what you want for dinner."

"A cheeseburger. And fries. With ketchup." Alec hated red meat. And ketchup. And anything unhealthy. "And a Coke." Soda. Another thing I haven't had in forever.

"You got it."

With each greasy, cheesy bite of food, the world's a little clearer. No longer in soft focus like it's been since my accident. I can't finish the meal, but I don't care. It was still the best food I've had in…a long time.

"What did he give me?" I ask quietly. "At the hospital…I don't remember what they said…"

Connor pulls a folded piece of paper from the back pocket of his Wranglers and spreads it out on the table. "Scopolamine, primarily, but also something called temazepam. They're used for motion sickness and insomnia, but in high enough doses, the two—hell, even one of them—can act a lot like rohypnol. The date rape drug?"

"Shit. Is that why everything's fuzzy?"

Running a hand through his short-cropped brown hair, Connor sighs. "You cracked your skull in two places when you fell. But the brain scans you had before Alec checked you out of the hospital didn't show any long-term damage. I talked to your attending physician two days ago, and he told Alec if you went to physical therapy and worked the program, you'd regain most of your mobility."

"So when you said I'd walk again…" I can't finish the sentence. Because it's been months. What if it's too late?

"There's a room waiting for you at a long-term rehab facility in Arlington," he says. "They're the best in the state. Psychological counseling, physical therapy, and top-notch security. I've sent a couple of my guys there. Including one who had a mob hit out on him. No one's getting to you at Thatcher House."

The idea of going somewhere new terrifies me, but I want out of this damn chair so badly I can taste it. "A room?"

"Well, it's more like a small apartment." He moves to one of the two beds in the room with an open suitcase I hadn't noticed before. Of course, I hadn't looked either. I'm used to not looking. Used to not thinking for myself. Used to letting Alec control everything. Pulling out a brochure, Connor hands it to me.

"I can't just...live with you for a while?" I hate how desperate I sound. We're not close. Hell, I don't even know what he does for a living beyond something for the government.

Connor shakes his head, but his eyes are soft. Almost apologetic. "I don't know the first thing about what you need, Quinton. Other than a hell of a lot of counseling and a team of doctors on your side. You'll get that at Thatcher House. And I'll check on you."

Rummaging in his suitcase again, he comes up with a brand new cell phone still in the box. "My number's already programmed in here. You can reach me twenty-four hours a day. And that phone isn't registered in your name. Or any name traceable to me. Mom...I'll bring her to visit you in a couple of weeks. But not until I'm sure she understands just how important it is that she never, *ever* breathe a word about you to Alec."

This entire day has been wave after wave of reality crashing down on me. I can't handle any more. When the first sob escapes, Connor scoots his chair close to mine and wraps his arms around me. "You're safe now, Q. And you're going to get better. I promise."

∼

THE STERILE GRAY walls in one of Thatcher House's three little meeting rooms feel like they're closing in on me. Across the table, my lawyer, Randall Sunstrom, removes a small stack of papers from a manilla folder.

"As we discussed, Quinton, this order of protection won't stop Mr. Harrow from harassing you. But it will make it a crime for him to do so. Whether or not the police choose to do anything about that crime...well..."

My stomach twists into knots. Oh, who am I kidding? It's been one giant knot since Connor first introduced me to Randall.

"Just need your signature."

My fingers are shaking so much, I drop the pen twice. As I pick it up for the third time, the meeting room door slams open, and I jerk, sending a spasm of pain from my back all the way down my legs.

"What the *hell* are we paying you for, Sunstrom?" Connor shouts, his massive presence sucking all the air from the room in a heartbeat.

"Excuse me?" he asks.

"You can't charge that bastard with anything? He kept Quinton prisoner for more than two months. He drugged him, locked him up in that condo, and kept him trapped in a wheelchair!"

Randall pushes to his feet, though he's at least six inches shorter than my brother. "Mr. Davis, as I told your brother, Mr. Harrow didn't technically break any laws."

"The hell he didn't!"

"Connor." My voice isn't much more than a whisper, and I can't look my brother in the face. But he stops and turns to me. "Randall's right."

"How? Q, you were barely lucid when I got you out of there."

"I never said no."

"What?" Dropping into a chair next to me, Connor rests his elbow on the table. "Explain."

Shame curls my shoulders inward, and I fidget with the RFID bracelet that opens the various doors in and out of the facility. "You read my journal."

"So? He's a sociopath. He doesn't have a conscience. That doesn't excuse what he did."

"Of course not!" When I raise my voice, Connor's eyes widen. I haven't yelled at him since I was a little kid. Back then, he could ignore me. "But I didn't say no." Memories hit me in flashes. Alec's voice. The taste of the pills on my tongue. Him lifting me out of bed and dumping me into the wheelchair. Every. Single. Day. Panic tightens cold fingers around my heart, and I pull out the little tin of Xanax I keep in the pocket of my sweatpants and swallow one dry.

Randall, thank God, clears his throat. "At no time did Mr. Harrow force Quinton to take medication against his will or stop him from leaving the condo. If Quinton had been in a long-term care facility, we might have a case for medical negligence. But not with their prior established relationship."

I flinch at the word. Relationship. I'll never trust someone with my heart again. I can walk now. Not well. Not for long. But one day, maybe I won't need the walker I used to shuffle down the hall from my room. The cane I use on my good days. The muscle relaxers.

Connor jerks to his feet and starts pacing the room. "Two months. That asshole had Quinton for two months. And the best you can do is a fucking restraining order."

"Connor, shut up." I flip through the paperwork and scrawl my signature next to Randall's little Post-it flags. It takes me several seconds to muster enough strength to press my hands to the table and push myself up. "It doesn't matter what happens to Alec. You made sure he'll never find me."

Randall opens his briefcase and removes a second stack of

papers. "Which brings me to the next order of business. Name change paperwork. Sign everywhere that's marked and as soon as I get to the courthouse in the morning, you'll officially be Quinton Silver, not Quinton Davis."

"Are you sure about this?" Connor rests his hand on my shoulder, giving it a gentle squeeze. "You shouldn't have to give up your name."

"It's safer," I whisper. "When I get out of here, I want to go somewhere he'll never find me. San Francisco. Seattle. Los Angeles. Start over. Help me do that. Please, Connor."

My brother wraps an arm around me, careful not to tip me off balance. "Whatever you need, Quinton. I wasn't there for you after the accident. I'll never make that mistake again."

CHAPTER FOUR

Present Day

Graham

A COLD BREEZE stirs the fallen leaves as I run hill repeats on Phinney Ridge in the dark of early morning. Why did I agree to this again?

Because you finally beat Inara on the climbing wall, and she was pissed.

The former Army Ranger sniper—and one of the team at Hidden Agenda K&R—challenged me to this torture. I owed her after the celebratory dance I did when I reached the ground.

Fog wraps around me, tinged with the scent of seawater, and when I turn the corner, the visibility drops to no more than fifty feet. It's disorienting, and a chunk of uneven sidewalk trips me up.

I hit the ground, scraping my palms, and my right knee lands in something...oh, fuck. Dog shit. The stench is overwhelming, and suddenly, I'm not in Seattle anymore. I'm trapped in an alley in San Francisco, four guys taking turns beating the crap out of me.

I can't move. Can't breathe. All I can hear are their taunts and slurs. Wrapping my arms around my head, I curl into a ball, trying to make myself as small as possible.

"Graham?"

Inara's voice cuts through my memories, and I jerk up to my hands and knees. "Here." My voice isn't steady. Neither are my legs, but I struggle to my feet as she jogs up to me.

"You okay?" Her nose wrinkles as she stops short. "What the fuck is that God-awful smell?"

"Some asshole not picking up after his dog. Take my name off the climbing wall leaderboard if you want, but I'm done." My hands burn, and I yank off my running cap and swipe it over the mess on my knee, then toss the ruined black fleece into the garbage can.

Inara's fingers wrap around my forearm, and I can't stop my whole body from going rigid. "What's wrong?"

"Nothing. Other than being covered in dog shit." I haven't told anyone at Hidden Agenda what happened to me eight years ago. Ryker—our team leader—probably knows. His background checks are so deep, I'm sure he even found out about that time in seventh grade I got detention for kissing another boy. The police report from the attack would be public record. But Inara? West? Ripper? Ry wouldn't tell them without telling me first.

She snorts. "Sure. Because I don't have any experience with men keeping secrets. I swear, you're as bad as Ry. Just with a better sense of humor."

Shaking off her hold, I take a step back. "Fine. You're right. It's not the dog shit. But it's not something I want to talk about either."

"Suit yourself." Inara swipes at her brow and pulls a bottle of water from her running belt. After a swig, she runs a hand through her hair and narrows her eyes at me. "You know we're family, right?"

The words sting. So does her tone. "It was a long time ago. I'm solid."

"You better be. This happens on mission, you could put us all at risk."

"I've been with Hidden Agenda almost three years. You don't trust me by now?" I keep my voice low. This neighborhood is a mix of apartments and condos on top of businesses, and the last thing I need is to wake the neighbors.

"I trust you with my life, Graham. That's the point. Family doesn't keep secrets. Not with what we do out there." Passing me the bottle, she pulls off her bandana and tosses that to me as well. "Clean yourself up before you get back in your car. Otherwise you'll be smelling that shit for a week."

She gives me a look that could melt a glacier, but there's warmth in her tone. Concern.

"Thanks. Give me some time?" As much as I don't want to admit my shame to *anyone*, I can't keep secrets from the team. From my family. And now that Inara knows this particular one can turn me into a shaking ball of fear in the middle of a Seattle sidewalk, she's right to press me on it.

Turning on her heel to head back down the hill, she stops, then looks back at me. "When you're ready, you know we'll listen. All of us. Any of us. It's when you keep everything shoved down so deep it can't escape that you're in trouble. Because it will. Every time. In the worst way possible." With one last meaningful glance, she finally takes off. "See you at tomorrow's workout, " she calls over her shoulder.

By the time I make it to my red Smart Car, my hands are actively throbbing. I must have missed a spot cleaning off my leg—even with the water bottle and bandana—because the smell's so bad, the only way I can make it back to my condo without throwing up is to roll all the windows down. In thirty degree weather.

An hour later, I pull on a pair of shorts and a t-shirt and crawl into bed. Logically, I know my extra-long shower where I rubbed my knee raw took care of the stench. But the one in my memories? That one's back, stronger than ever. It was all over me. My hands, my knees, in my ear. Mixed with blood and drying cum. All because a group of men decided I wasn't fit to call myself a member of the United States Coast Guard because I kissed a guy outside a bar on New Year's Eve. I didn't find out until a few months later that the four of them had been eyeing me for a couple of hours after I politely—but very firmly—told one of their female friends I batted for the other team. Seeing that kiss I shared with the bouncer? That set them off all over again, and they followed me to that alley to beat the shit out of me and "teach me a lesson."

I can't get warm, so I curl into a ball and bury my face in my pillow. Most days, I don't think about the attack anymore. Which makes the times I do pack even more of a punch.

Where I am now in my life? Everyone accepts me. Hell, Ryker, my boss at Hidden Agenda, a K&R firm he started after he left the Special Forces, didn't even blink when I told him I was gay.

Seattle's a great place for just about any lifestyle, and I've dated from time to time. Found a couple of guys where things lasted long enough to get to the fucking stage, and I'm good as long as no one asks me to bottom.

But when the memories come, there's not much I can do besides take my anxiety meds and hide away from the world. And wonder if I'll ever feel something other than broken.

CHAPTER FIVE

Graham

FRIDAY NIGHTS behind the bar at the Unicorn always leave my ears ringing. But when I'm not training or on mission, this gig is a good diversion. And if there's a party going on, I can make a solid five hundred in tips for a single night's work.

A little slice of normal in my world that's anything but. No one at the bar knows my history. My damage.

Plus, no one tries to kill me. Usually. There was that one bar fight last year... My shoulder still aches from time to time—especially when it rains.

A little after 2:00 a.m., the streets in the Capitol Hill neighborhood of Seattle are bustling. Tourists, local revelers, a handful of drunks... No one sleeps along the Pike/Pine corridor, the blocks full of bars, restaurants, and music venues are packed to the gills all weekend long.

After almost eight hours slinging drinks, all I want is a little peace and quiet, so I duck down a side street to avoid the crowds hanging out at Nectar Lounge. Weaving in and out of the throngs of people? I'm too tired for that, and Ry wants me at the warehouse at nine tomorrow. Or...today.

Two blocks off the main drag, it's almost quiet, and I pass by a darkened row of townhomes. An empty parking lot across the street is fenced off with construction signs announcing plans for a multi-story condo complex.

One of the reasons I love Seattle? A five minute walk can bring me from the heart of the city to a neighborhood that's almost suburbia. Deserted, all the residents either out partying or asleep. No traffic. No incessant bass beat. No sirens—for the moment. It's so peaceful, the rasp of a lock is louder than I expect. Tensing, I spin to face the center townhome, fists raised, ready to fight.

"Wait," a soft, male voice says from the darkness of the doorway. "Please...stop. I need help."

I stagger back. Memories I can't handle—not tonight, maybe not ever—try to push their way to the surface. Another dark space. My own plea for help—one that fell on uncaring ears. "Call 911 if it's an emergency, dude."

"It's not. To them." Desperation floods his tone, taking a hammer to the box I keep my emotions in. "There's a bag. In the yard. I can't get it."

Narrowing my gaze, I scan the little fenced-in area. Flat stones with unkempt grass between them form a haphazard path to the front porch where two short steps are covered by a thick piece of plywood to form a ramp.

The contents of a green canvas grocery bag spill out onto the stones. A carton of ice cream with the lid smashed, mint chip melting everywhere, a box of cereal, a tube of shaving cream...

"It's three feet from your door, man. You expect me to believe you can't reach it?"

"No." A hint of resignation mixes with shame. "But, I can't."

After a pause, he sighs. "Please. This isn't a trick or a prank." My eyes have adjusted so I can make out his shadow in the small crack of the doorway. "I'll lock up. Four separate locks. You should be able to hear each one. I swear—on my life—you're not in any danger from me. I won't hurt you. I couldn't...even if I wanted to. Just pick up the bag, set it on the porch, and go."

The door closes, followed by four distinct *thunks*.

Well, fuck. He sounds so sincere—and desperate—that I can't walk away.

"We help people. Anyone who can't help themselves. You understand me? We never leave a man behind." Ryker's words play on a loop in my head. The ones he said the day he hired me.

Opening the gate, I move slowly, scanning the yard for any threats. No trees. No shrubs. Nothing but dry grass and weeds. And inside, a man who needs help.

Down on one knee, I survey the grocery devastation. It's worse than I thought. A carton of eggs spilled open, four of them cracked and broken, two whole, but resting in mint chip goo. A pint of milk is warm to the touch, as is the block of cheddar cheese.

How long was this bag sitting here, anyway? Rescuing the unbroken eggs, I return them to the carton, tucking it in next to the shaving cream. But that move displaces a box of mac and cheese, and underneath?

The red and white prescription bag screams at me, the label too big *not* to read. Clonazepam. The same little yellow pills I keep in a plastic container in my back pocket. My panic attacks don't come often anymore, but when they do, they're more intense than ever.

Quickly, I shove the pills under a package of warm steak. It would have been easy to read the guy's name, but I've invaded his privacy enough, and if he's out of his meds...I'm not going to keep them from him for another second.

The porch is as unadorned as the yard. Except for a single sign at eye level.

Leave all packages directly in front of the door, ring the bell, and walk away. Occupant will not answer and cannot sign for anything.

Setting the bag down, I eye the video-enabled doorbell, then push the button. A chime sounds inside, and I turn, ready to walk away, when I hear an audible click.

"Thank you," the pained, soft voice says through the speaker. "I called the store earlier, but they wouldn't—"

"Do you need me to replace any of this stuff?" I ask. "You're down to eight eggs, your meat is probably spoiled, and I'm pretty sure your bread is...shit. I was going to say toast, but that's taking a bad pun way too far."

His laugh isn't relaxed, but some of his distress eases. "No. I'll...I'll get by. The guy who delivers on Saturdays isn't as much of a dick."

"This happens on the regular? Fuck, dude. You need to talk to a manager or something. You shouldn't have to pay to replace everything."

"It's okay. I'm used to it. Thank you. Really. Uh...?"

"Graham." Pausing, hoping to get his name, I stare at the solid wood door, the single, barred window. But there's only silence, so I shove one hand into my pocket and head down the ramp. I'm almost out of earshot when the locks *thunk,* one at a time, and the door opens slowly.

Silhouetted in a faint light, he's a little taller than I am. Maybe six-foot-two? Short, dark hair, a neatly trimmed beard. "Quinton," he says, then grunts as he bends down slowly to pick up the bag. "I'm Quinton."

There's a vulnerability to him, despite the broad chest and the well-muscled arms. His jeans are loose around his legs, and he moves carefully, taking two steps back so the glow from the interior light falls across his face.

He's drop dead gorgeous. Except for the fear so evident in his eyes.

"You're welcome. Quinton. Good night."

With a single nod, and maybe a half-smile, he shuts the door, and though I should go home, I turn on my heel and head in the opposite direction. The night manager at the grocery store is going to get an earful.

~

Quinton

As soon as I shuffle back into my kitchen, I paw through the bag for my meds. My anxiety has been on overdrive all day, and my hands are shaking.

Clementine, the little orange kitten I found half-starved to death on my front porch a month ago, curls around my ankles and squeaks, begging for a treat. I pop open the jar I keep on the counter and drop a small handful for her. The little thing curled up in my lap all afternoon, purring, and I think she's the only reason I didn't end up having a full-blown panic attack.

Over a pint of ice cream.

One year ago today, my brother saved my life. Rescued me from my ex who had me convinced I'd never walk again. Who was doing everything he could to keep me dependent on him, drugging me with a cocktail of meds that kept my thoughts so muddled, I couldn't see what he was doing to me.

Alec hated ice cream. When we started dating, he told me how bad it was for me. Lectured me for an hour about the horrors of dairy milk, of sugar, about how I should stick to popsicles. I wanted to make him happy. So, I gave up my favorite comfort food. For him. After that, it was coffee. Mexican food. Cookies. Beer.

Then my friends. My ability to walk. And finally, my freedom.

Today, all I wanted was a pint of mint chip and my damn pills. Instead, I have a mess to clean up. The crackers are destroyed, my bread practically mush after sitting in melted ice cream all afternoon, and everything perishable is spoiled. Almost three quarters of the order needs to go right in the dumpster. Outside. Where each step feels like climbing a mountain and I'm lucky if I don't hyperventilate until I pass out.

It takes me an hour to deal with the mess, and once I have the trash bagged up, I spend a good ten minutes watching the back door security camera. I shouldn't be so paranoid. I haven't heard a peep from Alec since Connor threatened to beat the shit out of him if he ever came near me again.

But between the agoraphobia I can't kick and the pain that plagues my every step, going outside—even though the dumpster is all of five feet away—is scarier than jumping out of a plane. Without a parachute.

At least it's flat. And well lit. I flip the three deadbolts, check the camera one more time, and then shuffle into the alley, my heart pounding. By the time I'm back inside, I feel like I just ran a marathon.

My left leg is starting to tingle, a sign I need to lie down, so I head for the motorized lift chair I had installed to carry me up to the second floor. If today were one of my good days, I could manage the stairs on my own. But after spending the past few hours with my entire body tense and shaking, there's no way I'll take the risk.

I lower myself into the chair, and Clementine jumps into my lap. Before I can flip the switch, my doorbell rings.

Pulling out my phone, I activate the camera.

It's Graham…standing on my porch with a grocery bag in his hand. What the…?

After a few seconds, he clears his throat. "Quinton? Um, you don't have to answer. But I know what it's like when all you want is ice cream." He hangs the bag on the door knob, smiles nervously, and then turns on his heel so precisely before he walks away, I think he must have been in the military.

Even if I had to crawl back to the door, I'd do it for a pint of mint chip. My left leg is dragging behind me by the time I flip the locks, and Graham is long gone. But the ice cream is still frozen, and he even got the same brand I ordered.

Who does that?

No one in my world.

I shouldn't risk this. Hell, he's a complete stranger. For all I know, he could have dropped off a pint of poison. Injected the carton with PCP or nicotine or drain cleaner. But something in his eyes earlier...I think he's a good guy. Even if I swore after getting away from Alec that I'd never trust my own judgement again.

Carefully spooning half a pint into a bowl, I smooth out the bag and prepare to stuff it in with all the other bags in the cabinet when the receipt falls out.

With his name on it.

Graham Tempelton.

He doesn't look like a Tempelton. He needs a tougher name. Grittier. And I should leave it the hell alone. But I'm not sure anyone's ever been this kind to me for no reason at all, and I wish I would've been fast enough to thank him.

Sinking into my massage chair, I turn on the heat and set it for the gentlest setting, then slide the table over so I can access my laptop. Clementine immediately joins me and her purr helps take the edge off my nerves as I type his name into the search box.

Well, crap. That wasn't hard. Graham Templeton has a one page website with his resume. Bartender. No. *Mixologist.* And there's an email address.

I don't know why I'm doing this. Since moving to Seattle, I haven't taken a single risk. Haven't talked to anyone outside my physical therapist, my psychiatrist, my housekeeper, and my brother.

And yet, I'm sending this stranger an email.

Graham,

You rescued my groceries, then bought me ice cream. No one's that nice. No one I know, anyway. I just wanted to say thanks. Today kind of sucked, and you made it better.

Q

The bowl is empty and I'm still staring at the screen. At the send button. Wondering why.

When I find the answer, I almost throw the laptop across the room. But then I'd need to buy another one, and even in Seattle, I can't get a system that meets my needs in under two days.

I'm lonely. So fucking lonely. One whole year of freedom, but outside of my shrink, I haven't had an honest conversation with anyone. I can't have one with Graham either. But the ice cream? This email? It's a sliver of connection. Even if it only lasts until the rest of the pint is gone, I'll take it.

Send.

CHAPTER SIX

Graham

THE SCENTS OF COFFEE, gun oil, and sweat are so familiar, they settle me every time I walk into Hidden Agenda's home base in a warehouse south of downtown Seattle. I'm late. My extra errand last night only took me thirty minutes, but after that, I stared at the ceiling for two hours.

Every time I closed my eyes, I saw Quinton's face. It's been a long time since a guy has caught my attention simply by existing. But something in his expression...He's haunted. Scared. Emotions I remember all too clearly.

Every moment of last night is burned into my brain.

Ryker McCabe, former Special Forces commander and my boss, never forgets a single fucking thing. Taught himself some shit about mind palaces and using mnemonics before he and his team were captured and tortured for fifteen months in a Taliban prison deep underground in the Hindu Kush. The man can remember the license plate number of the taxi cab that cut us off last year in Karachi, the exact layout of every single compound we've ever breached, and my best—and worst—time on the climbing wall.

And he's taught all of us enough of those tricks that I know I'll never forget Quinton's face, his voice, or his smile.

"Nice of you to join us," West drawls as he refills his coffee mug and snags a second from the cabinet for me. "You're lucky Ry's running late."

"What?" I scan the warehouse, convinced the former Navy SEAL is fucking with me, but Ryker isn't here. Inara's working through some yoga poses on a mat across the room, earbuds firmly in place, but the man who brought us all together? He's nowhere to be found. "Is he okay?"

West shrugs. "As far as I know. Saw him Thursday."

Inara rises with the grace of a dancer and pads over to the little kitchenette. "He texted me last night and asked me if I knew of anyone else we could bring in to Hidden Agenda. Maybe he and Dax are finally making good on their plans to grow the business?"

West tosses her a bottle of water from the fridge and jerks his head towards the boxing ring. "Well, Ry or no Ry, we still need to train. Which one of you am I taking down first?"

AT EXACTLY 9:45 A.M., Ryker strides through the door, looking like he hasn't slept in three days. I do a double-take, and West uses the opening to drive his shoulder into my abdomen, lunge, and flip me over his bent leg.

"Sloppy," Ryker says, his voice more gravely than usual.

"And you ambling in forty-five minutes late isn't?" I ask. I shake off West's outstretched hand, slap my palms down on the mat, and swing my legs behind me to put a good two feet of distance between the two of us as I jump up.

"Not bad recovery." West nods his approval, then ducks

between the ropes. "Ry, what the fuck? The last time you were late anywhere...was *never*."

"None of your goddamn business." He slams his coffee cup down and braces his hands on the counter. "Fuck."

West and Inara stand side-by-side, a united front, with me, the new guy—despite being here almost three years—well outside of the line of fire. Until West glances back at me with that one arched brow. I don't know how the man does it. Do they teach that look in BUD/S? The one that says "Do what I say right the fuck now or I'll kill you without breaking a sweat"?

I join them, and Inara elbows me in the side. *"What?"* I mouth until I see that she and West are mirror images of one another. Arms crossed over their chests, standing ramrod straight, twin expressions of resolve on their faces. *Seriously? Is this some sort of intervention? Oh my God. This is an intervention. A legitimate serious-as-fuck intervention.*

Ryker might be in charge of Hidden Agenda, but no one fucks with the SEAL. And Inara? She's got more long-range kills than any man currently on active duty. So I follow orders, adopting the same stance and expression, and wait.

"Want to try that again?" West asks. "Because family doesn't keep secrets and then claim it's nobody's fucking business."

Ry scrubs his face with his hands, then slowly and deliberately reaches for the coffee pot. "Don't ask. Just...give me some space with this."

"The last time you needed 'space' with something, you disappeared, then called Inara from *Russia*. I postponed my wedding. Inara had to drive six hours from the middle of fucking Iowa to get to the nearest base with a transport plane. So, no. You don't get 'space' to 'figure shit out' with us."

Ryker turns, and his normally ruddy complexion is so pale, the scars that cover the left side of his face stand out even more than usual. The three of us have to stare up at him—the dude's only a couple of inches short of seven feet tall, and shit. The look in his eyes is nothing but pure, unadulterated terror.

He reaches into his back pocket, pulls out a small piece of paper, and stares at it like it's in a foreign language—one of the seven he *doesn't* speak. And then he thrusts it at West.

"Holy fuck." The SEAL's voice takes on a reverent tone, and Inara draws in a sharp breath. It takes me a full three seconds to process what's in the photo.

"Wren's...?" I can't finish the sentence. Not when the man who's never been afraid of a single fucking thing is standing in front of me like the whole world just fell out from beneath his feet.

"Nine weeks," he says, nodding at the sonogram picture. "That's...where I was. At the doctor."

"Is she okay?" Inara asks. "It's...she's...healthy?" At West's pointed glare, she rolls her eyes. "I don't know anything about this shit. Do you? Either of you?"

I hold up my hands and take a step back. "I was halfway across the world when my sister was pregnant. Didn't come back until her son was almost two."

"The doc says Wren's fine. The...um..." Ry stares down at the black and white picture again and shakes his head.

"Baby?" West supplies.

"Yeah. It's...'tracking normally'?" Rubbing his bald head, he snorts. "I don't know what the fuck that means. But there's a heartbeat. And it was moving around."

The man's clearly in shock. I've never heard him so uncertain, so out of his element. Wren's his whole world. So much so that before he met her, he didn't think any of us should *have* lives outside of Hidden Agenda. Told me when I joined that I better not fall in love. Ever. Of course, less than a month later, Inara and Royce got together. West and Cam were a couple before West signed on to do this job, so Ry didn't have a say in that.

We stand around in awkward silence until I clear my throat. "Congratulations, Ryker. Ry. Sir."

Shit. Get it together, dude. This is your fucking boss.

Despite me sticking my foot in my mouth so deep I could kick my own ass—or maybe because of it—Ryker shakes off the mix of fear, wonder, and love that has him so bound up and laughs. "Jesus Fuck, Graham. You're part of this family whether you like it or not. You can drop the 'Sir' bullshit."

He doesn't hug anyone. Or high-five. Or even smile. I'm not sure he knows how. But he's lighter now. And when the photo's safely tucked back in his wallet, he leans against the counter and takes a long drag of his coffee. "Whenever we go on mission, I write Wren a letter. Drop 'em in the mail when we land. Easier, y'know? Then having *that* conversation?"

We all nod. Despite not having a serious relationship in... well...ever, I know what he means. The conversation about how we might not come home. About how what we do is dangerous as fuck. How no government in the world sanctions our work. How we could fail and every single one of us could just...disappear.

"When we went to get Trev..." He shakes his head again and stares up at the ceiling. "Of all the missions I've run—including every one the four of us have been on together—that was the least certain I've been that we'd make it back."

I don't know that I've ever heard Ry talk this much at one time unless he was giving orders.

"I asked her if she wanted...if she'd ever wanted..." A shrug, and he swallows hard. "Only time I've ever been this scared in my life was in Russia. Hell doesn't hold a fucking candle to this."

Moving almost as a unit, the three of us take positions around our tough-as-nails leader. Even though Ry's in charge, even though he's the reason we're all here, West is the glue that holds us together. Maybe it's his position—logistics. Infil and exfil. Strategy. Maybe it's his background as a SEAL team leader. Or maybe he's just better at talking about his feelings than the rest of us.

Whatever it is, Inara and me? We follow his lead. So when he claps Ry on the shoulder, we do too. You'd think it'd be awkward, but the man's shoulders are massive.

"You're not alone, Ry," West says, and under the reassuring tone, I think there's a small measure of longing. "No one in this family is *ever* alone."

THREE HOURS LATER, I'm flat on the concrete floor, covered in sweat, watching Ryker decimate West on the obstacle course. I came damn close to beating Inara, which is a victory of epic proportions for me. I'm younger than the rest of them by at least five years, but West and Ry live for this shit, and Inara? Her past haunts her. The guy I replaced on the team, Coop, was captured on a mission where she hesitated. Just for a second, but that was long enough. Everyone thought he was dead until he kidnapped Inara's husband, Royce, and almost killed him. So she pushes herself harder than any of us.

"Now who's late, frogman?" Ry taunts from the other end of the massive building where he just crawled out of a makeshift tunnel so narrow, I was certain he'd get stuck.

"Not me." West taps his stopwatch as he gets to his feet next to Ryker. "I was almost an hour into the workout when you showed up. This wasn't a fair fight."

"Life isn't fair." Grabbing a towel from the stack by the lockers, Ryker rubs the sweat from his bald head and drapes the white cloth around his neck. "Get used to it."

West says something I can't make out, but I'm pretty sure I wouldn't repeat it in polite company.

After draining half a bottle of water, Ryker tells us to hit the showers and take an hour before we start the mental portion of today's workout—a handful of new tactical challenges planning infil and exfil for locations generated at random by one of Wren's algorithms.

Late September in Seattle brings changing leaves, but also one last heat wave, and the warehouse is like a fucking sauna. So I turn the water all the way to cold and step under the spray.

This day is unfolding like some twisted form of reality. Every time we took even a five minute break, my thoughts turned to Quinton. I'm fantasizing about the guy, despite seeing him for less than five minutes, and Ryker McCabe, the toughest, meanest son of a bitch ever to come out of this country's army—or any other country's army for that matter—is going to have a kid?

All I need now is for Inara to hug me and we'll be in full-on bizarro world.

Despite the icy water, my dick still twitches to life as Quinton's face flashes behind my eyes. This is ridiculous. I'm never going to see the guy again. For all I know, he's not gay. Even if he were, I can't have a serious relationship. I don't want one.

I won't subject anyone to my random panic attacks, the nightmares that haunt me when I get low, my complete inability to let a guy top me—ever.

The occasional Tinder hookup has to be it for me. And if I didn't work for Hidden Agenda, I wouldn't even have that. At least with the resources we have access to, I can run a background check on any guy I might swipe right on *before* we meet up.

The dates are all the same. Drinks, then back to his place or a hotel room for a quick fuck where I top—non-negotiable—and then an apology the next day. Bartending's a hard job, no flexibility, grueling schedule, some shit like that. Once in a while, I try the truth: I'm not in a "relationship" sort of space right now and probably never will be, that sort of thing.

So why can't I stop thinking about Quinton?

By the time I'm dressed in black jeans and a t-shirt, I've mostly put him out of my mind. Until I check my email. It doesn't have my real name attached to it. Nor do the paychecks I get from the Unicorn. When I joined Hidden Agenda, I was new to Seattle, and Ryker insisted I let him set me up with a cover story. A whole public identity separate from my government-issued, had-since-birth name and social security number.

"Peck, what we do is both highly specialized and highly illegal. We get made, we're on every single watch list around the world in under fifteen minutes. Trouble on a mission? No one comes to save us. You want in, there's a price."

"What price?" I ask. Ryker McCabe is a legend. He survived Hell because he was too stubborn to die. Too tough to kill. Too determined to make it back home. Working with him? It's both unbelievably dangerous and the safest place I could ever be. Because based on the stories I've heard, he doesn't let anyone mess with his team.

"In public, from now until the end of fucking time, you give up the name Peck. I know a guy who can set you up with a brand new identity and cover. Something simple. A job that lets you take off at a moment's notice. Waiter. Substitute teacher. Because when someone needs us, we go. Middle of the night, Thanksgiving, Christmas... doesn't matter." He stares me down, his multi-hued eyes as hard as the rest of him. "I already have a SEAL and a former Ranger sniper who have ties to the community. If I could move this whole operation to London or Dubai and take them with me, I would. Start over. Give them new lives. But they won't leave, and I can't ask them to. You, however...you follow my rules. All of them. Including no relation-ships." He practically sneers the last word, and I clench my hands on my thighs under the table. "That a problem?"

"No, sir. Got no interest in relationships. Do I get to pick the new name and the profession? Or is that all you?"

"That's your only question?" His brows shoot up, and he sits back in his chair.

I shrug. "Waiting tables isn't my thing. Been there, done that. But I can mix drinks that'll knock your socks off."

With a snort, Ryker shakes his head then offers me his hand. "Bartending it is. Welcome to the team."

Becoming Graham Tempelton was ridiculously simple. A couple of photos taken against a white wall, a set of finger-prints, and a whole lot of cash, and in less than a week, I started looking for an apartment with my new name and applying for bartending gigs.

How the hell did Quinton find me?

I only told him my first name, and there are a lot of Grahams in this city. I'm halfway through a less than civil reply when I remember the ice cream. And the credit card I used to purchase it. I don't remember what I did with the receipt.

My second attempt at a message is a little less...intense. But I have to know if I compromised myself somehow. Or if Quinton—Q—is someone I should tell Ry and Wren about.

So, this is going to sound weird, but...how'd you find me?

Less than five minutes later, he replies.

You left the receipt in the bag. I Googled. Your website came right up. I'm sorry. I didn't mean to intrude. You won't hear from me again. - Q

Fuck.

Glancing around the warehouse, I check to make sure Ryker's not standing over my shoulder about to pounce. I probably look guilty as fuck. But he's on the phone, and I overhear him ask, "What do you need? West can run the drills—" And then a moment later, "I *know* it's just morning sickness. Doesn't mean I have to like it."

I can't wait to see him change a diaper.

Returning my focus to the screen, I try ten different replies before I settle on what I hope is the right one. I shouldn't care. But Q looked so lost standing at his door last night, and the idea that I hurt him doesn't sit well with me.

You said no one's ever been that nice to you? If that's the truth, you need better friends. And I'm sorry. I didn't mean to jump down your throat. I was just surprised you tracked me down, that's all. Did you get your groceries replaced?

-Graham

It's nothing. A quick, light message with an apology. Because whatever his deal is? I don't want to make it worse.

I rush to close down the browser as Ry strides over to the corner of the warehouse Wren and Ripper helped us turn into a tech hub, complete with workstations for each of us, a massive rack of servers, and a dedicated high-speed internet connection faster than anyone but the United States government.

But as the window disappears, another reply shows up, and the preview rattles me for reasons I can't take the time to unpack right now.

I gave up on friends a long time ago. And people in general. Thanks again for the ice cream. - Q

CHAPTER SEVEN

Quinton

A LITTLE AFTER NOON, my watch timer goes off, and I swat at it like it's a mosquito about to bite me. Clementine opens one eye from the little cat bed I put next to my computer monitor.

"No, it's not dinner time."

With a big sigh, she goes back to sleep. I swear, this kitten is the most melodramatic creature on the planet. But she's been my constant companion since I first rescued her, and when I freak out, she helps calm me down.

I need to get up. To move. No matter how much it hurts. When Connor saved me, I couldn't manage more than a couple of steps at a time. Now, on my good days, I can do almost everything I used to—except run and balance on one foot.

Today's not a good day, though, and I repeat one of the mantras that help keep me motivated when the pain's at its worst.

You're strong. You survived. Don't let him win.

An electric shock zings down my left leg as I brace myself

on the arms of the chair, forcing me to blow out a deep breath. My physical therapist would tell me to take a pain pill, but they make me feel loopy, and I can't let my judgement be compromised in any way.

The last time I took one, I found myself on *his* Facebook page. My intention? Make sure he was still living in Dallas. But I wasn't being careful, and almost hit the *message* button. I flushed all the pills down the toilet after that.

Another two minutes, and I'm standing. Wrapping my hands around the handles of my walker, I shuffle slowly and deliberately down the short hallway to the first floor bedroom. I converted the space into a home gym not long after moving in. Well, I didn't, but two of my PT's friends did.

Cursing at the treadmill as I climb on, I set it for the ridiculously low speed of two miles an hour and flip on the little television mounted on the wall.

One episode of *The Office* and I can stop.

Each step sends more sparks racing up and down my back and legs, but by the time the show's over, my muscles have loosened up enough that I'm almost steady.

"You'll never be a hundred percent again, Quinton," Jack, my rehab coordinator, says to me as I stare out the window at the rain. "But if you keep working the program when you get out of here, you can probably make it to a solid seventy."

"What the fuck is seventy percent?" I spit out. "Only falling three out of every ten steps? Because that's not acceptable. I want my life back."

My life. Back then—two months after I escaped Alec—I thought I'd *have* a life again. Snorting as I flip off the TV, I make it to the weight bench without the walker, and sink down to start working my quads.

After every exercise, I make notes in the little booklet I share with my current PT, Manny. He's the best in Seattle, and while I can barely afford him, he's one of the few therapists who offers in-home visits. I need to take back control of my own body. To feel something close to *normal* again. Alec didn't just steal months of my life. He robbed me of something even more precious.

Any hope of trusting myself—or anyone else—ever again.

THE CLIENT I've been working for this past month is thrilled with the website I built, and our final video call is tinged with a hint of sadness on my end. Each time I finish a project and say goodbye to these small glimpses into the outside world—into other people's worlds—I fight a new bout of depression. A fresh reminder that I'm alone and always will be.

At least I already have two new projects lined up that will carry me through the holidays. The idea of spending those dark months all alone—the short days, the endless nights— leaves me hollow.

If I were stronger...

No. Don't go there, Q.

"If you need anything else, Rebecca," I say, forcing my smile to match the client's expression on screen, "you know how to reach me."

"Quinton?" Her eyes narrow slightly, and she leans closer to her camera. "You take care of yourself now. I mean it. While I appreciate you making time for me on a Saturday, weekends should be for relaxing. I'm going to need your help again in February, and you'd better not still be so pale. Get some sun. Take a vacation. Anything but work yourself to death." Rebecca carries herself like a grandmother, despite not being much older than I am, and when she shakes her finger at me, I chuckle.

"I'll try. I promise. I have you all scheduled for the second

Monday in February, and I'll send over the contract by the end of next week. Don't forget to tell me when you announce the rebrand so I can help you spread the word."

We say our goodbyes, and before I shut down my workstation, my gaze flicks to my email.

Nothing new. Not from anyone I want to talk to, anyway.

Like Graham.

The words bounce around in my head before I can stop them. Followed quickly by self-loathing and frustration.

Well, maybe if you hadn't been a dick to him... For fuck's sake, Q. How would you feel if someone tracked you down from an ice cream receipt?

Answer? I would have fallen into a panic attack so severe, nothing would have been able to pull me out. Before I moved to Seattle, my brother and my lawyer helped set me up with a new identity. Quinton Davis disappeared, and Quinton Silver was "born." Along with a corporation—Silver Star Technologies—that signed the lease on this townhouse, pays the utilities, and handles all of my banking needs. There's no way Alec should ever be able to find me, but that doesn't stop me from looking over my shoulder—figuratively—every single day.

And yet, I tracked down a guy who didn't give me his last name just because he brought me ice cream. I should have known better. Hell, I shouldn't have messaged him at all. My time with Alec not only left me physically broken, it shrunk my world down to these four walls. I lost most of my friends to that asshole's lies. The few who stuck around? Or who led me to believe they stuck around? Well, I messaged one of them before I left the rehab facility for Seattle, and two days later, Alec showed up at Thatcher House, demanding to see me. The security guards called the police, but the officers didn't want to do a damn thing—even though he'd violated the restraining order I had against him.

"He didn't threaten you, Mr. Davis."

"The security guards had to subdue him! When he finally agreed to leave the building, he sat in his car across the street staring at Thatcher House for three hours. How is that not a threat?"

"Don't engage with him and you'll be fine."

I'm never going to *engage* with Alec again. But that means cutting off contact with anyone who might even *think* he's an okay guy. And narcissists? Sociopaths? They can fool almost anyone—for a while.

Shutting down my computer, I head for the kitchen. I can't even handle microwaving a frozen dinner tonight. After filling Clementine's bowl, I pull the rest of the mint chip out of the freezer and head upstairs. A Netflix marathon is all I have the energy for.

~

Graham

After eight fucking hours at Hidden Agenda running drill after drill after drill, all I want is a beer and a couple of slices of pizza from Big Mario's. And to get my head on straight.

Quinton's last email burned itself into my brain, and I can't stop thinking about him.

"I gave up on friends a long time ago. And people in general."

What the hell happened to this guy that he doesn't have friends? Or...anyone in his life?

The line at Big Mario's is out the door, so I pull out my phone and switch over to my email. I shouldn't reply. He probably wants to be left alone. But the pain in his voice last night, the raw desperation, the need...I can't ignore it. Or walk away. Not yet. Not without one more question. Or...three.

"Why? Why did you give up on people? On friends?"

Half an hour later, I code myself into my apartment. The

security system is more sophisticated than anything on the market today—courtesy of West's wife and computer genius, Cam Delgado.

Despite the tech, the building is old, which means large, spacious units. After my first couple of missions with Hidden Agenda, I moved into the top-floor east-facing space with almost fifteen hundred square feet and a view of the entire neighborhood.

Grabbing a bottle of Coke from the fridge, I sink down onto the couch with the pizza box. I ended up with a whole pie because...well...why the fuck not? After hours of grueling workouts this morning, I've earned it.

My phone dings with a new email, and when Quinton's name flashes across the screen, I almost choke on a sip of soda.

"Because my friends gave up on me."

Shit. I drop my second slice and thumb out a reply, then delete it. What do you say to a message like that?

I want to tell him that true friends don't give up on people. But then I think about Ripper. Ry and Dax thought he was dead. For six fucking years. They never would have given up on him had they known the truth, and it haunts them. Hell, Rip gave up and stopped fighting when his captor made him believe Ry and Dax had been killed.

Giving up isn't always a choice.

It takes me another full slice to decide what to say.

"Sometimes, people are complete dicks. But other times, they're up against a wall with no escape. Either way, you need new friends. Ones who stick around."

~

A LITTLE AFTER 10:00 p.m., I'm in bed with my laptop reviewing schematics for the new surveillance tech Cam, Royce, and

Wren have been working on for the past few months. Wireless cameras smaller than a pack of gum and a receiver that can fit on any standard bookcase. Pretty sophisticated stuff. We sent the first batch of them to Second Sight last week, and from what I hear, Ronan and Clive are using them on some op with Austin Pritchard.

Never expected Austin to reach out after Venezuela. Despite what he did for Ripper—giving him the Congressional Medal of Valor even after what Abdul Amir Faruk made him do—Austin never gave any indication he understood the meaning of family. He and Ry got into it more than once in that miserable hovel just outside of Caracas. But by the time we rescued Trevor, I think they'd found some sort of peace.

For the twentieth time tonight, I tab over to my email, and my heart starts to beat faster when I see Quinton's name.

"Are you offering?"

I can't tell if he's flirting or being sarcastic.

"To be your friend?"

The reply comes back almost immediately.

"Yes. Because I'm a shitshow, Graham. You seem like a nice guy. A really nice guy who should run away from me as fast as you can."

Well, fuck.

~

Quinton

Now I've done it. It's after midnight, and Graham hasn't replied to my last message. Not that I'm surprised. I *tried* to push him away after all. Guess I did a bang up job of it.

Seconds before I shut down the laptop for the night, my brother's name pops up on screen. Connor hasn't emailed me in months.

Quinton,

I couldn't sleep tonight. Something just felt...wrong. Went for a run around 10, and I'm pretty sure I saw Alec sitting in a car at the end of the block. He drove away before I could confirm it was him. If he's watching me, he obviously doesn't know where you are, and I'll make sure it stays that way. But be careful.

-Connor

My heart races, and I lurch into the bathroom and grab a Xanax. Alec has nothing but time. After the accident, he quit his job to "take care" of me. Even though it was my money supporting the both of us. When he lost access to my bank accounts, he went back to work at some day trading firm, but Connor—who's been keeping tabs on Alec ever since he rescued me—said he was fired after being served with the restraining order. The process server found him at his office, and his boss...well...apparently it didn't go over well.

Alec stalked Connor for two months. Until my brother threatened to beat the shit out of him.

The Xanax starts to take effect, but my back is locked up tight from the strain. My fingers aren't steady, but I send Connor a quick reply.

If you see him again, call the police. Get it on the record—even though they won't be able to do anything. I'm sorry you have to deal with this. - Q

I only have another five minutes before the meds *force* me to relax—by way of making me so loopy, the only thing I'll be able to do is sleep, but I email the last detective assigned to my case to give him an update. I don't even know if he's still working in Dallas. It's been a year, after all. But I have to try.

Alec won't hurt Connor. My brother's built like a tank, and thanks to his years in the army, he's got that scary-as-fuck look down pat. But stalking Connor is a way to get to me. To still hurt me even though we're half a country apart.

As I drift off to sleep, my thoughts fractured by the Xanax and exhaustion, I decide it's a very good thing I drove Graham away. He doesn't need to see what a complete mess I am. And if Alec does decide to try to find me again? Graham would just be one more target he could use to get to me.

CHAPTER EIGHT

Quinton

Despite how poorly I slept, I'm determined to have a good day. My next client project doesn't start for a full week, so I can spend every minute putting the finishing touches on my anti-anxiety app, Zen Oasis.

Alec convinced me I'd never be able to write code again, and if I'd stayed with him? I'd have given up my dream completely. But six months ago, my therapist suggested I start working on it again, and as soon as I opened up the old files, I realized how important it was for me to finish the damn thing. Not only because I think it'll help people, but because it's one final "fuck you" to the man who almost killed me.

Checking in with the beta testing group for Zen Oasis boosts my mood even more. They all love it, and while I have a few new bugs to fix, they're minor. If I can keep my own anxiety in check, I might be able to submit the final product to all the mobile app stores in just a few days.

The latest message waiting in my inbox would have me bouncing in my chair if my body were capable of it.

"This app is changing my life. Every time I've had an anxiety attack in the past week, I've played Zen Oasis, and it's kept me from landing in full-on panic mode. Thanks, Quinton!"

It's almost noon before I take a break, and when I open the front door to get yesterday's mail, sunlight warms my cheeks. For a moment, I stand perfectly still, braced against the door jamb, one foot inside, one foot on the porch. My heart rate spikes as a car passes by, and my instincts scream at me to get back inside.

It's only one more step to the mailbox. You can do this.

The street's quiet now, and Clementine lets out a yowl from the kitchen, demanding to be fed.

I didn't manage to get this far yesterday. Scanning the street one more time, seeing no one, I lift the lid of the antique mailbox, grab the pile of envelopes and junk mail inside, and rush —as best as I can—back to the safety behind my locked door.

Clementine ambles down the hall, stops halfway between me and the kitchen, sits, and watches me with that look only cats are capable of. The *Why aren't you feeding me? Don't you love me anymore?* look.

"I'm getting there, sweetie." And I am. Until I glance down at the catalog clutched in my hands. My stomach lurches, and my back hits the door before I sink down to the ground.

Rodeo Vibe Apparel

The guy on the cover is posing in profile, hands on his hips, dark blue denim molding to his ass, a flannel shirt open and clearly blowing in the breeze. It's the company's signature look. A variation of it graces every catalog they've ever sent, and I know because this was the *only* place Alec ever shopped. The only place he let *me* shop the whole time we were together.

I don't want to turn the catalog over. Don't want to see the address. And when I do? A sob sticks in my throat and I can't breathe.

It's addressed to me. Not my company. Me. By name. My *new* name. Quinton Silver.

There's no way Alec could have found me. I've been careful. So careful. But how else would the company get my name?

Clementine crawls into my lap and starts kneading my thigh, her purr so loud, I can hear it over my own wheezing. Scooping her up, I let her paws go to work on my shoulder, and she *mrrps* softly, rubbing her head against my cheek.

I never thought a cat could keep me from totally losing my shit, but this one...it's like she knows just what I need. Maybe because she was starving when I found her, soaked to the skin from a summer rainstorm. Or because I held her almost constantly for the first two days trying to keep her warm and get her to eat.

Whatever made her this way, I'm grateful as fuck. After a few minutes—and more than one wince as I really need to trim her nails—my chest loosens slightly and I think I'm strong enough to make it to the kitchen where I keep a stash of my anxiety medication.

"You'll look so good in this shirt, Quint."

"Your wardrobe needs some serious help."

"I am not moving all of those frumpy old man jeans into my place. You're getting new ones."

Flashbacks hit me with every step. All the times Alec put me down under the guise of trying to help me. The back-handed compliments. The gentle reproach. The *suggestions* that sounded encouraging, but really, were like death by a thousand cuts. Or a thousand criticisms.

I'm on autopilot as I pour some kibble into Clementine's bowl, and setting it down on the floor makes my back spasm. My appetite? Completely gone.

Sorting through the rest of my mail, I don't find anything else concerning. A notice to file my corporation's annual report, my quarterly tax notice, and the ValPack coupons sent to every single household in Seattle.

The catalog is the *only* item addressed to me. I want to shred it. To tear out each page, crumple them up—as violently as I can—and burn them. But though I might find a sliver of comfort doing so, it won't answer the most important question.

How did I get on their mailing list with this address? All of Quinton Silver's mail goes to a PO Box in Dallas. One my brother has checked every few weeks. If there's anything important, he packages it up and sends it to me here, but he always uses my company's name. Never mine.

I wish I could call Connor. Or...anyone. But my brother never answers his phone. He claims all I have to do is text him and he'll get back to me the moment he's free, but I don't want to bother him for something so...minor.

So I send him an email, then call Rodeo Vibe Apparel and ask them to remove me from their mailing list immediately.

After that, I give up on work for the day, stretch out in my massage chair with Clementine curled up next to me, and pop in my earbuds. My therapist keeps suggesting meditation, and though I feel like a failure at it, I try at least once a week.

As the peaceful music surrounds me and the heat starts to loosen my tight muscles, I will myself to relax.

You're safe. You have a kick-ass security system with cameras everywhere, and Alec's two thousand miles away.

I wish I believed my own self-talk. Because I don't know how else Rodeo Vibe would have gotten my address. But why now? And more importantly...what is my psychopathic ex going to do next?

AN HOUR LATER, I'm only slightly calmer, but at least my pain level is back to normal, so I spend the rest of the work day perfecting Zen Oasis. Fixing the last remaining bugs requires me to actually play the game, and that alone helps tamp down my anxiety.

Until the doorbell rings a little after six. Is the Universe just fucking with me? Or does she just have a sick sense of humor?

Pulling out my phone, I check the video feed, and my entire body flushes with heat.

Graham. Standing on my porch with a paper bag in one hand and an ice cream cone in the other. I'm mesmerized when he takes a lick, and my pants get a little tighter. No. A lot tighter. I shouldn't answer. He's a distraction. And if Alec is after me again, anything that stops me from focusing on my own safety is a huge risk.

But when he stares directly at the camera and smiles, any hope of ignoring him vanishes. So I tap the intercom button.

"What—" my voice isn't doing me any favors, so I clear my throat and try again. "What are you doing here?"

He takes another lick from the cone and shrugs. "Honestly, I don't know. But there's this place up the street, Sue's Scoops? Most days, there's a line out the door and around the corner. But they have an app, and you can order ahead." He lifts the cone slightly. "Thin Mint Chip. It's basically crushed up Girl Scout cookies with dark chocolate chips. I brought you some."

By this time, I'm at the front door, and my heart's pounding. Too fast and too hard. I don't do this. Don't talk to people face to face. Don't willingly invite anyone inside.

Resting my forehead against the wood, I pause, eyes on the screen in my hand.

It's just ice cream.

After you told him to run away.

He came back. With ice cream.

"Quinton?" Uncertainty pinches Graham's brows, creating this sexy little furrow. "There are two pints in here. I'll leave them on the porch."

Do something!

My inner voice, the one that warned me every fucking day to get away from Alec? It isn't telling me to run and hide now. It's screaming at me to do the exact opposite. Because this guy seems nice. And I could use...nice. Even if it's just for five minutes.

Graham sets the bag down, and I punch the button for the intercom. "Wait."

My hands shake as I flip the locks, and I take a couple of deep breaths so he won't see how panicked I truly am.

Just keep it together for a few minutes. Long enough to thank him. And to apologize for being suck a dick over email. Then you can go back to being...pathetic.

Words fail me with him so close. He's bigger than I thought. Wearing a black t-shirt stretched across a broad chest, ink peeking out from the sleeve to wind down his right arm. From what I can see, he's completely ripped. Like almost body-builder ripped.

Dude must get killer tips at the bar.

And then he takes another lick from that fucking ice cream cone. "Sorry," he says with a sheepish grin, and his cheeks flush. "Should have eaten faster."

"It's...you're...I mean...shit." I'm leaning against the door frame like it's the only thing keeping me upright—and it probably is.

"Want a bite?" He's still grinning as he offers me the cone. Whatever my face does in response must be horrible because Graham's smile falters. "More for me, then. These are for you." He offers me the bag, but I almost fall over taking a step forward.

And then his hand cups my elbow, his fingers warm and strong. "Whoa. You okay?"

"Fine. This is my normal." I should pull away, but fuck. I haven't been touched—outside of my PT and doctors—in over a year, and this guy even smells good. Like bay rum. But his gaze is full of questions, and I don't have any idea how much I can—or should—tell him. "Bad fall a little over a year ago. Couldn't walk for more than three months."

"Fuck, dude. That's why the groceries...?"

Yeah, let's go with that. Admitting to agoraphobia isn't exactly sexy.

"One of the reasons."

Pull away, Q. Before you do something you regret. Like invite him in.

I can't seem to move from the spot or do anything to dislodge his hand from my arm, and if I'm honest with myself, I don't want to. Fuck it.

"Do you, uh...want to come in? I should put the ice cream in the freezer."

Say no. Please say no.

Having him in my space is dangerous. But if I make him stand out on the porch any longer, he's going to keep licking that cone, and my heart is going to keep racing and...

"If it's okay. Or point me towards your kitchen and I can take care of the ice cream."

"I'm not an invalid." The words escape sharper than I intend, and Graham drops his hand. Shit. I cringe and blow out a breath. "Sorry. Reflex. The kitchen's straight back."

One advantage to letting him in? I get to watch his ass as he strides down the hall. As soon as he disappears, I shut the door and limp over to the couch.

Graham calls out, "Want a bowl?"

"Pretty sure you have at least two bites left in that cone. Or was that a limited-time offer?"

What the hell am I doing? Flirting?

His laugh carries, and dammit. I want to hear it again. "Fair enough."

I track every one of his steps back to the couch, and he stops in front of me, the cone held at the perfect angle for me to take a bite. This has to be one of the hottest things a guy's ever done, and as I taste the soft mint, I'm so turned on, it's actively painful.

"You can finish it, if you want." His voice is huskier now, deeper, and he's still standing there, but now there's a very distinctive bulge under his board.

Shit. I can't keep leading the guy on when there's no way I can legitimately start anything with him. "No. I'm good, thanks." Sitting back, I straighten my shoulders and try to regain a measure of composure while he polishes off the last two bites.

And then Clementine jumps into my lap, her tiny paws landing right on my not-so-limp dick. Hissing out a breath, I try not to let Graham see just how much pain I'm in—or why.

"Who's this?" he asks, crouching down to give the kitten a scritch behind her ears. The little traitor starts to purr, but all I can see is how close his hand is to my junk. How strong his fingers are. How gentle he's being with my kitten.

"Clementine. She's a little needy."

"She's certainly little." He stares from me to the cat and back again. "And cute."

I don't have a response. Not an appropriate one anyway. All the things running through my head? Variations of "you should go" and "I can't do this" and "she's cute, but you're breathtaking."

Fuck. I want him to go almost as much as I want him to stay, and from the look on his face, he's just as confused as I am.

After another minute, he stands and shoves his hands into his pockets with a frown. "Well, I guess that's it, then," he says. "Have a good night, Quinton. I'll see you around. Maybe." He turns, and by this point, I don't know which end is up.

"I'm sorry," I blurt out, grunting as I stand so we're mostly eye to eye. I have a couple of inches on him, though where I'm wiry and thin, he's the exact opposite. Solid. Strong. *Safe.*

He shakes his head, then runs a hand through his short, dark brown hair. "You don't owe me an apology. Or...anything. I ran by the ice cream shop earlier and I couldn't stop thinking about your email messages. I know what it's like to have your friends disappear on you. And I guess I wanted to tell you that."

Something flickers in his blue eyes. Darkness, pain, regret? I don't know him well enough to be sure. I want to, though.

"It was a dick move searching you out from your receipt. If someone had done that to me, I'd have freaked the fuck out. I didn't apologize well enough for it yesterday, and I should have."

"Why'd you do it?" Graham holds my gaze, and the intensity burning in his eyes unnerves me. And makes me want more. I don't think there's a dishonest bone in his body. He carries himself with pride. Honor, even. Shoulders back, legs slightly spread, hands still in his pockets.

"I don't know." His lips press together, and I rush to continue. "What I said about friends—and people in general—that's my life. Has been for a while now. And, what you did? Helping me? Coming back? It made me realize how fucked up that is."

"So what *do* you want? Because the vibe you're giving off is more than just 'let's be friends.'"

"It doesn't matter." The finality of the words is like a physical weight punching me in the gut, and I think Graham senses it too. "*Wanting?* Anything? That's a risk I can't take."

Graham's so close I feel the warmth radiating from his chest. "Risks are what make life worth living." Strong fingers cup the back of my head, his other hand molds to my hip, and then those firm lips are kissing me. Gently. He doesn't push. Doesn't demand. Doesn't try to take it deeper.

A moan vibrates in my chest, and I wrap my arms around

him. I can tell myself it's because I don't want to fall, but that's a lie. He's strong and solid and steady, but there's pain deep inside him too. Maybe he's as broken as I am.

If so, kissing him is a terrible idea. But do I stop? Hell, no.

Graham

Warning bells go off in my head, louder every second we stay locked together. But the noise Quinton makes, desperate and raw, and the solid pressure against my hip war with the fear I saw in his eyes the moment before I touched him.

I don't know a damn thing about his injuries, and if I let this go any further, I could hurt him, so I ease back just enough to meet his gaze.

And there's that look again. The one that says he wants to run. "I shouldn't have done that," I manage.

"Why not?" His arms fall from my waist, and he shuffles back a step or two, enough so he can brace a hand on the couch where the kitten is staring up at him, her tiny paws kneading the cushions like she's desperate to make him feel better.

"Because you're *terrified* right now. I'm good at reading people, Quinton. And even if I weren't? Clementine certainly is. And I won't kiss a guy who's scared of me. At least not a second time."

He flinches like I just slapped him, and fuck. If I didn't feel guilty enough already...

"I'm not scared of *you*," he says quietly. "I'm scared of everything else. I don't talk to people. I never invite anyone inside. But for some reason not only did I do both with you, I kissed you back." He shakes his head like he can't figure me—or himself—out.

Honesty, at least. I know when people lie to me. Got pretty

damn good at knowing after Ry, West, and Inara started teaching me the signs. Eye movements. Fidgeting. Slight changes in speech patterns. In tone of voice. In a person's sweat. Their respiration rate.

"So where do we go from here?" I can't just walk away. Not until I get some clarity. Or Quinton asks me to go.

"Well, I think we can probably skip the whole 'So, you're gay?' discussion."

I laugh, but it's a nervous laugh. One that does nothing to actually break the tension between us. "Good point. Though you could be bi. Not that it matters to me."

"I'm not."

"But you're still scared." I reach for him, and proving my point, he stiffens the instant my fingers brush his cheek. "If you don't even want me to touch you, this isn't going to work."

He lowers his gaze, and mine follows, landing on the rather obvious bulge in his loose pants. "Didn't think you were blind."

This time, I can't manage to do anything but ball my hands into fists and shove them into my pockets. "Fucking and touching are two different things. And while I've done the former more than once the past few years, that's not why I came here today. I haven't stopped thinking about you since we met. Not because I want a casual fuck, but because for some reason, you're the first person in a really long time I want to touch. To know. I'll take things as slow as you want, but you've got to give me *something*, Quinton. Talk to me."

He scrubs his hands over his face, and it's so obvious he's been hurt. Badly. By someone he trusted. If I could, I'd find the asshole and...well, probably do something I'd regret later.

"Slow." The word is barely audible, strained, and the plea in his voice? I'm not sure I can resist it. "I can try...slow."

He meets my gaze, and all those emotions I saw a moment ago are still there, but behind them, I think I see a glimmer of hope.

"I have to be at work in two hours. Shift at the Unicorn tonight. Let me give you my phone number, okay? Texting is slow. We can start there. Maybe work our way up to coffee."

He nods and passes me his phone. Once I add my number, I press the device back into his palm and let my hand linger on his for a long moment. "Text me so I have your number too?"

When he sends me an ice cream cone emoji, I chuckle and save the number. "You signed your email Q. Do you prefer that to Quinton? Or Quint?"

All of a sudden, he shuts down. Like a switch. Like someone slammed a lid, trapping all his emotions, everything that makes him a person, deep inside.

"Not Quint," he whispers. "Anything but Quint. Fuck. This...was a mistake. You should go. I'm a bad bet. Always have been, always will be. I'm sorry, Graham."

Quinton scoops up the kitten, holding her to his chest, and limps awkwardly to the door. He fumbles for the locks, only to realize they were all open, then mutters under his breath, "How could I have been so stupid?"

"Stupid? Q, Quinton, tell me what's wrong." I don't raise my voice. He's scared enough as it is.

"I can't. Please. Go."

Every protective instinct in me rears to life at the pain in his voice, but if I say anything, do anything but leave, I'll lose him forever. Hell, from the look in his eyes, I already have.

He shuts the door so quickly, it almost hits me in the ass, and I know I should walk away and never look back. But I can't.

"Q?" I press my palm to the door, hoping he can still hear me. "You know how to find me. Whatever I did wrong...fuck." There's nothing I can say to chase the abject terror from his eyes. "Just know I'm sorry."

My heart aches as I walk away from the closest thing to a romantic connection I've had with another man in years. I'm almost two blocks away when my eyes start to burn and a lump forms in my throat.

It's better this way. Ry and Dax want to expand Hidden Agenda, and that means a larger team. I don't need any more complications in my life. Especially one who's too scared to talk to me.

Then why, with every step I take, is my inner voice telling me I'm full of shit?

CHAPTER NINE

Quinton

"You know how to find me."

Sharp pain zings up my left leg, pulling me out of my thoughts. "Dammit, Manny."

"Scale of one to ten? How bad is it today?" my physical therapist asks. Despite the concern in his voice, he doesn't stop digging his knuckles into my hamstring. The man's a sadist. Of course, that's what I pay him for.

"Seven," I grunt. "It's been a good couple of days. Are you *trying* to ruin my streak?"

"I'm trying to maintain it, Mr. Silver." Pressing even harder, he waits until I yelp, then eases off a bit. "You know the only way to keep making progress is through hard work."

"Sadist."

"I prefer the term 'dedicated.'"

Shit. I said that out loud? I'm off my game. Unsurprising as I've been thinking about Graham nonstop for three days. I tried to text him. A dozen times or more. But I deleted every single one.

Despite replaying that kiss on a loop. In the shower. While jerking off.

"Sorry." I turn my head to catch his eye. "I know you're just doing your job."

"A job you pay me handsomely for." His dark hair falls over his forehead, and he studies me. "So what's got you so wound up?"

"Work."

"Yeah, right." He grabs a towel and wipes his hands. "You're done, kid. No more torture for today. Bonus, you get a break for the next two weeks. I'm taking a seminar on advanced kinesiology out in Atlanta, so I'll miss our next session. Don't suppose you'd let me send Carl?"

Panic crawls up my spine, and I roll over on his portable massage table, then struggle to sit up. "No. Only you." The idea of anyone else in my safe space terrifies me, even though I've known Manny for months now. "I can't—"

"Relax." Manny offers me his hand to help me off the table and steadies me until my legs agree to support me again. "You'll be fine for two weeks. Just keep up with your daily exercises. Listen to your body. Push yourself, but don't go overboard."

"Yeah. Okay." My heart is pounding, and shit. I should be better than this by now. Manny talks about Carl all the time. The guy rehabs all the local football and soccer players, and they've worked together for years. But I lurch into the bathroom, almost falling over on the way, and grab the prescription bottle with my low-dose anxiety meds. Ten minutes, and they'll kick in. Ten minutes, and I'll be okay again. Ten minutes, and I won't feel like I've lost control.

"Quinton?" Manny stands in the doorway, hands on his hips. "I know I should leave it alone. But you could save a hell of a lot of money if you'd let Carl work with you instead of me. You're more than a year post-injury. You're stable. Sure, you'll continue to make some modest improvements as long as you're consistent with your therapy, but you don't need someone with my credentials to get you there."

"I trust you." Those words...they're the hardest ones for me to say. Because I don't trust many people. Manny. Val, the woman who cleans my house every week, my therapist, and my brother, Connor. That's it. And while I may trust them, I'm not close to any of them—not even Connor. But he's the one who came to rescue me. He's the one who got me into Thatcher House and paid for all of my rehab. Not that he told me *how* he could afford that.

Manny blows out a long breath. "Fine. I won't bring it up again."

"I'll do my exercises while you're gone. No problem," I say, my hands still braced on the sink.

"It's not just your exercises. Part of your recovery is getting back out into the world. Going for a walk. Navigating the grocery store aisles. Going to a coffee shop. There are some things exercise can't do for you. Only real life can. Dealing with seams in the sidewalk. Avoiding puddles on linoleum floors. You know it rains a lot here, right?"

The damn pills aren't kicking in. Why aren't they kicking in?

Because it's only been three minutes, dumbass.

Clementine jumps up on the counter and nudges my hand with her tiny wet nose.

"I see that little one is doing well," Manny says. "She hid the last time I was here."

I had a therapy session with Manny two days after I found Clementine and I practically begged him to take her to the vet for me. Get her checked out. Make sure she was going to survive. The man went to the pet store, bought a carrier, and sat in a vet's waiting room for two hours after his last client. I panicked every minute until he came back with a very pissed off kitten, a certificate giving her a clean bill of health, two pounds of kitten food, a litter box, and a collar.

"I'm not sure she's forgiven you for kidnapping her and letting someone shove a thermometer up her ass." Joking helps diffuse a small bit of my anxiety, and Manny's chuckle chips away at it further.

"Fair enough. What did you name her again?"

"Clementine. My mom always used to buy those little Clementine oranges for Christmas. And she's the same exact color." I run my fingers along the kitten's back, and she arches and purrs under my touch. "Thanks for helping me with her."

Manny makes a vague *pshaw* sound. "I have a soft spot for animals. Especially ones that fit in my palm. But if I don't leave right now, I'm going to be late for the kids' class at Emerald City Krav Maga. At least *try* to get outside for a walk before I get back. Around the block. Just once."

I nod, even though I have no intention of doing it. Manny's a good guy. A great therapist—one of the best in the country. But he doesn't know me. Doesn't understand.

The door shuts with a finality I can't ignore. When he comes back, I'll either have to lie to him or admit the truth— that I'm never going to be able to go for a walk like a normal person. Or step inside a coffee shop without having a panic attack. Or let anyone close to me again.

Graham

I'm only the second to arrive. Ripper's sitting at Hidden Agenda's conference table, a cup of coffee at his elbow, peering at the computer screen and scowling.

"Rip? I didn't expect to see you here today."

He glances up briefly, then rolls his eyes. "Neither did I. But Ry damaged the hardline to his condo. I'm setting up a server farm here to handle some heavy processing Wren has running."

"Damaged...?" I pour myself a cup of the best damn coffee in Seattle—courtesy of West—and join him at the table.

"Uh, he's doing some construction." Ripper looks downright uncomfortable now and doesn't meet my gaze.

"Does this have something to do with the baby?"

Relief washes over him, and he sits back with a weak chuckle. "Thank fuck. I told him he couldn't keep this from the rest of you, but you know how well he listens to me. Or anyone."

"He told us last Saturday. Still can't believe it."

The man we rescued from a literal hole in Afghanistan studies me.

Jackson "Ripper" Richards served with Ryker and Dax in the Special Forces, but after six months of torture in Hell Mountain, a system of tunnels and caves deep under the Hindu Kush, Ripper disappeared. Taken by one of the tribal leaders, he was brainwashed, beaten, and forced to use his computer skills for the Taliban's gain. The world thought he was dead for six years. When we found him, he was so messed up, he didn't trust anyone. Fuck he didn't even believe that Ry and Dax were *real*.

"Something on your mind?" he asks.

Rip doesn't need to deal with my shit, so I wave him off and focus on my coffee. I haven't managed more than three hours sleep a night since that kiss with Quinton, and the urge to text him? It's almost overwhelming.

"Well, now I know you're fucked," Ripper says. "Spill it, kid."

"I'm only a few years younger than you, *probie*." He's the newest member of the team, and the only one who never leaves Seattle on a mission. When he joined us, the title of

Probie—slang for probationary—transferred from me to Ripper.

"I hate that term," he mutters. "I've got more experience in my thumb than you have in your whole body."

Despite his best effort to sound tough as nails, his tone holds a rare warmth reserved only for us and his wife, Cara. A part of him loves being hazed a little, because it reminds him that he's a part of something. That he's alive. Free. His own man.

He doesn't speak again, just sits back in his chair and stares at me like he knows I'm about to crack. And I am. His eyes are a pale blue, never at peace, never still. He's always checking his surroundings for threats, even here, one of the few places he *knows* he's safe.

"I met this guy…"

His brows arch, and a hint of a smile tugs at his lips. "Should have known. So? What's the problem?"

Taking another sip of coffee, I stare up at the ceiling and try to figure out how to put the "problem" into words. But I can't. At least, none that make any sense. "He's hiding. From me, from himself too, I think."

Ripper shuts the lid on his laptop and nods towards the kitchen. "I need more coffee. Start from the beginning."

HALF AN HOUR LATER, Ripper knows everything. Or, mostly everything. How we met. How Q's emails bounced from curt to dismissive to flirty and back again. How we kissed, and I thought we were finding some sort of middle ground when he shut down completely.

We've moved to the little sitting area. Two leather couches, a coffee table, pinball machine, and bean bag chair, along with a big screen TV. Almost like a second home. Albeit one with a boxing ring, climbing wall, and enough space to run an obstacle course the likes of which no endurance race in the world could top.

Ripper rubs the back of his neck and presses his lips together to form a thin line. That particular combo usually means he's having a flashback or reliving a bad memory—serious shit, as Inara likes to say.

"You remember that first night?" he asks, his voice rough.

I nod. I'll never forget it.

When we found him in Afghanistan, he was dehydrated, malnourished, and beaten to shit. The asshole who'd tortured him had left him to die in an old well where scorpions came out at night and stung him until he was delirious with pain from their venom.

"You were on watch. Pretty sure the guys thought I'd jump out the window if they left me alone. Not that I could have gotten myself out of bed."

"That was almost word for word what Ry said when he and Dax left me in charge."

There was also a *very* specific threat as to what would happen to me if I let my attention wander for even a second, but I keep that part to myself.

"You remember you had to help me," he swallows hard and won't meet my eyes, "take a piss?"

This time, I stay silent. He's working his way up to something, and with Ripper, these small moments of vulnerability are rare. I get the sense he's more open with Ry and Dax, with Cara, but not with West. Never with Inara. We're all family to him, but some of us, he keeps almost at arm's length. I thought I fell into that category too.

"I asked *you* to help because I didn't know you from Adam." Clearing his throat, he stares down at his boots. "Nothing seemed real. Until you offered me your cup of coffee. I hadn't had coffee in six years. Fucker only ever gave me tea, and whenever *he* brought it, there was something in it that messed with my head. Coffee? It made me think...maybe I really was out of that hole. Safe."

"Rip." I lean forward, elbows on my knees, careful not to get too close. The man doesn't like to be touched. None of them do. He, Dax, and Ry were tortured for so long that they don't trust anyone. Except the women they fell in love with. And each other. Hell, this is the most Ripper's said to me in over a year.

He shakes his head. "If Ry had been the one sitting next to that bed? I would have pissed myself before I asked him for help."

"Why? He's...he's your brother."

"In every way that counts, yeah. Doesn't make it any easier to admit you can't do something as simple as stand up. Or whip out your dick and hold it over a toilet." Ripper drains the last of his coffee as Ryker strides into the warehouse, the snap of the electronic door locks the only sign of his entry. Despite his size, he's utterly silent when he walks. As he pushes to his feet, Rip reaches out and rests his hand on my shoulder. "Graham, if this guy's been hurt before, if he's really as scared as you think he is? Try what you did with me. Don't ask him if he's okay. Ask him if he wants a cup of coffee."

FOR THE NEXT SIX HOURS, we put a group of five vets through a series of drills, actively *trying* to make them quit. Two of them do—an Army medic and a Naval Petty Officer. After West barking orders at them every five minutes, Ryker's intimidating stare, and Inara's prowess on the climbing wall, one of the washouts asks me if it's always this brutal.

I tell him to go run two miles and come back for another climb. His response? "Go fuck yourself, asshole."

With a laugh, I meet Ry's gaze across the warehouse and

shake my head. Five minutes later, Ry hands him a check for $1000—just for showing up—and warns him if he breathes a word of what happened here today, he'll regret ever being born.

A little after 6:00 p.m., Ryker shouts, "Shut it down. Everyone on the mats in five."

The three newbies, Caleb, Jonah, and Raelynn, head for the corner we use for yoga practice. The guys collapse in sweaty heaps, but Raelynn stands tall with her hands on her hips.

"You two pansy asses can't even bother to stand up? Sheeee-it. I'd rather be elbow-deep in a heifer's ass pullin' out a calf than goin' into the field with the two of you."

I take a step back when she casts a quick gaze at me, then turns to Caleb and Jonah. "That kid out classed both of you."

Inara barely manages to cover her laugh. Ryker's stone-faced as always, but something dark and dangerous simmers in West's eyes. "Graham's not a kid. He's a senior member of this team. One I trust with my life. And you'll show him some goddamn respect if you want to consider joining us."

Raelynn snaps her mouth shut and gives West a curt nod. "Yes, Sir."

With what might almost be a smile, Ryker steps forward. "The physical part of the interview's over. Next up...psychological testing and one-on-ones. If you want to take this step, there are updated NDAs on the conference table."

"We already signed one," Jonah protests.

Ryker stares him down until the former Marine looks appropriately chastised. "And you'll sign another. Because what comes next could land any one of us in worse shit than you've ever imagined. We clear?"

"Crystal, Sir," Caleb and Raelynn say sharply.

Jonah pushes up with a groan. "I had enough of this clandestine shit when I was deployed. I'm done." He refuses to take the grand West offers him for his time and grabs his keys and jacket from the temporary locker each potential was assigned when they walked in the door.

"I don't have to remind you what happens if you breathe a word of this to anyone," Ryker barks out.

"Then don't. Fuck off, McCabe. The government might think you're a hero, but I just think you're an asshole."

The door slams, and five seconds later, West, Inara, and I burst out laughing. Ryker turns to us, one brow raised. The other is bisected by a thick scar. "Care to explain?" he asks.

"The Marine's not wrong," West says as he cracks the seal on a bottle of water. "You are an asshole."

"Damn straight." Ryker jerks his head towards the conference table. "Well? If you two sorry sacks of shit want a chance to work with an asshole—and this asshole's team—get to signing."

CHAPTER TEN

Quinton

BEFORE I SHUT my laptop for the night, I check my old email—the one I used when I was with *him*. I have a whole folder of archived messages from Alec—evidence if I ever need it—and I use this account almost like a diary. A history of the hell I went through and how I escaped.

Composing an email to myself, I summarize the past few days. Connor's belief that Alec was outside his house, the catalog that showed up in my mailbox, and my fears that Alec hasn't given up on his quest to hurt me. To get revenge for what I did to him—leaving him, serving him with a restraining order, calling him out on his shit.

After I send the message to myself, establishing a record of my thoughts, I notice the chat bubble in the lower right corner. Oh, God. Somehow, the program showed me as online, and Alec sent me a message.

Don't read it. Just delete it.

I can't. As much as I want to...as much as I know I *should*, it's all evidence. But he doesn't need to know that I read the message. I have a program that blocks read receipts. Once that's active, I click on the notification and try to ignore the icy ball of panic in the pit of my stomach.

My dearest Quint,

It's been over a year since we've seen one another, and this message is long overdue. I had the best intentions. But that doesn't excuse what I did. I thought I knew better than the doctors. That no one could take care of you like I could. I felt horrible knowing you got hurt because of me, and everything I did...it was because I loved you.

After your brother took you from me, I was angry. But then I got help. I can see how much I hurt you now. And I'm sorry. I know it's too little, too late, but I miss you. You were the best thing to ever happen to me, and I wish I hadn't screwed it all up.

My sincerest apologies,

Alec

Suddenly, I'm a shuddering mess on the floor, my arms wrapped around my knees. The position stretches my tight muscles, but it's all I can do when I'm paralyzed, trapped in my memories of my time with *him*.

What the hell is he doing? And does he really think I'm going to believe his apology?

Sociopaths, psychopaths, narcissists, and many individuals with Antisocial Personality Disorder often don't feel genuine emotions. They can't. They are, however, experts at mimicking the emotions of others. They always say just the right thing at the right time because they're often incredibly smart and experts at reading their victims.

Before the night I planned to break up with Alec for good— the night everything changed—my therapist warned me repeatedly not to believe any crocodile tears Alec might shed. Being a sociopath isn't like having depression or anxiety. You can't take a pill and make the condition go away—or even control it. Some people do learn to live without the ability to understand or feel emotions. A rare few even manage *not* to be a danger to others. They have very strict rules they follow every day of their lives. When you don't feel pain, remorse, anguish, or joy, it's too easy to think of life as one giant game designed for you and you alone.

Alec is up to something. I know he signed me up for Rodeo Vibe. How else would they have gotten my name and address? And now...this? If he thinks I'll believe *anything* he says, he's an idiot. And Alec is not an idiot.

Focus, Q. You're safe here. The cameras, the security system, the bars on the windows, the locks...

But am I? He knows where I live. That I'm in Seattle. Hell, he probably knows that I live alone. That I'm vulnerable.

Clementine crawls into my lap, and I rock back and forth for an hour with her until I'm steady enough to get to my feet. If for no other reason than she needs dinner, and I won't deny her a meal—ever.

But no more than five minutes after she finishes the bowl of kibble, my security alarm goes off. Oh, God. What if...what if he was just toying with me with that email? He could be here right now.

Clementine bolts for the bedroom, probably to hide under the bed, while I lurch over to my computer. The alarm's coming from the rear exterior security door, but when I check the motion sensor and camera, everything's quiet. Rewinding five minutes, I replay the video. Nothing. Not even a rat scavenging in the dumpster or a stray dog.

Resetting the system, I force a deep breath. It was just a false alarm. A glitch.

And then it goes off again. I've been watching the video the whole time. Nothing's moved outside. It's not even windy. Maybe the batteries need to be replaced? I just changed them a month ago, but that's the only explanation that doesn't leave me panicked.

This is the best system money can buy. Emerald City Security has contracts all over the country, and Connor's used them for his job more than once—not that he'll tell me exactly how or why. But I vetted them thoroughly.

It has to be the batteries. I hate to get on the step stool and try to balance when I'm so shaky the world feels like it's vibrating, but I can do this.

Ten minutes later, batteries in my pocket, I check the cameras one last time. Courage is hard to come by—especially after reading Alec's message—but what choice do I have?

The alley's deserted, only a low hum of crowd noise from the Pike/Pine corridor a few blocks away. It's not much after 8:00 p.m., and the real parties won't get started until close to midnight.

The security door sensor is up high—on the top inside corner of the metal monstrosity, and I brace myself on the wall as I take one step, then another onto the step stool.

The doctors warned me that reaching over my head and arching my spine would be difficult for the rest of my life, but so far, I think I'm okay. Until I pull off the thin, plastic cover that hides the sensor battery. An electric shock zings down my arm, and a brackish dust burns my eyes. The first cough makes my equilibrium go to shit, and I miss the first step, landing hard on my weaker left leg.

The concrete rushes up to meet my ass, and my back spasms hard enough to draw a strained cry from my throat. I'm reduced to crawling back inside, and as soon as I slam the door and flip the only lock I can reach from the ground, I give up any semblance of pride and drop my head into my hands.

I'm a helpless, bumbling, *invalid*. And now, I'm so terrified, I don't know if I can get up, let alone go back out there to try again.

It's just a battery. What man can't change a damn battery? The alarm goes off for a third time, setting my nerves on edge. I don't know anyone in Seattle besides Manny and my housekeeper. Manny's in Atlanta, and I can't call my housekeeper this late.

"You know how to find me."

Graham's voice tears through my memories, and fuck. I've ached for a reason to text him all week, but this? How helpless, weak, and pathetic will he think I am? It doesn't matter. Because he's the only option I have left.

I fucked up with him on an epic scale, and there's no way I can fix it in a text. So I settle for something simple.

I need help. Can you come over? It won't take long. Ten minutes.

For all I know, he's working tonight and won't get off until the bars close. Or he's already asleep. But with the alarm blaring every five or six minutes, I only have two choices.

Turn the whole system off and watch the cameras all fucking night or leave it on, and enter my security code every time it goes off.

After I disable the sensors, I drag myself to the living room and lie down on the couch, phone in hand. If Graham does show up, hopefully I'll be able to make it to the front door.

I'd kill for a cup of coffee, but every time I move, my back protests, so I try to relax and stare at the night vision images. Nothing moves for ten minutes until one of the neighborhood cats ambles by, and then it's all quiet again.

Time ticks by in endless minutes that stretch out forever. Fifteen. Twenty. Graham's not coming. He's not even going to text me back. Clementine has settled at my feet, and she's kneading like her life depends on it.

Sitting up takes me a full five minutes, but I only locked one of the deadbolts on the back door. Even with the bars on the first floor windows, the security doors, and the cameras, I feel exposed. Vulnerable. Desperately and completely alone.

If I start some coffee, maybe I can give the batteries another go.

The doorbell rings before I can steel myself for the pain of standing, and I drop my phone. Then, forgetting just how fucked up I am, I try to reach for it and almost fall off the couch.

But at least I snag the hunk of glass and metal so I can check the camera.

He came. The sight of Graham, tense, shoulders hiked up, hands balled into fists, makes my breath catch in my throat, even as his name flies to my lips.

"Q? I'm here. Let me in."

Even his voice is strained. Determination and raw need override my shaking muscles until I can flip all four locks and open the door.

His hand on my arm is like a lifeline, warm and gentle, yet so strong, I know he'd never let me fall. "What is it?"

I should tell him. But the only words I can force out?

"You came."

His brows draw together. "Of course I came. I'm not a complete asshole. I was working. Had to get the manager to cover the rest of my shift. I should have texted you back, but as soon as I found him, I handed him my tip jar and...ran."

He ran. I want to cry. Or throw my arms around him and tell him how long it's been since anyone...*cared*. But that part of me died back in Dallas, and I can't do anything but stare at this gorgeous, kind man who should have blocked me from ever contacting him again.

"Q? Talk to me."

Words fail me, but I collapse against him, my arms winding around his waist, and he holds me. Just...holds me.

"Whatever it is...we can fix it. *I'll* fix it. If you let me." His fingers thread through my hair, and for a moment, I feel safe. Protected. Not afraid. And I wish I could stay in his arms forever.

～

Graham

Q's shaking, and I don't understand why.

I need help.

In the twenty-three minutes between seeing his message and knocking on his door, I went through a hundred worst-case scenarios. He'd hurt himself somehow. Or he'd been attacked. A break-in. A fall. Tripping over his cat.

"Tell me what's wrong," I say as I loosen my hold so I can meet his gaze.

He winces, pain etching deep lines at the corners of his mouth. "My alarm system..." Defeat mars his tone, and it makes my heart hurt. "The sensor on the back door...something's wrong with it. I tried to replace the battery, but..." He stares down at his feet. "I fell, and I can't...I can't fix it by myself."

"That's the problem? That's it?" From his flinch, I've said exactly the wrong thing. "Fuck. Q, I didn't mean it like that."

The distance between us is even greater now than it was an hour ago, and he tries to shake me off, but he's so obviously in pain, I stay close as he shuffles into the kitchen. The position lets me study his uneven gait. And appreciate his ass. Q's left leg is weaker than his right, and his foot drags a bit.

Digging into his pocket, he comes up with a handful of batteries, then nods towards the counter where a small sensor sits next to a folded set of instructions. "If the batteries don't fix the problem, that's a brand new sensor. The wires are color coded."

His fingers brush mine, but before I can even try to hold on, he jerks his hand away, his shoulders hunched.

Fuck. All I want to do is be close to him. To tell him it'll all be okay. But he's so worked up, he's shaking. "Do you have a stool?"

"I...left it outside. When I touched the old one, it shocked me. That's when I...when I fell." Staring down at his phone in his hands, he fiddles with the screen. "I can reboot the system once the new sensor's in place."

From the brief glance I caught, I think his system is the same one Cam designed for business-grade personal security. But the sensor he gave me is definitely *not* part of her system. A former army bomb disposal specialist and West's wife, she's a computer genius, but unlike Wren, who does most of her work on the dark web, Cam's job is completely above board and out in the open.

Q's about to come out of his skin, so I save the questions for later. "I'll take care of it. Sit down. Please. Do you need help?"

"No." His voice is no more than a whisper, and he limps back into the living room and sinks into his computer chair.

The step stool is right next to the door, and once I climb up, I can see the frayed wires sticking out of the back of the tiny sensor. They're covered by a fine layer of dust, and I frown.

This is why I carry a multi-tool everywhere I go. The pilers are shielded, and when I pull the sensor off the door and it lands in my palm, I hiss out a sharp breath. It's hot to the touch. Something is *definitely* wrong with it.

I duck back into the house for the replacement. "I don't trust this old sensor. Give me another minute or two." In the bright kitchen lights, I pause for a second to examine the wires. One is frayed, the yellow insulation almost melted away. Could be insect damage or an electrical fault, but working for Hidden Agenda has taught me to be suspicious of *everything*.

Installing the replacement only takes two minutes, and I make sure all three deadbolts are locked before I head into the living room and crouch next to Q's chair. "Try rebooting. That sensor was definitely worn out. Your batteries were practically smoking."

His muscles tense even more. "Smoking? That's not right. It's not even a year old..."

"Probably just some bug eating away at the insulation." I try to keep my voice light, because he's about five seconds away from losing his shit. His brown eyes are bloodshot and red-rimmed, and his chest stutters as he tries to click the button to reboot the system.

Draping my fingers over his, I guide the mouse where it needs to be. "Deep breath, Q. You're okay."

"N-no. I mean... Yes. I'm fine. Just need to lie down. Assuming this works."

"I won't leave until everything's fixed. I promise. I'm good at this shit. You're using a modified Emerald City Security system, right?" Now that I'm staring at the admin screen, I don't have to ask, but I also know he's spooked, big time, and I'm not ready to explain what I *really* do for a living.

He turns, his brow furrowed and his voice equal parts desperate and hopeful. "You know about this stuff? How?"

"The owner's a friend." It's close enough to the truth. Cam's family, through West, and we've worked together enough to call each other friends, despite her discomfort with people in general. If she could hide behind her computer all day, every day, I think she would.

"Oh." Q's cheeks and the back of his neck take on a reddish tinge, and he watches the screen. The system comes back online without any faults, and it's like all the tension melts from his body at once. "I..." He shakes his head and then scrubs his hands over his face. "I didn't have anyone else to call."

"Technically, you didn't *call* me." It's supposed to be a joke, a way to ease the mood and maybe get him to loosen up. But it has the opposite effect, and he forces his back straight, pushing the chair away from the desk—and away from me.

"Fine. I don't have *anyone* to call. Happy now?" Lurching to his feet, he steadies himself with one hand on the wall while he points to the front door. "Thanks for your help. I'll try not to need it again."

"For fuck's sake, Q." A pen and notepad lie next to his

mouse, and I write down a second phone number along with a five-digit code. Holding up my cell phone, I meet his gaze. "There are two SIM cards in here. The first...that's the number I gave you last week. The number you texted tonight. I was at the bar, and I couldn't just walk out until I had someone to cover for me. But the second SIM? The number I just wrote down?" I jab the paper for emphasis. "Anyone who calls it needs to enter this code when the exchange picks up. You do that, and no matter where I am—no matter what I'm doing—I'll answer immediately. You *always* have someone to call."

I should go. Walk out of his life and never look back. But I've already decided that's not going to happen. He's scared. Long-term fear and distrust. Someone hurt him in his past, and I know what that feels like.

Stopping right in front of him, I keep my arms at my sides, trying to appear as non-threatening as I can. It's no use. I'm two inches shorter than he is, but probably outweigh him by fifty pounds of muscle. When I started at Hidden Agenda, I couldn't do half the shit I can now—physically. But between West's Krav Maga training and Ryker's insane drills, I've bulked up a lot, and Q shies away from my gaze.

"I'm not the enemy here," I say softly. "You asked for my help first—with the groceries, remember?"

"I didn't have a choice." The words escape on a whisper, and there's that shame again, creeping up his neck, flushing his cheeks, causing him to stare down at the floor. At a pair of black Keds with orange laces peeking out from under the loose gray fleece pants. "I needed..."

"Meds. I get it." Fishing the plastic box out of my pocket, I show it to him. "Clonazepam, Hydroxyzine, and Xanax. You think you cornered the market on anxiety disorders or something?"

Finally, he meets my gaze, his brows pinched, confusion churning in his eyes. "You can't need those. You're...built."

"Built?" Now it's my turn to fight embarrassment. I'm strong, sure. But built? No. Ryker's built. Me? I'm just a kid from rural Michigan with a really good workout plan. And then I realize what I'm wearing. A tight black tank with the Unicorn Bar's logo and a pair of cargo pants. I don't *feel* like a badass, but I probably look like one at the moment. Assuming one *can* look like a badass with a pink sparkling unicorn in the center of their chest.

I offer him my hand. "Can we sit down and...I don't know. Start over?"

"Why?"

The question tears me up inside. He seriously has no idea why I want to get to know him. "Because you're brave as fuck, Q, and that's about the sexiest quality a guy can have in my book. Because when I kissed you, you kissed me back, and I haven't forgotten what that felt like. Do I need to keep going? I can."

"I'm not brave," he says with a shake of his head. "Why would you say that?"

This question, I understand. "Because I'm pretty sure you don't ever leave your house. You told me you didn't have anyone to call, so obviously you don't have friends in town. And yet you stopped me last week, in the middle of the night on an empty street. A guy you don't know, who's...to use your word...built... and asked for help. And then you did it again tonight. If that's not brave, I don't know what is."

My words sink in, slowly at first, but I can tell when they land hard. Q stands up a little straighter, still staring at my offered hand. And then he grabs on, his fingers cool and not entirely steady. "Okay. We can start over."

CHAPTER ELEVEN

Graham

FOR SEVERAL LONG MOMENTS, we stand in silence, Q holding my hand, looking like he's about to fall over.

"What now?" I ask.

"Don't you have to go back to work?"

Is the hope in his voice because he wants me to go or wants me to stay? Either way, I need to keep things light. Casual. Friendly. Q's had enough of the serious and heavy for one night. "Nope." I try for a smile that's more friendly than sexy. "My manager's covering the rest of my shift. It's only another hour or two anyway."

The relief on his face—it's both beautiful and heartbreaking. Leading me to the couch, he sinks down with a groan, and I'm close enough that his scent—fresh laundry soap, sandalwood, and something soft—washes over me. It's like coming home. Comforting in a way I didn't know I wanted.

He *needs* me. More importantly, he wants me. I can see it, even though he's trying to be strong.

Rubbing my palms over my thighs, I make a decision. If I

expect Q to trust me, I need to trust him as well. Ryker's going to kill me when he finds out, but until he rips me into a dozen pieces and buries them somewhere no one will ever find them, I'll be honest with this man next to me.

"I have to tell you something," I say, staring at the darkened television across from the couch. "My last name isn't Tempelton."

His entire body goes rigid, and he sucks in a sharp breath.

I turn and reach for his hands. "Hear me out? Please? You're the first guy in years I want to get to know—really know. And I won't start this off—start over—with anything other than the truth."

He doesn't respond, but he hasn't pulled away either. There's suspicion in his eyes, and it's not until he jerks a small nod that I relax a little.

"When I left the Coast Guard, I didn't know what the hell to do with my life. Then I heard about this former Special Forces badass who was looking for someone to join his team. Someone young, someone with no attachments, someone who didn't mind taking risks."

"His team? What kind of team?" Q asks, still tense.

"Well, it's not a dance troupe." I chuckle, but it sounds forced. Hell, it is. How do you tell someone you're a mercenary for hire? That you kill people. Deal with the worst of humanity? And that you have no plans of stopping or giving up this life for anything? "K&R."

He narrows his gaze. "What's K&R?"

"Kidnap and ransom." His eyes widen, and I rush to continue. "No. No. We don't *do* the kidnapping! We save people who get themselves in trouble. All over the world. That's my job, Q. And why I use a fake name online. Because what we do is dangerous and highly illegal."

I shouldn't be telling him any of this. But one thing I learned working with Ryker? How to read people. Quinton is a good guy. An *honest* guy. He's scared, and he's hiding a fuckton behind the walls around his heart. But I think he wants the same thing I do. Something real.

His pupils dilate, and his breath catches in his throat. "You...no. Nobody *does* that. No one but people on TV. In the movies. *Real* people don't *do* shit like that." By the time he finishes, his voice is hoarse and he's shaking.

Pulling him closer, I wrap my arm around his shoulders. "Q, listen to me. You're not in any danger. Not from me, and not because of me. Breathe, okay? In and out." He's close to falling over the edge into a full blown panic attack, and if I had to guess, it's not his first of the day.

"Do you kill people?" he asks.

"Yes. When I have to. Though I'm the youngest, and the others...I think they still try to protect me from it as much as they can. I'm the only one who didn't see actual combat in the military. But K&R is dangerous work, and my hands aren't clean."

"Oh, God. Why would you—?"

He pulls away, and my heart sinks down to my toes. Rising, I start to pace his living room. "Because since I signed on, we've saved twenty-six people. Without us, they'd be dead. The military and the government can't go places we can. We're the best at what we do, and we're...a family. I'd die for any one of them if I had to without a second thought."

I can't read him. His eyes, usually so expressive, are wide with shock. Fuck. This was a mistake. I've lost him. I knew the risks, but now...shit. I've ruined the fragile trust he gave me, and what's worse? I can't leave without making him understand how important it is that he never breathe a word of this to anyone.

With my hands shoved deep into my pockets, I shake my head. "I'm sorry, Quinton. My baggage is way too much to dump on you all at once. I'll leave, and you won't see me again.

But I need you to promise me that all of this—everything I've told you tonight—stays between us. This is life and death for me and everyone I call family."

"Stay," he whispers and pushes to his feet. But his legs give out, and I catch him, my arm banded around his waist.

"I don't understand. You heard me, right? That I kill people? Regularly?"

He nods, and I can't decipher the emotions swirling in his eyes. Until he lets out a sigh. "That's not what I meant when I asked why."

"Then what did you want to know?"

His fingers tighten on my biceps, and those brown eyes hold mine. "Why would you trust me with all this? You don't even know me."

"Because I want to know you. You're a good person. I can tell. I've been *trained* to be able to tell. But also...someone hurt you."

He flinches, and if I weren't sure he'd been through some shit before, I am now.

"You don't have to tell me about it. Not yet, anyway. But you need to know that you're safe with me."

"You should let me go," he whispers.

"Am I hurting you?" I slide my hand up and down his spine, checking for swelling, feeling his terror in every breath.

"No. But Graham, I'm broken. My life is a fucking mess, and I don't *just* mean my back."

I'd do anything to banish the pain from his eyes. "Do you trust me?"

"I haven't trusted anyone but my brother in over a year." I can barely hear his reply, and he won't look at me anymore.

"But do you trust *me*?" Cupping his cheek, I lean in and rest my forehead against his. "I told you about what I do because I want to see where this goes and we can't do that if we don't trust each other."

"What's your real name?" he asks.

"Graham Davidson Peck."

Quinton chokes out a laugh, but it's not one that reassures me even a fraction. "Not Tempelton, but Peck? Like Tempelton Peck? Face from The old A-Team tv show? You're trying to tell me you work for the A-Team?"

"Kind of? We help people when no one else can. Though we're not currently wanted by the government since we don't *officially* exist. And when your last name is really Peck, what better alias is there? My boss let me choose, and my parents and I would watch the A-Team every Friday night when I was a kid. Face—Templeton Peck—always knew what he was doing. I never do." It's my turn to blush, at least a little, and I breathe in Quinton's scent. Fuck. I want him like I haven't wanted anyone in years. Maybe...ever. He's still too spooked for anything but comfort, and I won't do a damn thing he's not ready for, but I don't want to leave him. "My mom is LuAnn, my dad is Davidson—David for short. They live in Ann Arbor. I have one sister—Jennifer."

He studies me, like he can't quite decide if I'm telling the truth. Eventually, he squeezes his eyes shut for a moment, and when he opens them again, I can tell he believes me. "My brother saved my life. But we almost never talk."

"How come?"

Shaking his head, he stammers, "I...not tonight."

"I won't pressure you. For anything. That's not my vibe. I just want to get to know you. When—if—you want that."

"Even if I'm so fucked up, I can't even step outside my front door?" The pain in his voice makes me want to hold him. All night. Every night. It's stupid—feeling this much this fast. But I can't help it.

"Your yard needs serious work. Can't say I blame you for not wanting to go out there. It still smells vaguely of mint chip."

Humor is my go-to. The defense mechanism I pull out

whenever things get too intense. But sometimes, it backfires in the most epic of ways, and I hold my breath until Quinton's lips curve into the barest hint of a smile.

"The store manager called me personally to apologize. Did you have something to do with that?" he asks.

Shrugging, I guide him back to the couch. He's letting me support more and more of his weight, and I think he needs to get off his feet. "Maybe. You had meds in there. And what? A hundred bucks' worth of food? The asshole needed to know what his people were doing. If I overstepped, I'm sorry."

"No. You were right. I suck at standing up for myself. Or...asking for what I want."

"Well, practice. With me." I lean against the arm of the sofa, intentionally putting some distance between us. "What do you want? Right now."

"I want you to stay."

The words seem to surprise him as much as they shock me. My brows shoot up, and half the blood in my body heads south, but apparently I have no poker face where he's concerned, because his cheeks turn a deep red and he holds up his hands.

"I didn't mean...*that*. Not tonight. Shit. This is why you should run, Graham. I'm so messed up I can't even explain—"

I wrap my arms around him and pull him close. "You don't have to."

The tension seeps out of him once he's settled against my chest, his legs tucked up under him. After a few minutes, his breathing changes, and shit. He's asleep.

What the hell do I do now? Stay on the couch with him all night? We'd both regret it in the morning. Despite how good it feels to have him in my arms.

After half an hour, when he still hasn't moved, I whisper, "Q? I'm going to take you upstairs, okay?"

He doesn't answer, and I slide my arm under his knees. Thank fuck for all those jump squats West insists we do every couple of days. Q's lighter than I expect, but still, it's awkward as fuck to stand without jostling him awake.

Peeking down the hall into the only other room on this floor, I find workout equipment, so his bedroom must be upstairs.

The large bed takes up most of the space, and I pull back the dark blue duvet and sheet and lay him down before taking off his shoes. I have no idea if I should go any further. Or where the fuck he wants *me* to stay.

The man's fastidious about his security. Whether I sleep on the couch or in here on the floor, I have to double check all the locks first. Four on the front door, three on the back. When I'm done, I glance at his computer, checking for any motion events over the past hour. It's all clear.

"Graham?" Q's panicked voice carries down the stairs, and I take them two at a time to get back to the bedroom. He's sitting up, white-knuckling the sheets.

"What's wrong?"

"I...didn't know if you were still here." He relaxes slightly, then meets my gaze, the plea obvious in his eyes. "Are you...staying?"

"I was just checking the locks." Shoving my hands into my pockets, I find the faulty sensor. "I can take the couch. But if you have an extra blanket—"

"The bed's big enough..."

Fuck. He's so hesitant. Like he expects me to be angry. Or to refuse. Sitting on the opposite side of the bed, I remove my boots and shove the security sensor into one, and my wallet, phone, and keys into the other.

When I turn back around, he's wriggling out of his sweat pants, revealing tight blue boxer briefs with pink hearts on them. It's fucking adorable, and makes me want him even more. One day...I hope he's ready for that.

"You can...um..." He gestures to my pants and pulls back the blankets.

"Are you sure?"

His eyes go glassy. "I can't...*do* anything." There's that shame again. The look that tells me he thinks he's too broken to be worth anyone's time. "Not tonight. My back hasn't stopped spasming for hours. But I miss...being held."

"Then I'll hold you. All night." Shedding my pants, I catch the appreciation flickering in his eyes. My briefs are a lot tighter than they were a few seconds ago, but I will myself to calm the fuck down.

I can't get under the covers fast enough, and when he turns so I can spoon him, I press a kiss to the back of his head. "I've got you."

His little sigh as he relaxes is beautiful, and I reach up and flip off the light on the table next to him.

I think I missed holding someone as much—if not more—than he missed being held. Because this? It feels...right.

CHAPTER TWELVE

Quinton

THE SHEETS next to me are cool to the touch, and I roll over with a groan, though my back feels better than it has in weeks.

Graham's not here. Shit. Did he leave? Is my door unlocked? Oh, God. The first guy I trusted in more than a year, the guy who saved my groceries and brought me ice cream…I should have known superheroes like that don't exist. And if they did, they certainly wouldn't have any interest in *me*.

After struggling into my pants, I limp down the stairs until I hear someone moving around in my kitchen.

He *did* stay. Either that or I'm royally fucked.

My left leg buckles on the last step, and I grab the railing.

"Whoa there," Graham says. "Careful."

He's shirtless, and I can't look away from his abs. Or the tattoo covering his left shoulder and arm.

I am the master of my fate and the captain of my soul.

I wish I had that confidence. "You stayed." It's all I can manage, and he frowns.

"Did you expect me to walk out in the middle of the night?"

He offers me a mug of coffee, and the scent helps clear my head.

"I...err...no. Maybe?" I'm not proud of how shaky my voice is. Or how wrong I was.

"Your last relationship must have been really shitty," he says with a shake of his head. "Either that or you lied when you said you trusted me."

"I didn't lie." The words slip out on a whisper, and I'm still holding onto the rail like my life depends on it. "He was a nightmare."

"Q, I'm sorry." His gaze softens, and he reaches out and skims his hand down my arm. "You didn't have much in your cabinets, but I think I can manage pancakes. If you're hungry—"

The coffee mug hits the floor, the hot liquid splashing onto my fleece pants.

"Shit!" Graham sets his cup down on the hall table, runs back to the kitchen, and grabs a dish towel. "Don't move. You could slip." Kneeling, he mops up the liquid and stares up at me. "What did I say? Or do?"

I can't answer him. Not until he stands right in front of me, all those muscles and ink and intense stare. Pain creases his brow, and he's so serious. So respectful.

"Quinton? Talk to me. Please?" Graham hasn't touched me, and as the seconds pass, the disappointment in his eyes only grows until his shoulders slump. "Let me get my stuff, and I'll go."

Before he can pass me on the stairs, I whisper, "Pancakes."

"What?"

We're only inches apart now. He's one step above me, and that puts us at eye level, which is why I drop my gaze to my feet. "Pancakes. My...my ex made them every day. And I hate them."

"What about waffles? Donuts? Scones? Ice cream?"

This amazing, considerate man is trying so hard, and I can't even look him in the eyes. All I can manage is to stare at his chin. The dark brown stubble, the dimple under his lower lip.

The firm line of his mouth shifts from worry to frustration. "I'm not him, Q. I won't hurt you. Won't force you to do anything you don't want."

"I never said anything—" Shit. I did. Last night. Not the details, but do they even matter? He knows my deepest fears, and he's actively trying to dispel them.

Graham eases down a step, giving me the height advantage. "I know the signs. Comes with my training. And years of therapy. You keep expecting me to be angry or shout or do *something* that scares you or hurts you so badly, you can't defend yourself. I'm not that guy."

"He broke me." The words stick in my throat, and only Clementine winding around my ankles keeps the panic from swallowing me whole.

Graham scoops her up and places her in my arms. "She was whining and basically climbing my leg until I put some kibble in her bowl."

"You fed my cat."

His brows furrow, and he curses under his breath. "I didn't mean to overstep. With any of it. Breakfast, Clementine, staying the night. I'll go."

Stop it, Q. Stop being a fucking coward.

Clementine head butts my chin, and she's purring so loudly, it's all I can hear.

"You didn't overstep." Digging deep for a fraction of an ounce of bravery, I reach for his hand. "You...took care of her."

Neither of us move or speak until Clementine wriggles out of my arms and sniffs at my damp pant leg. I can do this. Take one step towards a *normal* life.

"Breakfast comes with a lot of baggage. For me." Dropping my gaze, I try to force Alec's voice from my head. "I can do coffee."

"I'll make you a fresh cup."

~

Graham

If I don't get a move on, West is going to kick my ass. One of the newbies, Raelynn, is coming by for a crash course on some of our more *traditional* tech. Ryker's starting her and Caleb off at a snail's pace. Our fearless leader doesn't trust anyone. Not even after Raelynn's former CO called him personally.

West's message—the one I got moments after I woke up with Quinton still in my arms—told me to be at the warehouse at nine, and it's already 8:40 a.m. It's a damn good thing Q wakes up early. Or did today.

I left him with a slow, lingering kiss at his door, and an offer to bring pizza by for dinner. He agreed, and the prospect of seeing him again—even if it's just a meal—has me grinning. I don't care if West forces me to climb that fucking wall a hundred times today for showing up late, it'll be worth it.

Traffic is almost non-existent this early on a Saturday morning, though, and I park my tiny red SmartCar at the ware-house at exactly 8:58 a.m.

Raelynn's locking her bicycle up outside when I sling my duffel bag over my shoulder. "You rode here?"

She clips her helmet onto the crossbar and snorts. "No. I walked here all the way from White Center. Carried the bike on my head."

I probably deserved that.

"Sorry. Been kind of a weird morning. You can bring it inside, you know." Angling my head towards West's perfectly restored old pickup truck, I reach for the handle on the ware-house door. "Sampson's already in there."

"Didn't want to assume." She makes quick work of the lock,

then picks the bike up and balances the crossbar on her shoulder.

Following me into the warehouse, she scans the large space until I point to the far corner. "Over there's fine. Pretty sure one of those lockers has your name on it by now, so take a couple of minutes to stow your stuff and set your combination. Make it a good one."

Raelynn gives me the side eye as she sets the bike down. "A good one?"

I don't say another word as I head for the kitchen. Hell, I probably shouldn't have warned her at all, but when I joined up, I made my combo my mom's birthday, and a week later, *someone* had taken all my shit and filled my locker with packing peanuts.

My money's on West, but despite having zero sense of humor, Ry's the more likely culprit. He's so fanatical about security, he routinely tells all of us whenever we're not careful enough for his liking.

"You call this 'on time'?" West asks. "One more near miss and I'm going to padlock the coffee machine."

He's deadly serious, but he also cracks a smile as he pours me a cup. It's 9:00 a.m. on the dot. While yes, Raelynn and I are both *here*, that doesn't matter. We should have been ready to go by now. Instead, I'm expressing my deep and abiding loyalty to the SEAL and Hidden Agenda by moaning into the coffee mug.

"Want to explain that shirt?" he asks, one brow arched.

Oh, shit.

I meant to change the second I walked in here. Instead, I'm still wearing the black tee with the multi-colored sparkling unicorn emblazoned on the front. "Late night."

"As in one that didn't end at your apartment?" He snorts, then claps me on the back as he heads for the tech hub. "I've done a few walks of shame in my life, *Jimmy*. Never one quite that blatant."

We use code names in the field. Most of the time, I'm Golf. But since the mission to Venezuela to rescue Trevor—one of Dax's guys who got himself on the wrong side of the entire Venezuelan government—mine's been Jimmy Olsen.

"Give me two minutes." I don't dare set the coffee down. Given his mood today—surprisingly good—he'd spike it with salt to teach me a lesson about being on time. Instead, I rush over to my locker, enter the ridiculously long string of numbers on the keypad, and grab a fresh shirt, briefs, and a pair of basketball shorts.

"So, this is a thing," Raelynn drawls as I drop my pants.

"What?"

She's averting her eyes. Is she actively embarrassed by me taking my clothes off in front of her? All she can see is my ass.

"No individual bathrooms in the field." I shrug. "You served for almost ten years. Plus your time at the Air Force Academy. You can't tell me this is the first time a guy's stripped naked in front of you."

Some of her swagger and bravado fade away, and she turns back to her locker. "Hardly."

As soon as I'm dressed, I clear my throat. "Are we going to have a problem, Probie?"

"You did *not* just call me probie," she growls, her blue eyes blazing.

"I did. Because that's how things work here. You're the newest member of this team now—unless you royally fuck it up in the next couple of weeks. So, I'll ask you again. Are we going to have a problem? I may be a few years younger than you, but that doesn't mean I don't know my shit."

"It don't mean you need to throw yer weight around neither." Her Texas drawl thickens when she's upset, and she jams her hands on her hips. "Tryin' to intimidate the new recruit with the size of yer dick?"

That's what she thought this was?

Running a hand through my hair, I force out a long, slow breath. "Look, probie. I'm gay. And even if I weren't, that behavior isn't tolerated here. You're new. Maybe you think you need to prove yourself. Or be tougher than the rest of us, harder than the rest of us. But take some advice from someone who wore that Probie title for eighteen months. This is a family. The sooner you figure out how to trust that we've got each other's backs—all the time—the happier you'll be here."

Raelynn stares at me, her face a mask I can't read. All this posturing has left my coffee barely lukewarm, so I head to the kitchen for a refill, then join West. He's straddling a chair, his arms folded over the back of it, focusing all of his considerable staring power at Raelynn as she finishes up with her locker.

Without even blinking, he asks, "You get that all straightened out?"

"Yeah. Kind of surprised you didn't intervene, though."

He chuckles, which only enhances his unnerving stare. "You've earned your spot on this team, Graham. I stood up for you the other day so the newbies would understand the chain of command. But you don't need me to tell you what you already know. You belong here. And anyone who challenges that? They don't."

AFTER FOUR HOURS of simulation drills, West dismisses Raelynn. "Not bad instincts, Probie. Particularly where listening devices are concerned. At least in a sim environment. But your fine motor control needs work." He heads for one of the storage cabinets along the wall, punches in a sixteen-digit code, and when he turns back around, he's holding a game of Operation. "Practice with this."

"You have got to be fuckin' kiddin' me," Raelynn mutters. "A kids' game?"

"Don't laugh. My wife was an ordinance specialist in the army for years, and when she chose that specialty, this is how she trained. Once you can go an hour without triggering the buzzer, and try to do the same thing drunk." West rubs the light stubble covering his chin. "Gotta be prepared for anything. Even diffusing a bomb when you haven't slept for forty-eight hours. We stay alive because we train for anything."

"Yes, sir." She snaps to attention, preparing to salute, but West waves her off.

"We don't do that here. You call me West or Sampson. And no saluting. Because that's our other mission. To blend in. So get used to it."

Raelynn nods and heads for the lockers. Five minutes later, after she wheels her bike out the door, West shakes his head. "That one's got a stick up her ass the size of a two-by-four. But she graduated top of her class, and she's got a jacket full of commendations."

We've all read her file. Even though Ry had the final say over who we brought in and who we didn't, the five of us—West, Inara, Ripper, Ry, and me—sat in the lounge next to the kitchen for hours the other day, debating whether to hire Raelyn or Caleb. In the end, we decided to hire both of them, but Caleb landed himself in the hospital with appendicitis, so his training's delayed for a month until he heals up.

"You going to talk to her?" I ask, locking up the laptops.

"Not yet. We'll see if she comes around when we parachute into the middle of the Sinaloa jungle next week."

"What?" I stop in the middle of filling up my water bottle and glance back at the SEAL. "We're taking her on a mission? Already?"

"Fuck no." He pulls the tab on an energy drink can and chugs half of it. "Training only. I got one of the guys I know from BUD/S to set up a fake hostage rescue op. We'll see how she responds under pressure."

Forty-eight hours. For the first time, the idea of going on a training mission doesn't sit well with me.

"Something wrong?" West asks.

Shit. He never misses a damn thing. The man can read micro expressions just as well or better than Ry, and when he thinks you're hiding something, he won't stop until you break.

"Uh, that walk of shame? It wasn't a one night stand."

With a chuckle, he finishes the energy drink, crumples the can, and chucks it into the recycle bin from thirty feet away. "'Bout damn time. What's his name?"

"Quinton." Running a hand through my hair, I follow West to the couches and sink down across from him. "But it's new. *Really* new."

"That's not all you're worried about."

How does he *do* that? Always know when there's more to the story?

"He's been through some shit." I kick myself when that one eyebrow arches yet again. "I know, I know. But, West, he's actively afraid of something—no, scratch that. He's fucking terrified. The man has one of Cam's security systems for his townhouse."

"Overkill much? And expensive."

"One of the sensors went haywire last night, and Quinton called me to help him fix it. When I got there...he was seconds away from a panic attack, but every time I asked him what was wrong—I mean really wrong—he clammed up on me." I close my eyes and let my head fall against the back of the couch.

"You don't reason with a panic attack." Ripper's voice, tinged with a hint of a Texas drawl startles me, and I jerk, my eyes flying open to see him standing just behind West.

"When the fuck did you get here?"

"Maybe ten minutes ago? You said your guy's scared of something?" Rip sets down his small duffel bag and takes a seat next to West. Charlie, his German Shephard and constant companion, lies at his feet. "You can't fix it for him, Graham. Rule number one. It doesn't matter how many times you tell him he's safe...if you can't *show* him, you might as well be talking out your ass."

The days we spent with Ripper in a safehouse outside of Kabul are burned into my brain. He was so messed up after we got him out of that hole, he didn't know which end was up. More than once, Ry or Dax or Trevor had to calm him down, convince him he was truly free and not imagining the whole fucking thing.

And the hours I spent with him? Watching over him when the others slept? They gave me a front row seat to just how broken a man can be and still survive.

"I don't want to make anything worse for him." Defeat makes my shoulders slump, and I'm not even sure if I *should* pursue anything with Q.

"I got this," Rip says with a nod to West. "Cara told me you and Cam had somewhere to be tonight. Go on. The kid and I need to have a talk."

THE WAREHOUSE DOOR closes with a quiet *snick*, and Ripper leans down and ruffles the fur on top of Charlie's head. The German Shephard's tail thumps on the carpet, and I swear the dog looks like he's grinning.

"So...?" Rip asks.

"He texted me last night. His security system went haywire." I dig into my pocket for the faulty door sensor and drop it on the table between us. "I was working the bar, so I couldn't get there for almost twenty minutes. He was about to lose his shit."

Ripper's blue eyes darken, and he swallows hard enough I can hear it. Picking up the sensor, he turns it over in his hands, then pulls out his pocket knife and pries the case open. "That's some serious corrosion."

"Right? Can you tell if someone tampered with it?"

He squints, then brings the sensor to his nose. "I'm not sure. But you should have Cam take a look at it. It almost smells like vinegar, and that would definitely damage the wires, but not the shielding."

"That's what I thought too. And the wires were so hot they were almost smoking." Tucking the sensor away for later, I sink back against the cushions and stare up at the ceiling thirty feet above me. At the metal struts, the corrugated roof, the lights. "I stayed the night."

Ripper snorts. "Then what's the problem?"

What *is* the problem? That a guy I like needed me? Or that a guy I like didn't *want* to need me?

"The whole time, it was like he was fighting this war inside his head. Either he expected me to pull a Jekyll and Hyde and turn into a monster or he couldn't fathom why anyone would care about him."

If I didn't know Ripper so well, I would have missed his flinch. The hint of darkness clouding his blue eyes. Charlie sits up and lays his head on Rip's knee with a low, inquisitive sound.

"It's okay, buddy," Ripper says quietly and rests his hand on the back of Charlie's neck. He doesn't meet my gaze, staring somewhere over my shoulder instead. "I kicked Ry and Dax out of the hospital room in Boston a dozen times."

"I know."

Ripper's eyes cut to mine. "What?"

"I'm the one they called to stand watch while they went to Dax's gym and beat the shit out of one another."

"I never saw you." Tension hikes his shoulders up towards his ears, and he rubs the back of his neck. Charlie jumps up onto the sofa next to him, whining now, and Rip drapes an arm around the dog, holding him close.

"Rip? I'm sorry. I didn't spy on you or anything. Never even got close to the door. I was only there in case—"

"In case I lost my shit and tried to hurt someone?"

Now *I'm* the one who wants to avert my gaze. But I can't. Not after all he's been through. How hard he fought to come back. "In case you lost your shit and tried to hurt yourself."

If the man hadn't been sitting down, he would have fallen on his ass. Betrayal, horror, shame, anger...it's like he's going through the seven stages of grief in under a minute.

"They did the right thing," he whispers, so softly, I have to strain to catch the words. Patting his lap, he waits for Charlie to lie across his legs before he blows out a long, slow breath. "You saw how messed up I was those first few days. But it was worse back in Boston."

I don't ask why. Don't say a word. Ripper isn't one for long speeches. If he feels like talking, I'll let him. For as long as he wants.

"In that fancy-ass hospital, everything was *real*. Too real. Bright. Clean. Noisy. I dragged the bed into a corner and slept on the floor behind it." A hoarse, derisive laugh escapes his lips. "I barely had the strength to stand up, but I swore I'd kill anyone who tried to touch me."

Leaning forward, I balance my elbows on my knees. It's all I can do to offer him some comfort. To let him know he's not alone.

"The day I stopped kicking Ry and Dax out? The Fourth of July. The night before, there were a handful of fireworks. Kids' stuff. A few bottle rockets, M-80s. And I shut down. Couldn't move. Stayed awake all night, and when Ry came back the next morning, I wasn't...me anymore. I was *him* again."

Isaad. The person he'd been forced to become after months of torture. Beatings, drugs, days or weeks in that fucking well fighting off scorpions every night and burning up with fever. Living—existing—under the constant threat of death with no hope of escape.

"I didn't *want* to be Ripper. Because I knew everything I'd done, everything that had been done to me...I wasn't good enough to be...me anymore." Charlie gives his hand a lick, and Ripper leans down to bury his face in the dog's neck for a long moment. "That night, Ry and Dax sat on the floor with me. They didn't touch me. Didn't try to get me to talk. They found the movie *Bohemian Rhapsody* on TV, turned up the volume, and sang every fucking song. Pretty sure they played it a dozen times before the sun came up." Shaking his head, he finally meets my gaze. "What you're describing with your guy? What's his name?"

"Quinton."

"Whatever happened in Quinton's past? He's blaming himself for it. Probably thinks he deserved it. My money's on abuse. Long term. He's not going to trust you until he's good and ready. So, I'm going to ask you one question."

Ripper's grave tone makes me sit up straighter. "Anything."

"Is he worth waiting for?"

I think back to the previous night. How it felt to have Q relax against me. Fall asleep in my arms. How he settled a part of my soul I didn't think would ever find peace again.

The answer slips effortlessly from my lips. "Hell, yes."

CHAPTER THIRTEEN

Quinton

FOR THE HUNDREDTH TIME TODAY, I tap my phone screen, checking for messages. Graham promised to show up at seven with a pizza and beer, and I ordered a half-gallon of mint chip, a pack of condoms, and lube from the grocery store. I half expected the delivery guy to leave me some sort of lewd note about my sex life.

A little after four, my phone buzzes on the desk, startling Clementine. The kitten leaps out of her bed and her tail grows five sizes as she digs her claws into the back of the couch and makes the most non-threatening sound in the world. It's ridiculous how cute she is when she growls.

But given the number on my CallerID, she's not the only one with her hackles raised. "Connor? What's up?"

"I sent two of my guys to watch Asshole," he says, an edge to his voice I only hear when he talks about Alec. "He's been holed up in a motel on Galveston Drive for the past two days. Near as they can tell, he hasn't left the room since he checked in."

I blow out a breath. One I've been holding for almost a week now. "You're *sure* he's still in Dallas? And who are 'your guys'?"

Connor clears his throat. "Quinton, you know I can't talk about my job."

"That's all you ever say. I'm your brother, for fuck's sake. You took Alec's side when he claimed I was having a breakdown. After the accident, you ignored every one of my text messages begging you to talk to me. Then you show up at *his* apartment to rescue me, spend one night listening to me cry, dump me in a facility until I can walk again, move me out here, and…all but vanish. This is the first time we've spoken since."

"I didn't *vanish*, Q. I made sure you were safe, then I went home. The more contact you have with your past, the more danger you're in. Asshole is certifiable, and while he's probably too big of a coward to try anything serious, I'm never going to stop worrying."

With every word, the tension between us rises until I can't decide whether to hang up on him or scream at him. "I don't need you to worry," I say, each word carefully measured. "I need my brother."

"Clearly, you *did* need me to worry," Connor snaps. "Otherwise you wouldn't have gotten yourself tangled up with Asshole in the first place."

My voice fails me, and all I can think about is how I came home on a Friday night to find Alec and Connor posing as a united front during their "intervention." It doesn't matter that Alec is a master manipulator. It still hurt.

"Maybe if you'd believed me the first time I tried to tell you what Alec was doing, I would have left him before he destroyed my whole fucking life."

Jabbing the screen, I hang up on him. The only family connection I have, since Mom doesn't know where I am. She still thinks Alec is "such a nice guy." I know I'm being unfair.

Connor didn't even *get* my text messages after the accident. Alec made sure of that.

Clementine jumps onto the desk, and times like these, I think she's more empathetic than most human beings. She's kneading my forearm, yet still staring at the telephone monster like it'll turn on her any second.

And then the doorbell rings. It's too early for Graham to show up, and I'm not expecting any deliveries today. The sign's very clear.

Occupant will not answer or sign for any deliveries.

But the bell rings again. The camera shows a guy in the most generic delivery uniform ever. From the app on my phone, I activate the intercom. "Whatever it is, you can leave it by the door."

"I'm afraid I can't, sir. My instructions are to deliver it to the occupant personally." The man looks downright uncomfortable. Not that I blame him. He probably had to step over a melted and rotting puddle of mint chip to get to the door. The box in his hands can't be more than six inches on any side. Done up with a red ribbon.

"Who's the sender?"

"Seattle Floral Creations."

Flowers? Who the hell would send me flowers? Something doesn't feel right about this whole thing. Graham wouldn't do that. And even if he did, he's seen the sign. "Is there a card?"

Now the delivery guy just looks pissed. "No card, sir. Look, it's a prickly pear cactus. Do you want it or not?"

"Leave. I refuse the delivery. Just...go." I can barely get the words out. There's only one person who would send me a prickly pear cactus. Only one person who'd insist I receive it personally. Alec loved the damn things. Gave me one after our first date.

My hands shake as I text my brother.

You're sure he's still in Dallas?

Connor responds in under a minute.

Yes. Why?

He's messing with me. Signed me up for a catalog he used to love and just sent me a cactus—or tried to.

Even as I type the message, I can see how stupid it is. I don't have any proof it was him. A fucking catalog and a cactus?

My guys just verified he's in his hotel room watching TV. Sent one of the housekeeping staff to offer him fresh towels. He's definitely still in Dallas.

Then five minutes later, he sends another message.

I'll fly out tomorrow. We'll talk. About everything.

Big brother to the rescue. Again. But I don't need him to save me. Not this time. What I want more than anything? His respect. To just be my brother rather than my protector.

No. As long as he's still in Texas, I can take care of myself.

Three dots dance at the bottom of the screen, over and over and over again. But no message follows.

"We're okay by ourselves. Right, Clementine?" I stroke the kitten's soft fur and she rewards me by flopping over and letting me rub her belly.

I can do this. Even if Alec keeps harassing me, I can fight him now. I'm strong enough. At least...I hope I am.

Two hours later, I stare at my computer monitor, a silly grin plastered to my face. This has been my dream for three years. To help people like me. To do something *good* with my skills.

One click of the mouse, and Zen Oasis will be headed to all of the mobile app stores, and within a week, people will be able to buy it. For an entire year, I'd given up hope of ever making it this far. Hell, I'd given up hope for a lot of things.

Hitting that button? It's one more *fuck you* to the man who tried to take everything from me. But more than that? It's reassurance. Proof I survived.

I wish I had someone to celebrate with. Sure, Graham will be here in under an hour, and we'll have the "getting to know you" talk. But he won't understand how important this is to me. How big of a milestone it really is.

"You didn't win," I whisper, even though Alec can't hear me. The words still bring me peace. Satisfaction. Maybe even a hint of pride.

Maybe I can't walk to the grocery store or the coffee shop. Maybe I'll never be able to do those things. But this? This win means more to me than anything. I'm here. I deserve happiness. And maybe even...love.

~

Graham

This isn't like any other first date I've been on. Going to the guy's house? It's something you might expect to see on *Unsolved Mysteries* or *Dateline*. After one member of the couple disappears.

But Q isn't like anyone I've met before. And maybe this is more my speed. Maybe it has been all along.

He opens the door wearing a pair of khaki pants and a short-sleeved blue Henley, and it does things for his chest and arms that should be illegal. His cheeks redden the longer I stare without moving, until finally he clears his throat. "Um, do you want to come in?"

Hell, yes.

"Sorry. I was enjoying the view." The flush spreads down to his neck, and I carefully brush past him with the massive pizza box and six pack of lager. "Big Mario's is an institution in this neighborhood. But if you hate New York style pizza, there's another place around the corner we can try."

All four locks click into place, and Q joins me in the kitchen. "I appreciate pizza in all forms."

He's relaxed tonight in a way I haven't seen before, and I want to ask him what's changed, but I won't risk spooking him, so instead, I pass him a beer.

"To starting over?"

Q twists the top off the bottle and swallows hard. But he smiles, and it's about the best damn sight in the world. "To starting over."

WE'RE two beers in before we move beyond the superficial. Q designs websites for a living, work he can do from anywhere, graduated from Texas A&M, and a couple of years ago was working for a little weekly newspaper when he discovered the paper's owner was into child pornography.

"Shit. I remember that case." Draining the last of the beer, I relax, draping my arm over the back of the couch. "Seattle has a really popular weekly too—*The Stranger*—and when the bar's not busy, I read it between customers. The guy went to jail for at least fifteen years, right?"

"Seventeen. The judge knocked a few years off because he helped break up the ring that was distributing the images." Q rubs his palms on his khakis, his shoulders hiked up almost to his ears.

"Hey. Ease up." I lay my hand over his. "We don't have to talk about this. Or anything that makes you uncomfortable."

"It's not..." He lets out a frustrated sigh. "Everything makes me uncomfortable." Just as I'm about to offer to clean up the plates and our empty bottles, he adds, "Except this. You. Here."

He scoots closer so my arm is almost around his shoulders.

Fuck. I feel like I'm in some romanticized memory where I wasn't the only gay kid at my high school. One where I had the courage to pull a move this suave on a date.

"How long has it been?" I ask quietly.

"A year." He stares down at his knees, picking at an invisible piece of lint on his pants. "That was my last relationship. The...uh...the bad one."

Dammit. I can *feel* him withdraw, shrinking back inside this hard shell no one can penetrate just to keep himself safe. Playing with a lock of hair curling over his collar, I press my thigh to his. "I haven't dated in years. Did the Tinder thing here and there for a while. Always hated myself the next day. Until..." How much do I tell him? About my own past? About why I haven't had a relationship since that awful night eight years ago?

"Until?" The tremble in his voice makes me want to hold him and promise him that everything will be okay, but I don't make promises I can't keep. Learned that from Ryker and Wren. All I can offer him is the truth and hope it's enough.

"I found a family. Hidden Agenda. The people there—and in our partner company, Second Sight in Boston—they're like my brothers and sisters. Once I realized that? I stopped searching for meaning in anonymity."

I'm rambling. Hell, I don't even know if I'm making any sense.

"I've always had anxiety." Q slides his thumb over the label on the bottle of beer, then starts working a corner free, staring at it like it holds the secrets of the universe. "Only had a couple of boyfriends before...*him*. And after..." He shrugs. "Hard to meet anyone when you don't leave the house."

"You met me."

That cute little flush creeps up his neck again, warmth spreading under my fingers. He's still picking at the label, and I ease the bottle from his hand.

"Q? Before this goes any further—if that's what you want—I have to know your limits. Your triggers. Physical and emotional. I hurt you this morning, and I won't do that again."

The small shake of his head does nothing to reassure me. "I couldn't tell you all my triggers if you spent the next three full days listening to me." I'm about to ask him how we're supposed to move forward if he won't open up when he clears his throat. "Al-Alec was everything I thought I wanted in a boyfriend," Q says, his voice just above a whisper. "Until I realized what he was doing to me."

"Doing to you?" I force myself to remain calm. Because whatever Q's about to tell me? I have a feeling I'll want to hunt down this Alec asshole and beat him into next week.

"At first, it was little things. Convincing me I was only into the things *he* liked. Pancakes. Cider. Popsicles. Non-fat milk."

"Non-fat milk is just gray water."

His laugh puts a hairline crack in the tension between us, and he meets my gaze. I'd give anything to wipe that pain from his eyes. But if I've learned anything from Ry, West, Inara, and all the other members of our little family who've found their forevers over the years, it's that nothing ever takes the pain away. Relationships are forged when you can see *past* the pain. Accept it as part of the person you're with and love them anyway.

"After a few months, it got worse. A lot worse." His voice fades even more, and he blinks hard before he risks meeting my gaze again. "I know you're not him, Graham. This morning with the pancakes? I'm not proud of how I reacted. You were being nice, and my fucked up brain couldn't see past a single moment of fear to the guy standing in front of me offering me a cup of coffee. I'm getting better. Six months ago? I couldn't have let you in. Or called out to you in the first place. But, I'll never be the man I was before *him*."

"I don't want that man." Shifting to face him, I slide my

fingers up the back of his neck and tangle them in his hair. "I want this one."

The kiss starts out gentle, hesitant. Until I trace the seam of his lips with my tongue. Opening for me, he moans, the sound rumbling in his chest. Fuck. Why does he affect me so deeply? The first moment I saw him, I knew he was special. Now? I'm desperate for more, but there's a part of me that's terrified, too. Because after tonight, I'll never be the same again.

I urge him closer, sliding my arm under his knees to drape his legs over mine, putting his hard length in each reach of my free hand. Palming his erection through his khakis, I'm rewarded with another one of those deep, desperate sounds before I come up for air.

His fingers slide under my t-shirt, and it feels so damn good to be touched, I'd take him right here if I thought he was ready for that.

Now *he's* kissing *me*, and I'm not prepared for the intense rush of pure need shooting straight to my dick.

"Upstairs," he manages after I kiss him again, keeping up a rhythm between my tongue and the long strokes of my palm along his trapped length until we both have to stop and catch our breath.

"Are you sure?" Pulling away from him feels wrong, but before we end up naked, I have to tell him *my* limits. Cupping his cheek, I press a gentle kiss to those firm lips, but stop him from taking it any further. "I don't bottom, Q. I can't. Whatever we do...however far we go, it's the one thing I can't..." My breath stutters, my chest unbearably tight until his gaze locks onto mine.

"Graham." His eyes hold understanding—more than I deserve, more than I expected. Can he tell? Just how damaged I am? "I want you. You asked for my triggers, there's no way I'm not going to respect yours."

The gentle way he drapes his hand over mine, the slight

tremble in his fingers, and the roughness to his voice all make me want more than just tonight. We fit, somehow. Two broken people whose jagged edges align.

But it's too soon to think that, let alone say it. Maybe we've talked enough, though, because Q gets to his feet. And when he offers me his hand, I take it.

CHAPTER FOURTEEN

Quinton

After I've checked all the locks and Graham's cleaned up our plates, he stands at the foot of the stairs, hands shoved into the pockets of his jeans, looking about as unsure as I feel.

Except for the rather obvious bulge under the denim.

My back hasn't bothered me much all day, so I take his hand and lead him up to the bedroom. Where I promptly freeze. Because even though I was half naked with him last night, the reality of what we're about to do roots me to the spot.

"If you've changed your mind," he says, his arms winding around my waist, "I can go home. Or stay and hold you all night. Whatever you need."

"No." My protest escapes harsher than I intend, and for a second, I expect him to yell or chastise me, but when I turn, desire and respect swim in his eyes. "I want this. But there's so much you don't know..."

"About your injuries?" Guiding me to the bed, he sits next to me, one hand on my lower back, the other on my thigh. "Tell me how I won't hurt you."

"I broke three vertebrae. The bones healed, but injuries like mine...I have permanent nerve damage and neuropathy. Some parts of my back and legs are almost numb, others hurt like hell. I can't bend or twist or balance on one foot like most people. Physical therapy helps a lot, and I'm more flexible than I used to be, but I'll never be 100% again."

Graham leans in, curling his fingers around my neck and brushing his lips to mine. "If you're lying down...?"

More kisses. Down the curve of my shoulder. His other hand slides lower, flicking the button on my pants, palming my length, and I manage to whisper, "Yes...that...God."

His eyes lock on mine as he tugs at my khakis, easing them down my hips until he's kneeling on the floor. Every touch, every kiss...it's like I'm not broken. Like he actually *wants* me, despite my scars, my fears, my damage.

"Gotta get these jeans off before I risk permanent injury," he says, his voice tinged with both pleasure and pain. "Fuck." The single word, drawn out on a groan, makes my dick twitch and anticipation crawls up my spine when he's standing before me in only his briefs, a condom and packet of lube in his hand.

The way his muscles tense and flex, the anticipation lighting his eyes, his confidence and grace, despite his bulk... I'm mesmerized. I wish I had one ounce of his courage.

Because he's magnificent. Rugged and handsome, but also, somehow beautiful. Like he was sculpted from clay and brought to life from an artist's fantasy. Or from mine.

And then he does the sexiest fucking thing I could imagine. Crawls up the bed until he's next to me, cups the back of my head, and holds my gaze. "Tell me what you like."

What *I* like. Not what he needs. Not what he wants me to do. With those five words, he banishes all of my fears, all the ghosts that haunt me.

"It's been so long I don't know anymore." The admission costs me, and I try to look away from this man who's starred in more than one of my dreams the past week, but he slides his palm until it rests against my cheek, plants a gentle kiss to my lips, and shakes his head.

"Yes, you do. And whatever it is? You can tell me."

"I just…" Tears burn my eyes when I realize there's only one thing I want. That *nothing* else matters as long as I can have this *one* thing. "I want to look at you. I want to see you. The whole time. Face to face. Whatever we do, whatever we can or can't do with my back as fucked up as it is, I don't care. But I need to see you."

"Then you'll see me. No matter what." With a kiss to my palm, he seals his promise, and he's so earnest, so completely focused on me, that I start to think maybe…I can have this one night. This one, perfect night to get me through all the ones after.

Because soon, he'll start asking questions. About *Alec*. About why I didn't leave him sooner. About how I let myself be turned into a pathetic, drugged up, obedient zombie.

"Q? Are you sure about this?" Graham pauses, his fingers curled around the waistband of my briefs. I picked red today. Another rebellion against my past. Against Alec's hatred of anything but tighty whities. "If you're having second thoughts…"

Shit. Don't think about the future. Not yet.

I answer by covering his hand with mine and squeezing gently. "I'm not."

And then I'm bared to him, my cock throbbing and a drop of pre-cum glistening at the tip. Graham straddles me, dips his head, and swirls his tongue around my crown. That might be the sexiest thing anyone's ever done to me. "Is that okay?" he asks, his voice tight with need.

I can only nod, and then my God. He wraps his strong fingers around the base of my shaft and takes me slowly, like he's savoring each inch. His cheeks hollow, and I dig my heels into the mattress, pure, white hot need shooting through me.

Velvet lips, the heat of his mouth, and whatever he's doing with his tongue...I'm close. So close. "Graham."

He raises his eyes, keeping his promise. In that moment, I realize I asked him for the wrong thing. I don't need to see him. I need *him* to see *me*. And he does. With a throaty hum, he takes me even deeper, his free hand cupping my balls, and I can't hold on any longer.

The whole world slows, going soft and warm, and sheets rustle as Graham slides up my body and gathers me against him. "Come back to me, Q," he murmurs, his lips brushing my ear.

I'm trying, but I haven't felt this good in so long, I don't want it to end.

"Can I kiss you, baby?"

He's asking. Why is he asking? Blinking hard, I focus on his handsome face, his swollen lips, the eyes bright with need. Without hesitation, I pull him on top of me until we're locked together, and I taste myself on his tongue.

Graham gave me the choice. He's given me *every* choice.

"There you are," he manages when we come up for air. "Was worried for a minute. Was that okay?"

"That was...wow."

~

Graham

The gift Q gave me? It's beautiful. Letting go with such abandon, such joy...it's like he's never been allowed to be *free* before. I don't deserve this—or him—but that doesn't stop me from skimming my hand down his side and under one toned ass cheek.

His legs are thin—in stark contrast to his arms and chest, and a scar bisects his left hip. Pressing a kiss to the thick line, I watch his face, making sure I'm not hurting him or dredging up bad memories. One day, I hope he'll trust me enough to tell me everything.

"Put this under your ass," I say. "It'll relieve some of the pressure on your back."

He wriggles until his hips are slightly elevated, which affords me a beautiful view of his lithe, toned muscles and a chance to study how he moves. "Your right side is stronger? More flexible?"

"Y-yes." His eyes dart to the scar on his thigh, and I cup his chin, forcing his gaze back to mine.

"You don't have to hide from me, Q. I see you. And you're perfect."

Doubt shadows his gaze, and I slowly raise his right leg until it rests on my shoulder. "Still okay?"

A hint of apprehension lingers in his eyes until I suck two fingers into my mouth, and then his lips part, his breath catching in his chest.

The first time I brush his entrance with my slick fingers, he shudders, and a tiny moan escapes his lips. Massaging slowly, gently, I let him get used to the feel of me touching him *there*, watching for any sign of discomfort or pain.

His cock is already at half-mast again, precum leaking from the tip, and he's panting, trying to push his ass against me. "Graham, please..."

Grabbing the packet of lube, I spill a bit onto my finger, then circle his tight hole, gently increasing the pressure until I slip inside. His heat grabs me, and the whimper that escapes his lips holds so much pent up need, I wish I'd thought to do this earlier with my mouth wrapped around his cock.

Deeper now, I start to twist and stretch him gently, my gaze never leaving his face. "You're going to feel so fucking good wrapped around me," I say as I add a second finger, and I'm rewarded with a shudder and a choked moan.

I'm thicker than he is, but Q wins on length. God, I need this like I need my next breath. It's so much more than just a quick fuck, because he hasn't stopped looking at me either. Not once.

"Don't stop," he begs. The corners of his eyes crinkle with a hint of pain, and I ease back an inch, lessening the bend in his leg until all I can see is pleasure. He's ready for me—at least I hope he is—but I need to kiss him first.

Crushing my mouth to his, I don't know who wants this more. Q scores his teeth along my bottom lip, and fuck. I want to know what it feels like to have him suck me off. When I pull back so I can find the condom, he cups the back of my neck, holding me still. "You see me."

Those three words shatter my heart, because they're filled with such wonder. I swear, if I ever meet the asshole who hurt him, I'm going to make him pay for every terrible thing he did to this beautiful, strong, and haunted man.

"I see you." Repeating my promise, I slide the condom over my dick. I'm so on edge, I don't know how I'm going to last once I'm inside him. "Relax, Q. I'll go slow."

He hisses as my crown slips past the tight ring of muscle, and I cant my hips slowly, driving a little deeper each time. Despite having just found release a few minutes ago, he's hard again, and I take my slick fingers and wrap them around his shaft.

"Oh, God," he moans and tries to thrust into my palm.

"I've got you." Sliding my hand along his hard length in time with my hips, I know the second I bottom out and find his prostate. His body bucks, and his pupils go wide as he whimpers and moans, no longer capable of actual words.

I'm so fucking close, my entire body's coiled tighter than a spring, but watching Q's face, seeing how he's straining to hold on, to keep his gaze focused on me...it's beautiful. "Let...go..." I manage, and when he does, the intense spasms of his tight muscles around my dick send me over the edge right after him.

Q STARES AT ME, his brown eyes wide and slightly glassy as I ease myself out of him. "Stay here, baby. I'll be right back."

The term of endearment slips out, and he blinks, hard, uncertainty written all over his face. Too much, too soon. But a part of me doesn't care, because the connection I've found with him? The heat? The passion? We're not one and done. I want a lot more with him than just tonight.

With a warm, wet washcloth and towel in my hands, I return to the bed, but before I can finish, he stops me with his hand on mine. "I can do it."

"I know you *can*. But it's not weakness to let someone else take care of you a little. Especially not after...*that*. Because, whoa."

He chuckles, breaking this fresh tension between us, and when I'm done, we climb under the covers, and I wrap my arms around him. "Was that okay?" I ask.

"That was a hell of a lot better than 'okay.' That was amaz-ing." With a sigh, he snuggles closer. "Will you stay?"

Did he really think I was planning on leaving? After what we shared? "I'm not going anywhere. Not unless you ask me to."

Reaching up to turn off the light, he whispers, "Good. This...I've missed this."

"What?" His hair tickles my cheek as I press a kiss to the back of his neck. "Sex? Or—?"

"Being held. Being touched." His voice trembles slightly, and I tuck my legs up so they're against his. "I wanted to be alone for a long time, Graham. Needed it. Until I met you."

"You're not alone." As if to prove my point—or claim her

position in this house—Clementine jumps up onto the bed with a *mrrp,* curls up right next to Q's bent knees, and starts purring. "Pretty sure Clementine took offense at that."

"Nah," he says. "She just hates not being the center of attention."

In the dark, with the kitten's purr providing a constant, low backdrop, Q tells me how he found her. Wet, cold, probably only a few hours away from death. "I was in the middle of a panic attack. Checking the cameras every two or three minutes, completely unable to pull myself out of it, and then I heard her crying. She'd wedged herself against the front door, and I couldn't see her, but that little meow was so desperate, it helped me focus. The second I picked her up, she started purring, and didn't stop the whole rest of the night. I think she saved me as much as I saved her."

"A friend of mine has a dog like that. Ripper and Charlie are never far from one another, and the German Shepherd is the most perceptive animal I've ever known. Maybe one day, you can meet him. Them."

Q sucks in a sharp breath. "I...I can't go anywhere... outside...I don't. Please—" Clementine meows and starts kneading the bed even harder, like she knows he's upset, and I run my lips along the shell of his ear.

"I won't pressure you, baby." This time, I know exactly what I'm saying and why I'm saying it. I care for Quinton more than I've cared for anyone other than my family—both the one I was born into and the one I've found at Hidden Agenda, and whatever he needs, I'll give him. "If you never step foot outside these four walls again, I'll bring the world to you. Or keep it all away. Whatever you need to feel safe."

He falls silent, and though I have so many questions, I keep them to myself. We have time. For now, this is enough.

CHAPTER FIFTEEN

Quinton

THE SCENT of coffee wafts up the stairs, and a minute later, Graham saunters into the room, wearing only his briefs, and I stare at the man who rocked my entire world simply by *seeing* me.

"'Morning, gorgeous." He slides back into bed and passes me a mug. "How are you feeling? I didn't hurt you last night, did I?"

Taking a sip of coffee gives me a minute to choose my next words. "I have pain every day of my life, Graham. I probably always will. Even when I do everything right, there's a chance I'll wake up and it'll just be a bad day. So you can't worry every time I wince or limp or have to use the chair lift to get up or down the stairs."

He leans his head on my shoulder, a move that's surprisingly intimate, even after everything we shared last night. "I know a couple of guys with chronic pain. Ry—my boss at Hidden Agenda—is the toughest person I've ever met. But when he was in the Special Forces, he and his team were captured and tortured for fifteen months. The man knows exactly how many bones they broke, for fuck's sake. He powers through, but there are days I can tell."

We sit with our coffee in silence, our legs tangled together. "This morning? My pain's a four out of ten. On my best days, it's a two. On my worst, an eight. But those are rare."

"Q?" Graham sets his mug down and rests his hand on my thigh. "You told me *what* happened. But not *how*."

My shoulders hike up to my ears, and Graham shifts a little closer.

"I work with a Navy SEAL, an Army Ranger sniper, and a team leader for the Special Forces. You know the first thing each one of them taught me?"

I meet his gaze, those blue eyes so serious, yet full of compassion. I want to kiss that dimple under his lower lip and run my hands over his chest to trace each one of those defined muscles. But more than that, I want to *know* him. "What?"

"You trust your team. With anything. With everything. No lying. No secrets."

"And I'm 'your team'? We only met ten days ago."

"Q." He frames my face with his hands, and they're so warm and strong, I close my eyes and savor the moment. Until he kisses me, and I want to lose myself in him. With him. "I told you I didn't want this to be a casual fuck. I've had enough of those in my life."

"How many?" The question slips out before I can stop myself.

"Seven. Eight, maybe. Didn't exactly keep count of my Tinder hook-ups, but I don't think I had more than six of those." Dropping one hand so he can twine our fingers, he lifts his brows. "You?"

"You know my number," I say quietly. "Two before...and *him*."

"You've only dated three guys? Shit, Q. Why? You're gorgeous, smart—"

"Stop." I ease myself out of bed, bracing my hand on the wall until I find my balance. "I'm broken, Graham. Always have been. Even before Alec got a hold of me. Crowds. Traffic. Loud noises. I was only diagnosed with anxiety four years ago. No one wants to date a nut job who can't handle going out to a bar or a fancy restaurant. Concerts. Baseball games."

Graham scoots across the bed, his abs flexing with the movement. Then his arms wind around my waist and he presses his forehead to mine. "You're not broken, Q. And I don't care what your *number* is. The guys I fucked? They were a way to blow off steam. Before I found my place at Hidden Agenda. Before I knew who I was. And who I wanted to be."

My eyes burn, and the overwhelming emotion he stirs in me raises a lump in my throat. I'd give anything to have his confidence. His grace. To be as sure of who I am as he seems to be. But maybe...it doesn't matter. Because he's here. With me.

"This? What I think we're building?" he whispers. "It's real. And it sure as hell doesn't end when I walk out your front door in an hour. If the past few years have taught me anything, it's that the parts of us we think are broken? Those are the parts that make us who we are."

Graham

"I need to drive out to Ellensburg today to pick up five cases of MREs. It's a ninety minute drive. You could come with me?" We're in the shower, and I have my arm wrapped around Q's waist, holding him against me, his back to my front, as I slowly stroke up and down his shaft.

He stiffens, but not in the way I hope. "I can't. Graham..."

Turning, he stares down to where our bodies touch and chokes back a sob. "You know I don't go outside. Only to the dumpster, and even then...there are days I can't."

"Look at me, baby. Please?" I won't force him. Not to meet my gaze, not to go outside, not to do anything, and I desperately need him to understand that. "Quinton?"

Slowly, he raises his head, and his shame breaks my heart. "I'm not disappointed, not mad. It's just me in an SUV for three hours with a five minute stop. I thought it might be easier if you didn't have to be among people. If it were just the two of us."

Q's shaking now, and I turn him so the spray hits his back. With a shuddering breath, he buries his face in the curve of my neck. "It's still leaving the only place I feel safe. Before...Alec, I could go to a quiet bar or have a drink with friends. But he shrank my world down to nothing."

"How?"

Q flinches and pulls away, grabbing the shampoo and vigorously washing his hair. I think I've lost him until the words start to tumble from his lips so quickly, like he's trying to get them all out before he shuts down.

"Little things. Digs that my apartment was too small, it was too hard to find parking, so we always went to his place. He never let me pick when we ordered takeout. He'd put down my friends—not to their faces, but to me—and he never wanted to hang out with them. After a few months, I was so alone, and I thought...he convinced me...that I needed him. That he was the only one who understood me."

"Fuck, Q. That's straight up abuse. You know that, right?"

The look he shoots me over his shoulder makes me feel all of three inches tall. "No shit. But that's what abusers *do*. And Alec...it got so much worse than that."

There's only one way it could possibly be worse.

"Did he hit you?"

"No. Never." He slumps against the shower wall, his eyes closed. "Ever heard the term gaslighting?"

Warning bells go off in my head. Images of Ripper in the days after we rescued him. Ry used the term a time or two. "Yeah. It's making you doubt your own judgment, right?"

"Not exactly." After a shuddering breath, he swipes a sudsy trail of shampoo from his forehead. "Gaslighting is when an abuser makes you question your own sanity." He returns to scrubbing his hair like he's trying to scour the memories from his head, and I gently cover his hands with mine. This strong, brave, man crumbles in my arms, hoarse, choking sobs wracking his body, and I hold him so he won't fall. The water's starting to cool by the time he gets it all out, and I ease him out of the shower and wrap him in a towel before drying myself off and leading him back to the bed.

Q huddles under the blankets shivering while I sit next to him. I'm ready to tell him he doesn't need to say another word when he clears his throat. "Alec doesn't feel emotions like normal people do. No remorse, no guilt, no compassion. Life is one big *game* to him. One he always has to win. And I tried to leave him, but after I fell..."

Another wave of tears and he curls onto his side. Clementine wedges herself under his chin, and I take my own position at his back so I can hold him.

"How *did* you get out?" I ask when his sobs fade.

"My brother. If it weren't for Connor..." He swipes at his cheeks, brushing away the tears, and buries his face in Clementine's fur. "Alec took everything from me. And now, I don't know how to find myself again."

I'd give anything to reassure him. To tell him he's already found himself in so many ways, taken back so much of his life. But instead, I say nothing. Just hold him so he knows he's not alone.

AN HOUR LATER, he flips open the locks one at a time. He's tense. Has been ever since he told me about Alec, but I at least got him to smile when I found one of Clementine's toys and had her leaping and doing backflips as she chased a ball with a bell inside.

The morning sun brightens his front porch, and the way he's looking at it—the longing in his eyes—it breaks me. "How far can you go?" I ask softly, my hand clasped around his.

"Two steps. Just to the mailbox."

"In three, you'd be in the sun." I cross the threshold, still holding his hand, our arms outstretched. "I'd like to kiss you in the sun. But only if you want that too."

Q's lips press together in a hard, thin line. I expect him to shake his head, but before I can return to his side to say goodbye to him properly, *he* joins *me*.

His breath stutters in his chest, and I rest my free hand over his heart. "You can do this, baby. One more? Together?"

His nod does something to my heart. I can't describe it, except to say it's warm and reassuring and *right*.

We move as one, and when the sun hits his face, the corners of his lips tug up slightly. Sliding my hand from his chest up to his neck, I thread my fingers through his hair and kiss him so thoroughly, my dick rockets to attention, straining against my zipper.

He's breathless too by the time my phone buzzes in my pocket. Likely West wondering where the hell I am and why I haven't picked up Hidden Agenda's SUV yet. "I have to go," I say against his lips. "And I have to cover for one of the other bartenders at the Unicorn for the next two nights. But I want to see you again. Soon."

Q rests his forehead against mine. "I'd like that."

My phone rings again, and I roll my eyes. "If I don't get

going, West will have my ass. Text me. Any time. Or call. You decide what you want to do on Tuesday night, and I'll make it happen. Okay?"

He nods as I release him and walk backwards down the ramp. I might be falling for this guy. Harder than I thought possible. Because watching him stand in the sun? Seeing the pure joy on his face as he tips his head and basks in the warm light? It feels an awful lot like what I always imagined love to be.

CHAPTER SIXTEEN

Quinton

THOSE FEW MINUTES in the sun? Pure joy. Until I scanned the street and saw a blond, bearded man turn the corner and stare at me, his phone pressed to his ear.

It doesn't matter that I've never seen him before. That after five seconds, he continues walking without giving me a second look. I'm still too panicked to do anything but lurch back inside, slam the door, and flip all the locks before my chest is so tight, it's hard to breathe.

The day is mostly a lost cause. Other than feeding Clementine and throwing her favorite fishy toy every time she drops it in my lap, I can't manage to focus on anything but binge watching *Parks and Recreation*.

Graham texts me a handful of times, sending me pictures of the vast emptiness only an hour outside of Seattle. It's beautiful, in a haunting sort of way, and I wish I were strong enough to see it.

By the time the sun sets, I feel almost normal again, and I sink into my massage chair with my laptop to check my email.

"Oh my God." Zen Oasis is already live on all the mobile app stores, and the sales numbers... It's a good thing I'm sitting down. They're in the thousands. After only a day.

My dream—the one I gave up on for so long—is coming true, and my eyes burn as I blink back tears. Clementine *mrrps* from where she's curled up at my feet, and I reach down to rub her belly. "You know what a big deal this is, sweetie? It means he didn't win. I did."

Running some sales projections, I can't believe what I'm seeing. If they're even *close* to accurate, I should be able to cover my living expenses within three months *and* have enough money left to pay my brother back.

Alec ran up close to ten thousand dollars in debt on my credit cards, and Connor wiped the slate clean, paid for the rehab facility, and pre-paid six months of rent on this place. Hell, he covered the cost of the chair lift and the kick ass security system too.

I protested everything, but he waved me off. "I let you down," he said every time I tried to refuse. "Let me make it up to you."

If only he understood that all I needed was to have my brother back.

I'm so excited, I email him to share the good news. I doubt he'll respond anytime soon. His job—whatever it is—often takes him "off the grid" for days. His words, not mine. It's got to be something with the government, but he'll never tell me.

Focusing on anything when I'm this excited is damn near impossible, and as perceptive as Clementine is, I need connection. Someone to share this moment with me.

As if the universe can hear my thoughts, my phone buzzes with a text from Graham.

Busy night. Was so late getting back from Ellensburg, I'll have to unpack all the MREs tomorrow. After running drills for three hours. It'll be a miracle if I'm still standing for my next shift. Just wanted to let you know I was thinking about you, and I can't wait to see you on Tuesday.

He signs the message with a heart emoji. I can't *not* reply.

"Need to celebrate on Tuesday. Zen Oasis, the app I've been working on for three years is already live and it's selling! Alec tried to take that from me too. Kept me from working on it, told me it'd never be successful. But he was wrong, and I need to keep telling myself he was wrong about a lot of things."

My phone buzzes with a response in under five minutes.

"Holy shit, Q. That's amazing. I just downloaded it. I can't play around with it at work unless the crowds magically disappear, but you can bet your ass I'll check it out when I get off."

All my excitement evaporates in a heartbeat—replaced by anxiety. Graham's important to me. More important than I realized until just now. And if he pays attention to everything I put into Zen Oasis, he'll see how my mind works—and maybe, how truly fucked up I am. Oh, God. What if this was a huge mistake?

But then he sends me another message. With a photo.

"Can't wait to congratulate you properly."

I almost choke when I see the picture. Taken from chest height, it shows his Unicorn tank top molded to his sculpted abs and a bulge clearly visible under his tight, black pants.

"Did you just send me a clothed dick pic?"

His reply is only six words, but it still sends a fair bit of blood straight to my cock. *"Best I could do. For now."*

I don't understand why he wants me. Or how the hell he was still single when we met. But with every text, every touch, every moment of understanding he shows me, I think maybe I've found one of the good ones. And maybe I'll be strong enough to eventually tell him everything.

～

I'M HALFWAY through a website proposal for a new client the next afternoon when my doorbell rings.

Huh. The grocery delivery guy is actually on time today. Watching the video feed until he's back on the sidewalk, I flip the locks and step outside. Fully outside. I don't even think about it because in one of those bags? Ingredients for my favorite dessert. Double chocolate cake. It's one of the few things I can cook, and Alec hated chocolate.

The idea of making it for Graham—for the two of us—distracted me from my overwhelming fear of going outside, and I squint up at the sun. I made it three steps yesterday. Maybe today, I can take four.

One at a time. I don't want Clementine to get out, so I shut the door behind me, another leap of faith, and shuffle towards the ramp. I'm not fast. I never will be. Today's a solid five on the pain scale. But I'm steady. And when my feet are firmly on the ramp, I pull out my phone and take a picture of them.

My shoes are pristine. Black Converse that have never seen dirt—or concrete—and for the first time, I think maybe I should order some Scotchgard in case I ever make it all the way to the street.

Texting Graham before I go back inside, I send him the photo.

"At this rate, it'll be months before I can meet your friends. But...know that I want to."

I don't expect him to respond right away. He said as much when he texted me *"Good Morning"* a little after nine. But just knowing that I took this step—and did it on my own—leaves me smiling all the way back into the house and into the kitchen with the groceries.

Dark chocolate, powdered sugar, butter...I'm practically salivating. I'm not sure how my back will handle standing at the counter long enough to not only bake a cake, but also mix up a batch of frosting, but I'm going to try.

Distracted, I don't look at the six-pack until it's clear of the bag. And then the cardboard carrier slips from my grasp. At least one bottle shatters, and the scent...it makes me sick.

"No, no, no." I have to clean it up. Get the stench of the sweet rhubarb and pear cider out of my kitchen. Oh, God. It's on my shoes. The black Converse aren't pristine any more, and they never will be again.

Clementine *mrrps* as she pads towards the kitchen, and I shout, "Get back! Stay out of here!"

Yelling at my sweet, innocent kitten only makes me feel worse, and she bolts up the stairs. She's never done a single thing wrong. Doesn't even scratch the couch. But...the cider. It was Alec's favorite. His only vice. At least according to him. Well, that and popsicles. Raspberry popsicles. I paw through the bags, and fuck. There they are.

Alec did this. Despite the overwhelming smell and the nausea crawling up my throat, I have to know how these got in the bag. My hand shakes as I dial the store's number, and I hang up and try three more times before I can navigate their fucking multiple choice menu to connect with their home delivery department.

"Can I help you?" a pleasant female voice asks.

"I...uh. The delivery for Silver Star Technologies? There's s-something wr-wrong with it. Two things I didn't order." My voice cracks, and I'm shaking, leaning against the counter, staring down at the bottles of cider littering the floor.

"Can I have the order number?" All business now, the woman taps on a keyboard as I read her the ten-digit code. "Okay, there it is. Looks like two items: a six-pack of cider and a box of raspberry popsicles were added twenty minutes ago. The request came by email from a 'Quinton Silver.'"

Graham

The music pumping through the speakers mounted high on the walls at Hidden Agenda helps keep me focused. Restocking the MREs is everyone's least favorite task, and this month, I drew the short straw. Twice. That drive to Ellensburg is boring as fuck.

Every time I stop moving, I see Q's face as he stood on his front porch yesterday morning. Equal parts triumph and terror. The third box done, I pull out my phone.

"I hope you're having a better day than I am. Are we still on for tomorrow? I could cook you dinner?"

The little dots at the bottom of the screen dance for so long, I worry he's about to shut down on me, so I rush to add, *"At your place."*

He stops typing for a few seconds, and I hold my breath. If I fucked up somehow, I'll kick myself into next week.

"Okay."

That's it? One word? Now I know something's off. West and Inara are working out, and Ry's with Wren, who's having so much morning sickness she needed IV fluids the previous night. Raelynn should be here in an hour, but Inara's handling her training today—getting her up to speed on Royce's GPS tracking app.

As soon as I'm outside and it's quiet, I call Q. It takes him four rings to answer, and when he does, his voice is rougher than I've ever heard it.

"Did I do something wrong?" I ask. "If tomorrow's too soon for you, I can wait. Whatever you need."

He's quiet for several seconds. "It's not you."

"Then what?" I wish I could see his face, but I have a feeling he'd say no to FaceTime.

"Bad anxiety day. Really, Graham, I'm fine. Just a mix-up

with the groceries again. I'm handling it. I'll...I'll text you later, okay?"

"Sure. I'll be working, but I'll have my phone on me. If you need anything—"

He's gone before I finish the sentence, and fuck. This is more than a bad anxiety day. This is serious PTSD shit. I know the signs. I've lived them.

The only problem? We're so new, I don't know how much I can—or should—push. Too much, and I'll overstep. He'll shut down on me. Possibly for good. Too little, and he suffers alone.

Back inside, West and Inara are sparring, and I head into the kitchen for a cup of coffee. I should see if Ripper's around. And if he'll talk to me. There are days he still goes dark—even on Ry. But he's so much better than he used to be. Even jokes around once in a while. And he might have more experience than anyone else with Q's brand of trauma. As well as mine.

In the boxing ring, West flips Inara onto her back and jabs his fist within half an inch of her windpipe. "You're distracted," he says. "Everything okay?"

"Royce had three seizures last night," she says as West offers her a hand to help her up. "He doesn't want to up his meds."

"He's not driving, right?"

Inara snorts. "Hell, no. That's what Lyft is for. It's just hard watching him struggle to form words when I know switching up his meds would help."

The SEAL tosses her a towel and rubs a second over the back of his neck. "You work with the most stubborn man on the entire planet. And you're surprised when Royce acts like a typical guy?"

"No. Doesn't mean I have to like it, though." Inara ducks out of the ring. "He's been working so hard with Cam and Wren on the new surveillance equipment, he hasn't taken a night off in weeks."

"They're almost done, aren't they?" I ask. Only one box left to unpack. The fancy beef stew variety with the brownies West always saves for Cam.

"Thank God," West says. "After this overnight training, Cam and I are taking a few days up in Snoqualmie. You and Royce should get away." He glances over at me. "You too. Take your guy somewhere."

The look on my face must reveal a hell of a lot more than I think it should, because West narrows his eyes. "Trouble in paradise already?"

"No." I set the mug down and tug on a few short strands of hair. "He doesn't leave his house."

"At all?" West joins me in the kitchen and cracks open a bottle of water. "Agoraphobia?"

"Something like that. He had a crazy ex who did a number on him. Tried to control everything he did, cut him off from his friends—Q said the guy didn't feel emotions. That everything —the gaslighting, the abuse, and whatever he's not telling me about yet—was all a game to this asshole."

"Antisocial Personality Disorder? Or just a complete sociopath?" When I nod, West frowns, and his eyes unfocus for a breath. "I knew a guy—Anton something or other. He washed out of BUD/S because he literally gave zero fucks about any of us. SEALs are a team. You don't get your trident by leaving a man behind. That asshole almost killed three of us in training and never felt an ounce of remorse. He couldn't. If your guy—Q?"

"Quinton."

"If his ex is like Anton, Quinton's probably lucky he got out with a shred of sanity."

Fuck. I need to do a hell of a lot of reading. Draining the rest of my coffee, I rinse out the mug and brace my hands on the sink. "I just called him, and he's off. Whatever triggered him was bad. And we're so new, I'm not sure if I should beg off work and go check on him or let him deal with it on his own."

"What does your gut say?" West asks.

"It says I need to finish stocking that last case of MREs. Because otherwise, I'm going directly to his place to make him talk to me, and I think that would just make things worse. I'll text him before I clock in at the Unicorn and decide then."

West claps a hand on my shoulder and jerks his head towards the door. "Get out of here. Go see him or at least take an hour or two and get your head on straight. I'll finish the MREs. But every brownie you get on our training mission? You save for Cam."

CHAPTER SEVENTEEN

Graham

GET MY HEAD ON STRAIGHT? West's intentions were spot on, but there's no fucking way I'll be able to sort out all these emotions battling for dominance in the three hours before I'm due at the bar.

So I park myself on my couch with my laptop.

What makes a person a sociopath?

Scrolling through dozens of search results, I read everything that seems reputable. Then I move on to the other term Q and West used.

What is Antisocial Personality Disorder?

"People with antisocial personality disorder play mind games to control the people around them, often feeling no remorse at all for their actions. To many, they can appear charismatic and charming, which makes it easier for them to draw their victims into their trap."

Q survived someone like this? And he's healed enough to trust me? That alone is a fucking miracle.

My watch alarm reminds me I have to get ready for my shift,

but I bookmark half a dozen links to read on my downtime—assuming it's a quiet night. Mondays usually are, though.

I don't have any more clarity on how to proceed with Q, but as I pull on a light jacket and head down the stairs, I know one thing for certain. His trust is a gift, and I need to make sure he knows how much I cherish it—and him.

And that means telling him what happened to me eight years ago.

~

Quinton

Even after mopping the floors, washing my clothes and shoes, and lighting a candle, the disgusting stench of cider lingers in my kitchen.

I had to ask for the grocery store manager to get them to forward me the email that came in adding the cider and popsicles to my order, and after a little electronic detective work, I was able to confirm that the message was sent from an IP address in Texas, not Seattle.

It's possible Alec learned how to spoof his location, but while he's incredibly smart and cunning, he wouldn't hide if he *were* in town. And if he'd left that hotel room, my brother would have called.

It's well after midnight, but I can't sleep. My back aches, my left leg is numb, and I couldn't keep down the cereal I had for dinner. So I'm lying in my massage chair with the heat turned up to maximum and Clementine curled on my lap, purring.

"I'm sorry I yelled at you, sweetie," I whisper. Pulling out my phone, I stare at the last text I sent Graham a little before ten.

"I'm sorry. I still want to see you tomorrow. Maybe dinner and a movie in bed?"

He hasn't responded.

I should go upstairs. Lie down, even if I'm just staring at the ceiling all night long. Hell, I should have done that hours ago. Instead, I've stalked Alec's social media pages off and on, told my latest client that I needed another day for his proposal, and checked my security system a hundred times.

Why would he come after me now? It has to be the app. I renamed it after I escaped him, but he saw most of the designs when we were together, and it wouldn't be hard for him to set up a Google alert for new anti-anxiety apps.

Is this all about money? He's probably one of the smartest people I've ever met, but he can't hold down a job for long. After a few months, those around him figure out he's an emotional black hole, and he gets himself fired.

He needs someone to bankroll his life of takeout, online shopping, and gaming. My therapist told me that sociopaths, narcissists, and those with true antisocial personality disorder always have an eye on their *next* victim in case their *current* victim wises up to their lies.

During the months we spent together, he'd often tell me about other people in his life who'd wronged him. How he'd been betrayed time and time again.

"My last serious relationship ended when I forgot to send flowers for his birthday," he tells me on one of our first dates. "My dad had just died, and I flew to Utah for the funeral. James couldn't get the time off of work, so I went alone. But when I got back, he screamed at me for hours. How could I forget his special day? Why didn't I care about him?" Alec shakes his head, tears shining in his eyes. "He didn't care that I was hurting too."

Those stories—and he had a hundred of them—were designed to trap me. He prayed on my empathy, my anxiety, my desperate need to find my place in this world, twisting and turning all of my fears against me.

I know he moved in with another guy not long after I left the rehab center, but his social media went suspiciously quiet.

Even now, all I can see from an anonymous web browser are random memes and the occasional picture of downtown Dallas.

My phone buzzes, and I glance at the screen. Graham.

"I'm two blocks away with a pint of mint chip and an order of deep fried Oreos from the bar. If you're still up, can I see you?"

I shouldn't reply. There's no way I'm good company. But I shut him out so completely after the grocery delivery, and I need to make that right.

Which is why five minutes later, he's standing in front of me, minus his usual confidence. And holding a bag that's easily half grease stains.

"Are you okay?" he asks.

"Not really." If I want something real with Graham, I can't keep hiding from him. It might destroy me to tell him everything, but maybe tonight it'll be enough for me to let him know I want to. "I was a jerk earlier. I'm sorry."

"You don't have to apologize. I understand what it's like when the anxiety hits you so hard you can't even breathe. I won't judge you for that."

"Everything about me is broken! I *hate* it when people say they understand what I'm going through, because they don't!" Even as I say the words, I know I'm being more of an ass than I was this afternoon, but I can't stop myself.

Graham's lips flatten, his shoulders curving inward slightly. "I didn't leave the Coast Guard because I wanted to," he says, his voice low, with an edge that warns me this isn't a good story. "On New Year's, four guys jumped me outside a nightclub. What they did..." He swallows hard and stares down at his black boots. "There was a police report, and once that got out? Everyone I served with knew I was gay. There were complaints before I even got out of the hospital. A medical discharge was the best option. I spent months reliving that night every time I closed my eyes. The nightmares still come for me when I get low."

Oh, fuck. How could I have been so insensitive? The urge to fold him into my embrace and tell him it's all going to be okay is tamped down by the shame in his eyes. "That's why you don't—can't—bottom."

"Yeah."

I've been feeling sorry for myself all day. Hell, for a year now. Has it made me so blind, I can't see anyone else's pain?

He clears his throat and after a moment, meets my gaze. "What I said the other day? About being broken? We're all broken, Q. From the day we're born. When the right person comes along? You know because they accept all your broken pieces. All the jagged edges, the scars, and the pain. They see you for who you are, and they love you anyway."

A single tear carves a hot trail down my cheek, and Graham reaches up and wipes it away, his hand not entirely steady. I lean into the touch and curl my fingers around his, then press a kiss to his palm. "I want to tell you. I do. I just..."

"Shh." He closes the short distance between us, holding our joined hands to his heart. "I didn't come here to demand an explanation. Or to 'fix' you. I came because you don't have to face this—or anything—alone. Not unless you want to."

We don't move until Clementine meows and stretches up on her hind legs to sniff at the bag clutched in Graham's fist.

"Oh, no you don't," he says with a tight chuckle. "This would *definitely* not be good for you."

"It's not good for us either." Inhaling deeply, I catch the scent of fried cookies and my stomach growls. "But I don't think that should stop us. Will you stay? At least long enough to eat with me?"

Some of his strain eases, and in his eyes, all I see now is understanding. "I'll stay as long as you want."

~

Graham

Until just now, I didn't realize how scared I'd been to tell Q about the attack.

Other than my parents and one former boyfriend—who broke things off with me immediately—I haven't told anyone. Though Ry's background checks are so thorough, it's likely he dug up the police report. If he does know, he hasn't let on, and while I *think* Ripper might have some idea, he'll never press me about it. Not after what he's been through.

Quinton and I shared that pint of ice cream and the deep-fried Oreos, but he was in a lot of pain, so I left him to try to sleep in his massage chair. Back in my own bed, I only got three hours before my memories woke me, and unable to calm myself down, I returned to my laptop to read more about anti-social personality disorder.

At least he texted me a few hours ago. Another picture of him on his porch. Or...his feet anyway. Today, he made it halfway down the ramp, farther than he's ever gone before.

Balancing the grocery bag on my hip, I ring the bell and try not to worry that my admission will change things between us. That he'll see me differently, treat me like I'm damaged goods, or worse...won't want to touch me at all. We didn't cuddle last night. Just held hands. Kissed goodnight.

He's smiling when he answers. Scratch that, he's practically beaming as he steps back to let me in. "What's got you in such a great mood?" I ask. I ache to kiss him, but a part of me deep down needs *him* to make the first move.

Jazz spills from his computer speakers, and I catch the scent of chocolate wafting from the kitchen.

"Look." He shows me his phone, open to the mobile app store, and the Zen Oasis icon has a shiny, golden #1 banner in the corner. Along with three hundred five-star reviews. Before I can say a word, he wraps his arms around me, angles his head, and presses his lips to mine.

He's not timid. Not afraid. His hard length juts against me, and the tight ball of nerves I've carried around since last night starts to ease.

"You're amazing," I whisper in his ear when he finally breaks off the kiss. "If I didn't need to start cooking, I'd take you upstairs right now."

"I can wait to eat." The raw need in his voice is enough to make my cock ache, and I release him.

"Go upstairs then. I'll put the steaks in the fridge and be right there."

~

CANDLES FLICKER along the top of Q's dresser, and he stands by the bed, still blushing, his arousal tenting his black pants.

Please let this still...work.

I know he wants me. Or, at least wants me to want *him*. But if he hesitates touching me, I'm terrified it'll fracture our connection beyond repair.

"What's your pain level today?" I ask, sliding my arms around him and running my hands up and down his back.

"I'm not fragile, darlin'," he murmurs, then tangles his fingers in my hair and twists just enough to make me groan. Slanting his lips to mine, he tastes me, at first hesitant, then with bold strokes of his tongue and a deep moan.

This confidence? It's like he found another small piece of himself that he'd lost to his ex's abuse. And it's sexy as hell.

Grabbing his soft, peach Henley, I pull it over his head, and the sight of his lithe, toned muscles makes my heart beat faster. A lock of hair falls across his forehead, and I brush it away. "You are so fucking gorgeous," I whisper, trailing kisses along his collar bone, to the hollow of his throat below his Adam's apple, and all the way up to his shoulder.

"Graham..." His hands move almost desperately, loosening my belt, then fumbling with the buttons on the only dress shirt I own. I wanted tonight to be special, and from the way his breath escapes in short pants and the look in his eyes, he felt the same. "I don't deserve someone like you."

"Don't ever say that again." I don't know how I keep my tone gentle, but the words are harsh enough. In this moment, nothing in the world is more important than reassuring him. Not even freeing my very hard, very insistent erection. I'm in awe of him, and by God, he's going to know it all the way to his soul by the time I'm done loving him tonight. "You deserve every good thing you've ever wanted and more."

"I..."

Silencing him with my lips, I toe off my shoes and shed my pants while he finishes with my shirt. I want us both naked, want to kiss, lick, and touch every inch of him, and let him know how far and how fast I've fallen.

"Make yourself comfortable, baby. We might be here a while."

WATCHING Q COME? It's a sight I'll never get enough of. This time, I played with his ass as I sucked him off, and the way he writhed as he shot his load down my throat was the hottest thing I've ever seen.

I'm hard as a rock, but he's still shuddering, his eyes half-lidded and hazy with pleasure.

"Come here," I say as I wrap my arms around him and draw the covers over us. "You're so fucking beautiful when you let go."

"I wish I could..." Q's words fade away, and he buries his face against my neck.

"What?" After a beat, when he doesn't move, I press a kiss to the top of his head. "Q? You never have to be ashamed with me. I hope you know that."

His eyes are clear when he finally raises his head, but his shoulders tense. "I wish I could do that to you. I wish my back didn't stop me from—"

"You want to give me a blow job?"

He jerks, then nods. "I used to love it. Before. But I can't really kneel and move like that anymore."

Sitting up, I study him for a long moment. "You don't have to. Do you have a couple of extra pillows?"

Five minutes later, with Quinton slouched against the headboard, I kneel in front of him, one hand braced against the wall, the other cupping the back of his head. A drop of precum leaks from my crown, and Q tries to sit up to get closer to me, but I tighten my fingers in his hair. "The only work you have to do, baby, is with that tongue of yours. Got it?"

He nods, licks his lips, and wraps one hand around the base of my shaft as I push slowly into the heat of his mouth. His lips wrap around me, and he moans deep in his throat.

"I'll go slow. If you need to stop, hold up your hand." The only risk with me in control is that Q can't pull back if he gags or needs air. But the look on his face? It's pure bliss as he stares up at me.

All the quad and glute exercises West tortures us with? I'll never complain again. Otherwise, I'm not sure I could do this.

"Oh, God. Right there," I groan. He can do things with his tongue no one's ever tried with me before, and fuck.

His cheeks hollow time and time again, and he trails his fingers over my abs. "Grab my ass, Q."

The words escape before I realize what I'm saying, and his

brows arch in a silent question while his tongue swirls and slides over my shaft.

"I trust you, baby."

Reaching for me, he curls his hands around my hips. He's careful. Gentle, even. And I think maybe...one day, I could let him do more.

My balls tighten, and I can't look away from this man I think I'm falling for. "Quinton...fuck. I'm so close..."

He makes a low rumbling sound, almost a purr, and it's enough to send me falling off the cliff into an ocean of pleasure.

CHAPTER EIGHTEEN

Quinton

My DINING ROOM table is the size of a postage stamp, which just makes dinner all the more intimate. I'm still riding the high of what we just shared, of the trust he put in me.

We sit side by side, digging into steak, crispy potatoes, and salad, with a bottle of wine between us, sharing bits and pieces of our days.

It sounds like nothing special. But these little stories, the boring, run of the mill stuff? This is everything I've never had. Alec didn't listen to me. Never asked questions. Graham does.

And when he talks? He doesn't craft every sentence to make me feel less than.

"Ry—he's in charge of Hidden Agenda—is freaking out over leaving his wife for two days. The same guy who told me at my first interview: 'No relationships. You do this work, you stay single.' Then he went and fell in love."

"Why is he upset? You said you went all over the world for jobs." I cut another piece of steak, perfectly medium rare, and it hits me—hard—that Graham risks his life every time he goes on a mission. My stomach flips at the thought, and I set my knife down. "This isn't any *more* dangerous than usual, is it?"

All his attention is focused on his plate, but he snaps his head up at the concern in my tone. "No. It's just a training mission. But Wren's pregnant. When he told us..." He shakes his head, and I can feel the affection he has for these people he calls family. "Ryker's...well, picture the Rock, but a good six inches taller, a hell of a lot meaner, and covered in tattoos and scars. The baddest badass to ever walk the earth. But when he pulled out that sonogram picture, it was like the whole world fell out from under him and he couldn't figure out which way was up."

"Is he going to retire?"

With a snort, Graham picks up his wine glass. "Fuck no." After a healthy sip, he sobers. "Ryker spent fifteen months being tortured in a Taliban prison deep underground. They broke fifty-three bones, burned him, blinded Dax, and handed Ripper over to the sickest bastard since Bin Laden. The army thought all three of them were dead. They'd stopped looking completely until Rip got a signal out right before the fuckers sent him to that fucker, Faruk."

He shakes his head and lifts his gaze to mine. "Ryker will do this job until he can't anymore. So will the rest of us. Because we really are the best at what we do, and we don't give up. On *anyone.*"

For a full minute, maybe two, the only sounds around us are the clink of silverware and Clementine's occasional playful *meow* as she bats one of her toys around in the living room.

I'm not an idiot. I know Graham wasn't only talking about the people his team rescues. He was also talking about *me.*

After a healthy sip of wine, I clear my throat. "Alec sent me a message the other day."

My voice sounds thin, even to my own ears, and before I can regroup, Graham's fork clatters against the plate, and his whole body stiffens. This is him in full protector mode, and it's both reassuring and a little scary at the same time. "What?"

"He's messing with me." I can't look at Graham, so I focus on a grain of salt on the side of my plate. Now that I've admitted a part of my truth, I don't want any more secrets between us. "When we were together, he refused to buy beer or ice cream. If he found them in my fridge, he'd toss them. He made me switch to cider and popsicles. 'Healthier,' he said."

Next to me, Graham clutches the edge of the table, his knuckles white, and when I risk a glance at his face, I find a mix of pain and outrage in his eyes. "He doesn't get a say in what—"

I cover his hand with mine. "There's more. Please? Let me get it all out before I lose my nerve."

Linking our fingers, he nods, but I can tell he's barely holding it together. "Yesterday...I was such an ass to you because he called the grocery store and had them add a six pack of his favorite cider and a box of popsicles to my order."

That's enough to send Graham over the edge, and he pushes to his feet. "I thought he was back in Texas. Q, if he's in town—"

"He's not." I rest my hand on the back of his now-vacant chair and wait for him to sit back down. He does, but with the way his jaw ticks, I'm worried he's going to crack a tooth. "After he emailed me, I told my brother. I don't know what Connor does for a living, but I think it's something with the govern-ment, because he said he had two of 'his guys' watching Alec, and confirmed he's still in Dallas. Connor will call me if that changes."

Graham doesn't look convinced. "I thought you weren't close with your brother."

"I'm not. We don't...talk. But he saved my life. If he says Alec is still in Dallas, he's still in Dallas."

With a heavy sigh, Graham takes my hands, his gaze fixed on our linked fingers. For the first time tonight, I can't read him, and a hint of anxiety rears up inside me. "Q, I did some research on antisocial personality disorder. That's what Alec has, right?"

He glances up at me quickly, then looks away. I nod, amazed he thought to look it up. "That, and he's a classic narcissist and a sociopath. The combination..." Memories hit me before I can stop them, and tears spring to my eyes. "I think...if Connor hadn't gotten me out of there, he would have killed me eventually."

"How?" He scoots his chair close enough our knees touch. The contact renders me speechless, and he sighs. "You're important to me, Quinton. I know it hasn't been that long, and I wouldn't blame you one bit if you kicked me out for saying this, but..." He leans forward, and the scent of bay rum comforts me. "I've never felt this way about anyone."

"Graham..."

"Dammit. I know it's too soon, but I'm leaving tomorrow night for at least thirty-six hours. How can I do that knowing Alec is still fixated on you?"

Surging forward, I cup the back of his neck and pull him in for a desperate, searing kiss. He opens for me, and I can taste it all on his lips. The future I thought I'd never have. With him. Breathless, I break the connection, resting my forehead against his. "It's not too soon. It should be. You're right. But it's not. You make me feel like *me* again."

"You're trying to distract me," he whispers. "It's not going to work."

"No?" My hand slides up his thigh, but he stops me, brings our joined hands to his heart, and holds them there.

"I know there's more, Q. And I know I'm not going to like it. Will you tell me?" His breath whispers over my cheek, and fuck. I want to. But once I do, nothing will ever be the same again, and for just a few more minutes, I want the illusion. The normalcy. Just two people, sharing one of the best meals I've had in ages, building something I hope won't crumble into dust in the light of day.

"You put a lot of effort into dinner, darlin'. And I haven't had steak this good in a long time. The rest of it...I think we're going to need cake. A hell of a lot of cake."

I see the battle raging in his eyes. The need to know. The need to fix whatever's wrong. Or at least fight it. Beat it to a bloody pulp. But a moment later, his gaze softens.

"No more talk about that asshole until cake? That, I can do." Tipping his head, he kisses me. It's just a quick peck, but with the promise of so much more. "There's nothing I wouldn't do for you, baby. Even if it kills me."

AFTER THE DISHES are done and I cut us a ridiculously large slice of chocolate cake, we move to the couch. "I half expected you to toss the cake into the trash," Graham says with a small smile. "Hell, I thought about doing it myself. But that won't make the past go away. Tell me the rest of it?"

My stomach twists into a knot, and I pat the cushion until Clementine jumps into my lap. "After three months together, Alec took things too far. I was starting to see through his lies. I found a new therapist, and she helped me understand what he was doing to me." The kitten kneads my thigh, and I play with a tuft of her soft fur. "I left him. For almost a month. I called it a break, told him I needed some space to figure shit out. Either he gave it to me, or I was done. So he did."

"But you went back." Anger simmers in his eyes, and I stare at the cake I spent hours on.

"I didn't buy this, you know. And it's not from a box." Digging a spoon into the cake, I offer it to him, and he relaxes slightly as he savors the bite.

"Holy fuck, Q. You made this from scratch?"

There's a spot of frosting at the corner of his lips, and I reach over to snag it with my finger. The only way for me to get through the rest of this story? Breaking it up with sex. Or at least the promise of sex.

"My mom taught me. This is her Christmas Eve dessert." I focus on Clementine's tiny paws that never seem to stop moving. "I haven't had it in almost three years."

"Keep talking, baby. I'm on to your game now. Distract me with cake so I don't freak the fuck out about what that asshole did to you." Graham scoops up another bite and fixes his gaze on me. Completely. I can't hide anymore. And I don't want to.

"I was going to meet up with him to break things off. To tell him I never wanted to see him again. But he texted me at the last minute and gave me an address I'd never been to before. I thought neutral ground would be better. That I'd be stronger there. So I agreed. Turns out, he'd signed a lease on an apartment *for us*. Exactly the type of place he knew I'd love."

"Fucker," Graham mutters.

I offer him a weak smile. "Connor won't use his name. Just calls him Asshole."

"Your brother and I would probably get along just fine."

They would. Or...will. I hope.

"What happened when you got there?" Graham prods gently, shifting close enough our thighs touch.

"I told him we were through. That I was leaving him. But he was so sure we were meant to be..." The lump in my throat makes it hard to get the words out, but with Graham so close I can smell him—all woodsy and strong—I swallow hard and close my eyes. "He tried to kiss me, then he was undoing my pants..."

Graham makes a sound I can only describe as a growl. Low. Threatening. Deadly.

"I tried to get away, but I didn't want to turn my back on him. He'd scared me. Really scared me. I didn't even see the stairs. The whole building was industrial. Concrete and glass. Didn't realize I was so close."

"Oh, my God. That's how you got hurt? You could have died." He sets the plate down and wraps his arms around me.

"There's more," I whisper.

"I want to tell you to stop. Right now." We're both shaking, and Graham presses a hard kiss to my neck before drawing back just enough to hold my gaze. "But that's not going to help either of us."

"I was in the hospital for ten days, I think. Surgeries, pain meds...I was a mess. But Alec...he took care of everything. Never left my side. I was so doped up, and I thought..." Swallowing the nausea crawling up the back of my throat, I focus on Clementine's purr and the warmth of the man sitting next to me. "The two months after the accident...they're fuzzy. But Alec convinced me to sign over power of attorney to him. He moved me into that apartment. Right next to where I'd fallen. He told me the doctors didn't think I'd ever walk again. That I was confused all the time because I'd suffered permanent brain damage."

I know the moment Graham figures it out. His hands ball into fists, knuckles cracking, and a vein at his temple starts to throb.

"I'm pretty sure he started drugging me before I even left the hospital." Tears well in my eyes and I shrug, because what else can I do? "Alec took over my entire life. He responded to every email, every text message I got, pretending to be me, and eventually Connor caught on. Started trying to find me. He went to my old apartment, picked up a box of things my landlord had kept—including my journal. My brother hunted down the 911 report from the night I fell to get the address where Alec had me. He showed up one morning, punched Alec in the face, and carried me out of there."

I'm crying now, silent tears that land on Clementine's fur,

and she pops her head up with an inquisitive little *mrrp*. Graham rises and stalks into the downstairs bathroom, and I hope to God I haven't lost him admitting how incredibly weak and stupid I was for so long.

But a minute later, armed with a handful of tissues, he sinks back down and folds me—and Clementine—into his arms. "You are the bravest person I've ever met, Q. And I work with honest-to-God heroes every day."

"You're not...mad?" I swipe at my cheeks, unwilling to look at him.

"Oh, I'm fucking pissed. At Asshole. If he *ever* threatens you again, if he sends you another email, messes with your groceries, calls you, or God-forbid, shows up here, I will make him regret the day he was born. But shit, baby. You thought I'd be mad at *you*?"

"*I'm* mad at me. For not seeing who he was sooner. For falling down those stairs. For not fighting harder."

"You survived. Escaped. You built yourself a new life all on your own, and every single day you work to make it the life you want. I could never be mad at you for that." Graham cups my cheek, skating his thumb just under my eye to catch another tear. "You're a fucking miracle, Quinton."

CHAPTER NINETEEN

Graham

"ARE you *sure* you'll be okay if Asshole tries anything?" I ask, my arms wrapped around Q's waist as we stand on his porch a little before 10:00 a.m. the next morning.

The sun bathes us in warmth and lightens a few wisps of hair that fall over his forehead. "He's two thousand miles away, darlin'. He can email or call or send me cases of cider, and the worst thing that's going to happen to me is a panic attack. Or several."

"Is that supposed to make me feel better?" Cupping the back of his neck, I press soft kisses along his jaw and up to his ear. "Cam and Royce can come by and check on you. They're both army vets, and I trust them with my life. Plus, Cam built that security system you have."

Q shakes his head and stands up a little straighter. Despite his wince, he says today's a good day, with his pain only three out of ten, and the hours we spent the previous night talking seem to have lightened the burden of shame he carried since the accident. "For a year now, my therapist has been telling me that my worst enemy isn't Alec. It's my *fear* of Alec. I always thought she was full of shit, but I understand now. I've come too far to even *think* of going back to him, so all his antics? The worst they can do is trigger memories."

"That's not nothing." I squeeze my eyes shut, hearing the taunts of the men who attacked me all those years ago, and my stomach twists into a knot.

And then he's rubbing *my* back. Comforting *me* when all I want to do is protect him. "No, it's not nothing. But I'm stronger now than I've ever been." His firm mouth presses to mine, and with a bold stroke of his tongue against the seam of my lips, he begs for more, and I let him in, tasting the coffee we shared, a hint of his toothpaste, and...home. "As much as I love y—err, having you here, being with you...I need to know I can be alone too. Go be a badass in the jungle, and by the time you come back, maybe I'll be able to meet you at the corner."

"I'd like that." Sliding my hands under his shirt, I graze two of the longer scars that run along his spine. He survived injuries and abuse that could have easily killed him, and I need to remember that. I want the possibility for a life with this man, and that means not treating him like he's broken. "Just promise me one thing."

"Anything." His breathy reply makes my heart beat a little faster, and fuck. I'm so far gone over him, I ache to tell him, but when I do, I'm going to do it right.

"Memorize that code I gave you. If you need me—or need anyone—that code guarantees your message goes straight to Wren. And she can reach us over comms any time."

Q's smile lights up his brown eyes. Leaning in, his lips brushing my ear, he rattles off the code and adds, "Be safe, darlin'. And come back to me."

～

Transport planes are one of the worst ways to travel. Loud, cold, and uncomfortable. Canvas bench seats with a mesh backing. Our rucks are strapped in next to us, easily fifty pounds each. The engine noise makes it impossible to talk without headsets, and even then, the urge to shout is hard to resist.

Raelynn looks a little green, and Inara elbows her in the side. "When was the last time you jumped out of a plane?"

"Five years ago. Promised myself I'd never do it again."

West hands each of us a tablet. "Updated scans of the compound. The target was moved overnight. He's now underground, dead center, with six hostiles guarding him. It's a four-hour hike from the safest drop point. We'll set up eight kilometers from the compound, then split up into two teams. Romeo and Indigo take first watch while Golf, Lima, and I catch some shuteye."

"No more Jimmy Olsen and Steve Rogers?" I joke.

Ryker—Romeo for this mission—shoots me a look that could knock this plane right out of the sky. "Those are only in play when we're in public. The alphabet's simpler. Get over it." He waits a beat, then adds, "Jimmy."

The pilot breaks in. "Fifteen minutes to drop site."

"Gear up," Ryker orders, and we stow the tablets inside specially made pockets in our rucks, then spend the next ten minutes checking and double checking every hook, clip, carabiner, and strap on our own gear and each other's before West opens the side cargo door.

Six hours on this fucking plane, eight hiking, another six spent on recon and rest, up to four hours for the actual mission —if we're lucky—and another six hour flight home. At best, it'll be twenty-four hours before I talk to Q, and it's eating me up inside.

Ryker hasn't said a word about being away from Wren, but I know Ripper and Cara are checking on her often. She refused to stay with them overnight—saying she had to be close to her equipment if we needed her.

But after West, Raelynn, and Inara jump and it's just me and Ry left, he meets my gaze. Even through his goggles, I can see the strain in his eyes. He doesn't like this any more than I do.

With a nod, I follow the rest of my team, a canopy of dark green trees below us and nothing but the early evening sky above.

~

Quinton

After Graham left, I stretched out in my massage chair and tried to figure out why he would want me. Why he kept coming back every time I pushed him away.

The answer hit me like a punch to the gut. We fit. I pushed him away time and time again because I expected him to suddenly turn into Alec. But he won't. Because he's more than just a good man. So much more.

Graham gives me hope. That maybe I can be more too. More than a victim. More than an agoraphobic, weak, terrified shell of a man. That maybe...I can be as brave as he is.

I spend most of the day making minor tweaks to Zen Oasis, but now, my back is telling me I need to move. Clementine's been pestering me for more food, so I fill her bowl with kibble and head for the treadmill.

Less than five minutes into my workout, I stop the belt and grab my phone. This is ridiculous. I made it all the way down the ramp this morning with Graham. I can do it again. It's still light outside.

As brave as I *think* I am, my balance is still shit, so I fish a cane out of the closet.

Just in case.

I hate the damn thing, but it's a hell of a lot easier than the walker. "I'll be back in ten minutes, sweetie," I say when the kitten parks herself in the middle of the hallway and stares at me like I've lost my mind. "You'll be fine."

Despite my assurances, she gives me a long, plaintive meow as I flip the locks then start laughing before I get the door open. I've never needed my house keys before. I'm surprised I even know where they are, but after a few minutes, I find them in the junk drawer in the kitchen.

The sun's starting to go down, and the townhouse casts a shadow halfway across the street. Everything's quiet. It's way too early for the spillover from the bars to be anywhere around.

I'm safe. And for once...almost steady. Last night changed me in ways I never imagined possible. Alec doesn't control my life anymore, and while I don't think I'll ever forgive myself completely for not seeing through his lies from the beginning, I know *exactly* who he is now.

At the bottom of the ramp, I look up and down the street. It's quieter to the right. There's even a little community park on the corner. Only a single bench with one tall oak tree behind it, but that tiny oasis represents everything I've missed since the accident.

Freedom. Peace. The simple joy of sitting outside in early fall enjoying the fresh air.

One step at a time. Past the vague greenish outline of mint chip on the flagstones. To the fence. Through the gate.

Anxiety twists in my gut, but I take a deep breath and will it away. I can do this. With my phone in one hand and the cane in the other, I reach the end of my little yard. It's all of ten feet from the house, but it feels like ten miles for how big of an accomplishment this is.

My left leg wobbles, sending my heart rate shooting

skyward, but I don't fall. "You're almost there, Q. Twenty, thirty more steps."

I'm going to text Graham from that bench and tell him what I should have told him this morning. What I almost told him. That I'm falling in love with him.

Alec used to tell me he loved me ten times a day or more. So often and with such fervor, I started to say it back even though every time, the words took another piece of my soul with them.

With Graham...they don't. My little slip up this morning? As soon as I caught myself, I felt the difference. Loving Graham? It won't *take* anything from me. It'll give me back the one thing I didn't realize I'd lost. Hope.

Ten more steps. A bird perched on the back of the bench takes flight when it sees me, and for a moment, my eyes burn at how much life I've missed this past year. One of the local tech companies offers an app that changes my phone screen to a different Seattle photo every day, and I've seen how beautiful this city is. But this is the first time I've experienced it for myself.

When I reach the bench and ease myself down, my legs are shaking. So are my hands. But I unlock my phone and spend a full two minutes finding the right angle to capture my legs, the bench, and the grass all at the same time.

"I'm slow as fuck. But when you get back, give me ten minutes' notice, and I'll meet you on this bench. I have something important to tell you, and I want to do it right here."

I end the message with a heart emoji, then add a second and a third for good measure before I hit send. It's sappy and geeky and probably overkill, but I'm just so damn happy I'm floating.

The snap of a twig startles me, and my cane falls to the ground. Before I can pick it up, a shadow falls across my legs. "He's a scrawny one," a voice I don't know says with a heavy Texas drawl.

Snapping my head up, I frown. I know this guy. Blond hair. Beard. He saw me the other day. Was watching me.

Something cold and sticky presses to my neck, and a hand covers my mouth. Alec's stale breath ghosts over my cheek from behind me. "I've missed you, Quint. It's time to go home."

CHAPTER TWENTY

Quinton

Move. Do something.

But I can't. I can't even breathe.

Alec drops his hand from my mouth, but I only manage a weak, "Help," before he skirts the bench, and the blond guy sits next to me and wraps his arm tightly around my shoulders.

"Not a smart idea, Quint." Pulling his jacket open, Alec nods at the gun in a holster on his hip.

Oh, fuck. He's going to kill me.

"This is Dennis, by the way. You remember, him, don't you? From the cactus delivery? The one you *refused*?"

I turn my head just enough to give Dennis a sideways glance, and the look in his eyes terrifies me. Unlike Alec, whose eyes have always been dead and unfeeling, Dennis is enjoying this.

My skin tingles where Alec slapped my neck, and when I realize why, my entire body goes cold. Scopolamine. The patch is only an inch on each side, but when Connor brought me to the ER after saving me, they tested the one I was wearing and found out it was five times stronger than a normal patch. If I don't get it off in the next few minutes, I won't be able to think straight.

Alec bends down so we're face to face. "You ruined me, Quint. So now, I'm going to return the favor. I hope you enjoyed kissing that tattooed body builder this morning. Because you'll never see him again." He holds out his hand, and three white pills rest in his palm. "It's time for your meds. Take these so we can go. Dennis and I have a whole new life planned out, and it's time we got to it."

"I'm nnnot going anywhere with yyouu." Fuck. If I'm slurring my words after just a minute or two, I'm in deep shit. I jerk my hand up to try to peel off the patch, but Alec grabs my wrist and twists my arm, hard. The shock makes me cry out until Dennis punches me in the stomach.

I double over, struggling to draw in a breath, and that's when Alec's fist slams into my spine. It's like an electric shock from my neck all the way down my legs, and my vision tunnels. Someone yanks me to my feet—Dennis, I think—and then Alec's arm snakes around my waist like he's supporting a friend who's had one too many.

Flashes of the sidewalk pass by. A sliding door opens with a metallic sound, and then I'm falling. When I hit the floor, I roll over in a vain attempt to get up, but the door slams shut and then Dennis straddles me, grabbing my hands and forcing them over my head.

Metal clicks, cold around my wrists, and I can't lower my arms. "What arrre you doingggg?"

Alec chuckles. "Like I said, Quint. We're taking you with us. But we can't trust you. Not anymore. So you're going to ride back here. And you're going to take your meds. We have a long drive ahead of us. By the time we've reached our destination, maybe you'll be in a better mood."

Tangling his fingers in my hair, Alec lifts my head, shoves the pills into my mouth, and presses a bottle of water to my lips.

"Swallow. Now," he snarls.

Choking and kicking my legs weakly, I try to spit out the drugs, but Dennis pinches my nose, and I don't have a choice. The pills go down, and I'm screwed. I'll never get away from them, and if they're taking me out of state...

We really are the best at what we do, and we don't give up. On anyone.

Graham might not give up on me, but he'll have to find me first. My entire world is spinning now, and it's hard to focus. Where are they taking me? Texas? Or Utah? Alec grew up there. I think.

Twisting my head sends shooting pains down my back, but I catch a brief glimpse of my hands. There's a hasp on the floor of the van, and a padlock secures the handcuffs in place.

Dennis binds my ankles with duct tape, and Alec pats my thigh. "That should hold you for a while." He flashes me a smile. "If you're good and stay quiet, I won't have to gag you. But if you try to scream, you won't like the consequences."

Getting to his feet, Alec grabs a blanket and drapes it over me, covering me from head to toe. I start to wheeze, the panic gripping me so strong, I might never escape it again. Until he pulls the dark wool away with a soft *tsking* sound. "Sorry, Quint. There's one thing I forgot to do." Sliding his hand into my left pocket, he withdraws my phone along with my house keys. "These things are so fucking trackable these days. But I see you disabled the facial scan. What's your passcode?"

"Fuck you."

His fingers wrap around my throat. I can still breathe, but he's letting me know that could change in an instant. "You know I'll win in the end. You never could resist my special drug cocktail. You'll give me anything I ask for soon." Tossing the keys to Dennis, Alec smiles up at the man. "Go get his laptop.

That's it. Don't touch anything else and lock up when you're done. I'll send the bodybuilder a message so he won't think anything of Quint going dark for a while."

Oh, God. No. Clementine. She'll hide. She doesn't trust anyone—except Graham and Manny. I have to hold on to that hope.

After the door slams shut, Alec grabs my chin hard enough to leave bruises. "Passcode. Now, you piece of shit. Fighting me is useless. I'll have it all soon anyway. Bank accounts, passwords, a new power of attorney. Dennis is a decorated member of the Dallas Police Department. Or was until he retired last week. He'll be happy to testify about your mental state when we have our video conference with the judge in a few days. You're only delaying the inevitable. And pissing me off."

Giving up—giving in—takes another piece of my soul, and tears well in my eyes. "Seven, nine, one, four, five, two, two."

Alec fiddles with the phone for a few seconds, then pulls out his own. "There we are. Your messages and calls will ring on my cell, and this old thing...well, it's useless now."

After he powers it off and removes the SIM card, he drops the phone next to me, picks up a tire iron lying in the corner of the van, and smashes the device into pieces.

My last tether to the life I built lies shattered just beyond my grasp.

Dennis climbs into the passenger seat, holding up my laptop like a prize. "Got it, love of my life," he declares, and Alec blows him a kiss.

"You're amazing," he says sweetly, then pulls the heavy blanket over me, shrouding me in darkness and smothering heat. A few seconds later, the engine rumbles to life.

I start to sob. I'm chained on the hard, metal floor of a van, barely able to breathe and dizzy as fuck, while Alec and his latest conquest laugh at me. At how easy it was. How easy *I* made it for them to steal me away.

My mind wanders, coherent thoughts slipping from my grasp. Flashes of Graham's face behind my eyes. Memories of him kissing me. The van rattles over a bumpy road, and my back spasms, the pain consuming me.

If I drift off, let the drugs take me away, it'll be easier. I won't hurt any more. Or...I won't care. That's better. Right?

The rhythm of the road changes, smooths out. We're speeding away from my life. From my freedom. Soon, even if Graham does find me, there won't be anything left of me to save.

Graham

The brutal hike through the mountains left us all with little energy—or desire—to talk, and as soon as we made camp, West, Raelynn, and I stretched out under a makeshift tent and were out in seconds. One of the benefits of this job? I can sleep anywhere. At the drop of a hat. Unless I'm battling bad memories. But even with as much shit as I've seen with Hidden Agenda, the only time I ever had a nightmare on mission? When we rescued Ripper.

Two hours later, West heats up a metal French Press with a fucking blowtorch—the man cannot and will not function without coffee—and pours me a cup. He and Ryker outdid themselves. This is as physically difficult as any mission we've been on, and while that's the point—planning for the worst case scenario—all this time stuck in my own head isn't doing me any favors.

I dreamed of Q, but instead of kissing him, of worshipping his body, of hearing him shout my name with his—or my—release, I was trapped out here in the jungle, he was the target we were sent here to rescue, and we were too late.

"Spill it," West says quietly as we check the perimeter. "Whatever's been eating at you since we left base."

"You were right. About Q's ex having Antisocial Personality Disorder."

"Shit. Sorry, man."

Raelynn jogs over, her steps nearly silent in the mossy, damp underbrush. A few tendrils of blond hair stick to her forehead, and she wipes her eyes with her sleeve. "It's hotter than a cow's teat down here. How the fuck do you two still look daisy fresh?"

"There's a reason the warehouse is never the same temperature two days in a row. If you can train in those conditions, you can survive in these," West says. "Any movement?"

"Quiet as a church mouse. Got some broken branches two hundred meters east-northeast, though. Someone's been here besides us in the past forty-eight hours." Taking a pull from her canteen, she peers off into the distance. "I can take another look if you two were in the middle of somethin'."

"No secrets here." I lift the binoculars and focus in on our target location. From this far away, it's little more than a square patch of land with three buildings and tall, razor-wire fencing surrounding it. "My boyfriend's ex is messing with him. Sending him emails, having shit delivered to his house..."

West stiffens and grabs my forearm. "He's escalating?"

The SEAL's concern ratchets up my own. "Yeah. But Q's brother has guys watching the asshole and says he's still in Dallas. Just hate not being there—or being able to do anything."

Tapping his earbud, West connects his comms to Wren back in Seattle. "Whiskey to Base."

"Base here." It's not Wren who answers, but Ripper, and a muscle in West's jaw starts to tick.

"Where's Juliet?" he snaps.

"Sleeping. Mission wasn't supposed to start for another half hour, so I offered to be on standby. She's fine. Relax."

West blows out a breath. "Sorry. This isn't mission related. Golf needs some intel." Turning to me, he asks, "You know the asshole's name?"

"Alec. That's all I've got. Except he lives in Dallas, and there should be some sort of restraining order against him filed by a Quinton Silver that's a little over a year old."

"Anything official should be relatively easy to track down," Rip says. "What's this about?"

"This Alec shitstain is harassing Golf's guy. It's probably nothing, but in your downtime, find out everything you can about him. Including his current location. If it's anywhere other than Texas, we need to know ASAP." West rubs the back of his neck and glances down at the watch clipped to his chest. "Romeo will connect in twenty-three minutes, and I don't have to tell you what'll happen if Juliet doesn't answer."

"No, you don't." The sound Ripper makes might be a laugh, but he so rarely loosens up enough to joke around that I'm not sure. "Base out."

I dig a protein bar out of one of my pockets and tear the wrapper, despite the ball of fear currently lodged in my throat. "Probably nothing?"

"Almost definitely nothing. But I never ignore a gut instinct." West adjusts his rifle and jerks his head towards to the makeshift shelter. "Let's go before Ry gets twitchy. You *know* he's going to make the probie pack up all our gear."

I offer a tight chuckle and follow West as he picks his way over the dense underbrush. I hope his gut instinct is wrong. Because I'm falling in love with Q, and if Alec is anywhere other than Dallas, I need to get back to Seattle right fucking now.

∾

Quinton

"Hand me a candy bar, lover," Alec says from somewhere far away.

A candy bar? He doesn't eat sweets.

Nothing makes any sense. I can't move, can't see, and something thick and oppressive covers my face. My shoulders and wrists ache, and I have to pee. Every few seconds, the raw agony of a back spasm obliterates all rational thought.

A gun. Alec forcing me to swallow a handful of pills. I turn my head, and the patch on my neck pulls at my skin. Dennis. The hatred in the blond man's eyes.

No...

"You're sure he's going to cooperate?" Dennis asks.

Focus, Q. Listen.

It's my only hope. I have to stay present. To find some way to get a message to Graham and let him know what's happened to me. But it's so hard. I just want to sleep.

"...get to the house, we can do whatever we want to him. Have to keep his face pretty for the judge, but get enough of the scopolamine and temazepam into him, and he'll be putty in our hands. And if not, a couple of days chained up in the basement will do the trick."

"Can't we just make him OD and be done with it?"

"No!" Alec snarls. "He's going to pay for what he did to me. To both of us."

I can't listen anymore. It's too hard. He's so angry.

Let me die.

The thought shouldn't bring me peace. I want to *live*. To see Graham again. To cuddle Clementine and even suffer through one of Manny's torturous therapy sessions. But it would be so easy to just give in. No more pain. If I could just...let go.

～

A JOLT STARTLES ME AWAKE—NOT that I remember falling asleep. It's cold. My wrists burn, and I can't see. Why can't I see?

Blanket. Alec. Drugs. My mind struggles to put the pieces together. He's going to break me. Make me pay for leaving him.

Fight him, Q. You're stronger now.

Except, he doesn't have to break me this time. All he has to do is convince a judge that I'm not mentally sound, and he'll get access to my money. That's all he's after. That and control. He gets his rocks off making others do exactly what he wants.

The van slows and hits a pothole, and I stifle a whimper.

"Rest stop time!" Alec announces. "I'll take our passenger. You keep watch. If any other cars pull off the highway, come get me."

"Will do," Dennis replies, his voice full of puppy dog like adoration.

The side door opens with a snap, and I jerk, the handcuffs sending sparks of pain all along my wrists. "Now, if you're really good, Quint, maybe I'll give you something to eat before we set off again."

He moves around me for a couple of minutes, and I drift in and out, only vague fleeting thoughts I can't quite grasp floating through my head.

Fresh air hits my face as the blanket slides away, and I blink hard. It's dark outside, a single street light illuminating an empty parking lot and a plain, squat concrete building. Alec unlocks the wrist cuffs from the ring on the floor, cuts the duct tape binding my ankles, and then half drags, half carries me until I'm sitting in a wheelchair.

"Nnnoooo." I want to fight him, but I'm too weak, in too much pain, and he slaps my cheek lightly.

"Shut up. The rest stop is deserted, and there's no one to hear you scream, but if you make another sound, I'll gag you anyway." He throws a blanket over my bound hands and pushes a baseball cap low over my forehead to hide my face.

The world around me spins and tilts, but the fresh air helps me focus. Until he steers me into a large, accessible stall in the men's bathroom and reaches for my belt.

"Don't!" The idea of his hands on me is so repulsive, I want to vomit.

"Quiet," he hisses. "Like I'd ever fuck you again. I don't need to. You disgust me. But I don't want my van smelling like piss for the next five hours. So you're going to shut the fuck up, and I'm going to pull down your pants."

We're back at the van less than five minutes later, and he practically throws me out of the chair onto the floor. "Please," I beg as he yanks my hands over my head. "Don't. It hurts too much."

"It won't after your next dose of meds." His face swims in and out of focus, but I think he's smiling as he pulls out a pill bottle. "Open up."

I shake my head, and his fingers dig into my jaw. As soon as he forces the pills past my lips, I spit them out. The snarl he makes sends a cold shiver down my spine, and my cheek explodes in pain, his fist snapping my head to the side as he laughs.

"Remember, Quint. I don't need to be nice to you. I just need to keep you compliant and *relatively* unmarked for the next few weeks until all the legal shit is taken care of. After that, a quick overdose or maybe a shot of insulin? Doesn't matter. No one's going to care that you're gone."

"Connor," I whisper.

"Your brother isn't in a position to help you anymore." Dennis sounds almost gleeful as he pries my jaw open.

Alec dumps the pills back into my mouth and then presses a strip of duct tape over my lips. I scream, but my words are lost behind the tape.

What did you do to Connor, asshole?

Thrashing earns me another punch to my side, and then

someone tapes my ankles again, tucks the blanket all around me, and the engine rumbles to life. The taste of the meds dissolving on my tongue is familiar and overwhelmingly bitter, and I wheeze, fighting for every breath.

Memories mix with reality until I can't tell what's real anymore.

Graham. Graham is real.

But with the next pothole, I lose my train of thought, and I can't remember what it was I was holding on to. Or why.

CHAPTER TWENTY-ONE

Graham

THANK fuck Ryker didn't want to be away from Wren any longer than absolutely necessary. As soon as we rescued the "hostage," one of a team of seven former members of the *Cuerpo de Fuerzas Especiales*—Mexican Special Forces who helped us stage this mission—Ry called in a transport helicopter to pick us up. The trip to Culiacán only took twenty minutes, and the plane carrying us back to Seattle is twice as fast as the piece of shit we rode to get here. Also a hell of a lot nicer. Actual seats. With cushions.

It's a little after 7:00 a.m. back home, and before we take off from Culiacán, I turn on my phone. Q's message fills the screen, and holy shit. That's the little park on the corner of his street. He did it.

"I'm slow as fuck. But when you get back, give me ten minutes' notice, and I'll meet you on this bench. I have something important to tell you, and I want to do it right here."

He might be up already, and even though I probably *should* wait to reply, I can't help myself.

"We land around nine-thirty. I need a shower—trust me—but I'll meet you on that bench at ten."

The little *read* notice appears next to the message, but he doesn't reply. Odd. Maybe I woke him up?

Ryker taps his ear. "Alpha Team to Base. We're on the transpo about to head home. I'll contact you on our private channel in a few minutes." Circling his finger in the air, he signals the pilot to take off before moving to the back of the plane to talk to his wife.

West and Inara are asleep in seconds, and Raelynn pulls out a small notebook and starts writing. Her instincts were spot on in the field, but she needs to learn how to trust her team. Unsurprising as she barely knows any of us. Ryker or West will give her "the talk" when we get back. Remind her that going off on her own could get her—or any of us—killed, and then assign her climbing wall drills for a solid week. Or worse. Make her clean the whole warehouse.

I've done it. It's *not* fun.

Despite how worn out I am, every time I close my eyes, I see the picture of Q sitting on that little bench. I'll message him again in an hour. Until then, I'll fantasize about how good it's going to feel to kiss him outside in the sun.

THE ENGINES CHANGE pitch as we start our descent, and I'm still staring at my phone. I've texted Q two more times, and he's read both of them, but hasn't responded. Worry makes my shoulders ache—though hiking more than ten kilometers carrying fifty pounds of gear didn't help.

The city comes into view, and the device in my ear beeps. "Base to Alpha Team. Ry? Is Graham on comms?" Wren's stressed, her voice tight, the all-business tone she adopts for missions gone. And she used our names.

I sit up straight. "I'm here, Wren. What's wrong?"

"Cam called me a few minutes ago. That motion sensor you left at the warehouse? It was tampered with. Deliberately."

"Fuck me." My phone slips out of my hands, and I scramble to pick it up and unlock it so I can text Q again when I hear Ripper's voice.

"There's more. Alec Harrow. Took too long to find his name because Quinton Silver didn't file the restraining order. Quinton Davis did. Then legally changed his name to Quinton Silver a week later. The affidavit states Harrow messed with Quinton's prescribed medication daily for a period of at least eight weeks after an accident that left him unable to walk. The tox screen performed at the Fort Worth ER on the day Quinton *escaped* from Harrow's *care*? Scopolamine, temazepam, Oxy, Valium..." Ripper clears his throat. "Wren...I can't..."

"Rip. Brother, meet me on the private channel," Ry says sharply. "West...?"

"Yeah. Go." West unbuckles his seat belt and slides across the aisle to sit next to me. Panic makes it hard to breathe. I need my meds and paw through my ruck in search of the little plastic box until West blocks me with an arm across my chest. "Stop. I'll find them. Wren needs Q's cell number so she can make sure he's still in Seattle."

The SEAL's order carries weight, and I rattle off the digits without thinking. West presses my pill case into my hands, followed by a bottle of water. The Clonazepam won't compromise my judgement, but it'll keep me calm enough to think. Once it kicks in.

Until I hear Wren's voice. "I can't get a ping. Last known location was within half a mile of his place, but that was last night around 6:00 p.m."

The plane touches down, and within two minutes, we're in an SUV, West behind the wheel, Inara on the phone to Royce *and* Cam, trying to access Q's security system remotely.

"He customized the hell out of this thing," Cam mutters over the speaker. "Your man's a fucking genius."

He is. All I can do is stare at the picture of him on that park bench and pray he just forgot to charge his phone. But I know better. He'd *never* forget. It's his lifeline.

"I'm hacking into the traffic cameras within four blocks of his last known location now," Wren says. "The city of Seattle just upgraded their system last week, so it's going to take me fifteen or twenty minutes."

We're only five minutes away from Q's house, and he still hasn't responded to any of my texts.

Ryker—sitting in the third row seat—pulls up the floorboard, withdraws a metal ammo box, and pries it open. "Live rounds. Load 'em up. Now. Pistols only. It's the middle of the goddamn morning, and if anyone calls us in, we're fucked."

I'm out of the SUV before it even stops moving. "Q?" Pounding on the door and ringing the bell at the same time, I already know. He's not going to answer me. I just don't know why. Is he injured? Lying on the floor unable to get up? Or—?

"Probie? You're with me. Around back," Ry says as he strides away. "West? Breach on my mark."

"Wait. Don't break down the doors. Please." I grab West's arm. "He's obsessive about his security. I can't...if he's not in there, I can't leave his home unprotected. It would kill him."

"You heard the man," Ry mutters over comms. "Time to see who's faster at picking locks."

West already has tools in hand while Inara and I take up positions on each side of the door, weapons at the ready. In under a minute, both doors pop open. "Beta team, go high," Ry says quietly, and as I take the stairs two at a time, Ryker sweeps through the kitchen.

Q's bedroom is pristine—as usual. The bed's made, and his toothbrush is dry as a bone. He hasn't been here in at least twelve hours.

"Clear," West calls from the second bedroom.

"What the fuck? Graham, get your ass down here." Ryker's voice carries an odd tone, and I holster my weapon and head for the stairs. Inara, just ahead of me, starts laughing, and I can't think of a single fucking thing that could possibly be funny in this situation.

Until I reach the landing. Ry stands on the other side of the couch, weapon drawn and pointed at the floor, all six-foot-eleven inches of him perfectly still as a little orange ball of fur clings to his tactical vest, meowing plaintively.

"Alpha Team, what the fudgecicles is going on?" Wren asks in my ear.

West almost doubles over with his own rich laughter, pulls out his phone, and snaps a picture. "Check your phone, Base."

"Fudgecicles?" Raelynn asks. "Is this some kind of code y'all forgot to teach me?"

"Wren gets creative with her cursing," Inara replies.

Clementine is practically yowling now, kneading Ry's neck and butting her tiny head against his chin. "Come here, sweetie," I say softly as I reach for her.

In an acrobatic feat only a cat could pull off, she leaps from Ryker's shoulder, twists in mid-air, and lands square in the center of my chest, where I cradle her and coo softly. "It'll be okay. We'll find him. You're hungry, aren't you?"

Sweeping my gaze around the room at my family, I hold on to Q's kitten like she's all that's keeping me upright. "He'd never leave her. Clementine's as important to him as Charlie is to Ripper. Alec took him. I don't know how I know, but I know." My voice cracks, and my legs feel like jelly.

West grabs one of the chairs at Q's little table and shoves it under me before I fall. "Base, if you have any idea where that sorry excuse for a pig fucker is, we need it. Now. Probie? Upstairs. Find a suitcase, duffel bag, or hell, even a pillow case and pack a couple full changes of clothes for Quinton. Inara?

Find his laptop and pull all the cameras. We need those memory cards. Ry? You're on transpo. Get us a plane ready and waiting—something fast. We need Ripper at the warehouse as soon as Cara can get him there."

"Where the fuck do you think I am?" Rip replies.

"At my place. With Wren." Ry's tone leaves no doubt he's pissed as hell, and both Wren and Ripper start talking at once until he growls, "Rip, you better have a goddamned explanation for this."

"You cut your bandwidth in half when you took a sledge-hammer to your wall without thinking, asshole. The second we realized this was a big fucking deal, I called Cara. She's back with Wren now."

"I was alone for all of twenty minutes, Ry. And I'm *fine*. Stop being an over-protective Neanderthal and focus."

Only Wren could get away with talking to him like that, and Ryker's eyes widen for a second before he shakes his head. "I'll get us a plane."

Satisfied, West crouches down next to me as the rest of the team gets to work. "What does the cat need and where is it? We'll bring her to the warehouse."

I rattle off the list: litter box, carrier, food, her bed, a couple of toys, and West collects everything while I gently stroke Clementine's back. "He'd kill me if I left you here alone, you know."

She *mrrps* and finds one of the larger pockets in my tactical vest, pawing at the flap until I open it and let her crawl inside.

I should have known. Should have insisted he let me station someone outside his place. Every one of my instincts was screaming at me when I kissed him goodbye yesterday morning.

He was sure Alec was still in Texas. His brother would have called.

Tapping my earpiece, I clear my throat. "Rip? Q has a brother. Connor."

"Shit. Right. You said the brother had men watching Harrow?"

"Yeah. So either Alec got to Connor, or he's working with someone."

Ripper swears under his breath. "On it."

"No laptop," Inara says as she kneels in front of me. "Anywhere he'd lock it up?"

Turning, I scan Q's living room. His mouse is on the floor under the desk. "He doesn't leave his house. It should be right there." Pointing, I shake my head softly and squeeze my eyes shut. "Alec has it. And him."

I can't voice my next thought.

How long until he breaks Q completely?

Quinton

The van door opens, startling me awake. Voices surround me, but they sound like they're coming from underwater.

When did I fall asleep? Why can't I move?

Strange sounds. Metal. Footsteps. Laughter.

"Get the door open, lover." That voice. I know that voice. Hate it.

Light floods my eyes, and I struggle to focus. The air is hot and dry, and I catch a glimpse of prairie, vast and wide and open. A fence in the distance. Then a shadow blocking my vision.

Panic floods my limbs, and I whimper as Alec drags me out of the van and throws me into a wheelchair. My legs are numb. My ankles bound together. Fuck. Bits and pieces of the last however many hours come back to me, but then we're moving and my stomach pitches.

Through a door. Air conditioning cooling my cheeks. He rolls me so fast, I can't see anything but a blur. But I think we pass through a big room, then down a hall. We stop abruptly, and Alec locks the wheels, grabs my bound wrists, and tosses me over his shoulder.

Stairs. Bouncing. My stomach pitching, bile burning the back of my throat. No A/C down here, and it's stuffy. "The room's all ready, Alec."

Room? What room? And who...? Alec's new lover. Dave? Don? *Dennis.*

I land on a mattress, then Alec's face comes into soft focus. "Bring the chair down, lover," he calls over his shoulder.

I don't need the wheelchair.

But I do. My legs are numb. My arms too.

Alec yanks the tape from my lips, the pain clearing some of the fog from my thoughts. "Why?" I croak, my mouth so dry, my tongue sticks to the roof of my mouth.

His stare holds nothing but pure contempt and rage, and he pulls a notepad and pen from his pocket and drops them on my thighs. "Write down the name of your bank and your login information. Plus the password for your computer."

"No." I can't give him *anything.* He'll use it against me. But as the small room starts to come into focus, any hope I had vanishes. No windows. A shower, toilet, and sink in one corner —all at the right height for someone in a wheelchair.

Alec rolls his eyes. "Are you really going to fight me, Quint? Another couple of days and the scopolamine and temazepam will have built up in your system and you'll do anything I ask. If you don't make me wait, your last few weeks could be almost... pleasant. Otherwise..."

He leaves the threat hanging, and I curl onto my side away from him.

"Your stupid little app is a bestseller. And you're going to sign everything over to me."

"Fuck. You. Not...the same...guy you...gaslit. Asshole."

Alec grabs my chin, leaving fresh bruises on top of the ones he gave me back in the van. "You will be. And no one's coming to save you this time." He waves his phone screen in front of my face too fast for me to see. "Took care of big brother before I flew out to Seattle. Or...had Dennis's friends take care of him. It'll be a miracle if anyone finds him before the elements or his injuries do him in."

I lunge for the phone, but topple over, my balance lost to fear and whatever drugs he gave me. "What...did you...do?"

The phone screen is right in front of my face now. My brother lies on an expanse of dirt wearing only his boxers, his face bloody, eyes closed, right arm broken, and blood pooling under him.

"Billy—I have you to thank for him, baby—was a cop. He came to enforce the order of protection you filed against me. We had a good six months before Billy decided life wasn't worth living."

I try to wriggle away from Alec, horror making my entire body tremble. "You killed him..."

Alec snorts. "Actually, I didn't. That was all on Billy. He did some bad shit before he met me. But his buddies on the force? Including Dennis? Well, they were happy to help me out when I told them Connor had been the one to push Billy off that roof." Tucking his phone away, Alec shakes the pill container. "Time for your meds. Then a nap. Need you looking better than *this* before the competency hearing in two days. It's online, by the way. So don't get any ideas about leaving me. You're never doing that again."

I should fight him. Try to push him away when he shoves the pills into my mouth and tells me to swallow them dry.

But I can't. He hurt Connor. He stole me from my life so

easily. No one but Graham will miss me, and no matter how good his team is...they'll never find me.

In two days, Alec will have me so drugged up I'll be a zombie. The judge will happily give him power of attorney, and then, he'll get access to everything.

Tears tumble down my cheeks as Alec unlocks the handcuffs and cuts the tape around my ankles.

"Clean yourself up. You smell disgusting. I'll be back with food in a few hours." At the door, he plasters on that fake smile. "And if you try to remove that patch behind your ear, I'll just make you a stronger one and tie you to the bed until you're a drooling, incontinent idiot. So leave it the fuck alone."

The *thunk* of the lock is so loud, I flinch. Or maybe that's the drugs kicking in. My legs won't hold me, and there's no way I can maneuver myself into the wheelchair, so I crawl towards the little bathroom in the corner. With every passing minute, my world shrinks a little more.

Please, Graham. Just take care of Clementine.

Each breath is harder. The air thicker. The plain, gray walls warp and ripple. Clawing my way to my knees, I turn on the shower and struggle to remove my pants and briefs. I won't be good for anything in a few minutes, and I have to keep fighting as long as I can.

As I sink down onto my ass under the spray, I pull my shirt halfway over my head and stick my finger down my throat. My stomach is empty except for bile, so maybe he won't notice. The water washes away the vaguely yellow liquid with at least half an undissolved pill, and I relish in my tiny victory. Even if it might be the last one I ever have.

CHAPTER TWENTY-TWO

Graham

I'M NUMB, and only Clementine's purr against my chest is keeping me in the here and now. The drive back to the warehouse passes in a haze, my team talking around me, planning, occasionally asking me questions I don't know how to answer.

Where would Alec take Q?

Why come after him now?

Can Q fight back?

Ryker elbows me in the side. "Graham? Did you hear me?"

Shaking my head, I focus on the man next to me. He has partial heterochromia in both eyes, patches of green, hazel, and blue swirled together, and the colors—along with the intensity of his stare—make it impossible *not* to listen to him.

"*Someone's* read your texts to him, right?"

"Yeah." Pulling out my phone, I unlock it and pass it to Ry. "If his anxiety is off the charts, sometimes he doesn't respond to me right away, but...it's after ten. We were supposed to meet at the little park at the end of his street twenty minutes ago."

My boss's massive fingers fly over the on-screen keyboard

for a minute before he passes the phone back to me. "Add something uniquely *you*. Something this Harrow asshole wouldn't notice, but Q would."

It's like he's speaking a foreign language, and for a moment I just stare at the screen. Q's gone. He might already be dead.

But if he's alive, he needs you.

Pushing the panic aside, I take a breath and follow orders.

Quint? I waited at the park. Knocked on your door too. I'm worried. This isn't like you. Please text me back or I'm going to call the police. My whole family's in town, and they want to meet you.

I send up a silent prayer as I hit *Send*.

Two minutes later, as West pulls into the warehouse parking lot, the reply comes in.

Need some time alone. Everything's moving way too fast. I'm fine, and I'll call you in a couple of days.

Any shred of doubt I was holding onto evaporates into thin air.

"That's not him. He *hates* the name Quint. It's what Alec calls him."

Ry nods grimly, shoving at the door as the SUV coasts to a stop. I follow my team into the warehouse on shaky legs, one hand cupping Clementine and the other gripping my phone so tightly, I'm in danger of cracking it.

"Tell me you've got something." West dumps his rucksack next to the table Ripper's working at and starts peeling off his tactical gear while Inara motions for Raelynn to follow her to the supply cabinets. Ry taps his ear on the way to the showers, and starts demanding an update on the plane he requested.

Charlie trots over to me and presses his entire body against my legs. With a tiny *mrrp*, Clementine pops her head out of my pocket and stares at the dog for a minute, then lets out a plaintive *meow*.

"He's not going to hurt you, sweetie," I murmur, but she

doesn't need my reassurance. She's purring like a little freight train.

Ripper leans back in his chair. "Still working on a location. Quinton's place isn't visible on any traffic cameras. Neither is the park, but we caught the same gray panel van circling the area more than once in the past three days. The plates were a dead end. Stolen a little over a week ago outside of Las Vegas."

"What about Connor?" I ask. Needing to keep busy, I unpack Clementine's litter box, food and water bowls, then set the fluffy round pillow on one of the couches in the little sitting area.

"He's FBI. But they will 'neither confirm nor deny' that he works for them. At least according to Pritchard. He's calling in a few favors to see if someone from the local office can track the guy down."

West claps his hand on my shoulder. "Take a shower. Change into civvies and clear your head. It's going to take us at least another thirty minutes to gear up and hopefully by then, we'll know where we're going."

I start to protest, but he silences me with a single look. "That's an order."

~

EVERY SEAT on this private plane is plush, pristine leather. I don't know how many favors Ryker called in, but this beauty was ready and waiting for us when we arrived at Boeing Field ten minutes ago.

"We got a location," Ripper says over comms as West hauls the last of our gear on board. "There's a three bedroom house registered to a Leslie Harrow in northern Utah. Sits in the center of five acres of nothing. Over the past three months, two construction companies have filed permits for that address to modify the basement, adding plumbing for a shower, toilet, and sink and dividing the space into two rooms."

I drop my head into my hands. My hair is still damp, and I grab fistfuls of it and pull, hard, using the pain to keep me focused.

Ripper rattles off the coordinates, and Ryker presses a call button to relay them to the pilot. This plane has a fucking *call button*. Takeoff is smooth and quick, and my ears pop as we climb to cruising altitude.

"Detailed map as well as a floor plan headed to your tablets now. Harrow has a virtual appointment with a judge in Salt Lake City in two days. Case is listed as a conservatorship hearing."

"Fuck. He'll have access to Q's money, be able to make all of his medical decisions, and keep everyone else away from him. For the rest of his life." I punch the back of the seat in front of me. It's so soft, it doesn't even sting. Q's worst nightmare was falling under Alec's control again. Not being able to defend himself. Being drugged, locked away, losing the freedom he'd found this past year.

"This asshole is putting a hell of a lot of work in here," Inara says. "Is Q loaded or something?"

"He created an app that shot to the top of the mobile stores just a couple of days ago," I say.

"Holy shit." Inara whistles. "That's serious cash if it stays there."

"Zen Oasis?" Wren asks. She's still running comms from the condo she and Ryker share not far from downtown. Her anxiety attacks are worse than mine ever were, so I'm not surprised she knows about Q's app. "Spitsnacks. I recognized his company name—vaguely—but it didn't register why until now."

"He can't get into Q's accounts until after the hearing, right?" I ask.

"Not unless Q gives him the information. But Graham..." Wren sighs, and I finish her thought.

"If he's drugging Q like he was before, he might already have what he needs." Another, much worse thought steals my breath. "If he does...why would he even keep Q alive?"

I start to hyperventilate, and then Ryker's in front of me, unbuckling my seat belt, jerking me to my feet, and steering me to the back of the plane.

"Down. On your ass. Head between your knees," he orders. "Right fucking now. Q's going to need you once we get him out of there, and if you fall apart on him now, you'll be compromised in the field."

"Ryker." Ripper breaks in over comms. "I got this."

"No, Rip. Don't put yourself through—"

"I've already *been* through it. And a whole lot more. Go." My earbud beeps, switching us over to the private channel, and Ripper asks, "Is he gone?"

Ryker's already back up front with the rest of the team, each of them with their tablets in hand. "Yeah."

"Do you love Q?"

It's not the question I expect Ripper to ask. Hell, I didn't expect the man to try to talk me through this particular panic attack at all. But though he's the quietest member of our team, at the moment, his voice carries the same authority Ry and West have simply by existing.

"Yes."

"Does he love you?"

"Yes." I'd bet my life that's what he wanted to tell me on that bench. The bench we should be sitting on right now.

"Then...as fucked up as this sounds, it doesn't matter. That sad sack of shit with maggots for brains is going to try to break him."

"Not...helping," I wheeze.

"Not finished, dumbass." Anger and disgust war for dominance in his voice, and he swears under his breath. "That combination of drugs in Q's blood work...that *specific* combination...I know what it does."

"Oh...God. Rip." Before we pulled him out of that hole in Afghanistan, West and Trevor ran down the basics of how psychopaths like Amir Abdul Faruk break people. Drugs. Isolation. Intense pain followed by kindness. Keep the target off balance, never knowing which way is up. Do that long enough, even the strongest man—or woman—will break.

"When you get him out of there, he's not going to know which end is up. But he'll know *you*. You're his constant, Graham. His tether to reality. So you're going to do whatever you need to do and compartmentalize all the shit threatening to drown you so you can be there for him."

"I don't know how."

"Yeah, you do. Because those first couple of days after Ry pulled me out of that hole? When I didn't believe anything was real? That's what you did for me."

∼

Quinton

The *thunk* of the door lock is so loud, I jerk and force my eyes open. The ceiling is nothing but plain, gray cement, and the air is stuffy and cool. I'm in a bed, but it's not mine. Rough sheets. The smell of bleach.

"Time for your meds."

Alec. He breezes in and sets a tray on the bedside table. I blink up at him, at the bright smile, the gray eyes. I shouldn't be here. I left him. Escaped. Didn't I?

"I brought you lunch. Grilled cheese, a cup of tea, and your meds." The pills tumble into my palm. Three of them. Just like always. "Drink up." Holding the cup of tea close to my lips, he waits, eyebrows raised. "*Now*, Quint."

This side of him, the edge to his voice? It scares me, and I try to set the pills down, but he stops me.

"You need these. You know you do."

"I don't." My words are slow, but when I try to sit up straighter, my back spasms, and agony shoots down my legs. Gasping, I double over, and Alec shoves the pills into my mouth, grabs my hair to pull my head back, and pours some of the tea down my throat.

I swallow before I realize what's happening. Deep down, I *know* I should fight him, but I'm so confused.

"Drink. The whole fucking thing," he snaps and hands me the tea. "Right now."

The threat is clear. If I don't, he'll just force me, so I collapse back against the pillows and drain the cup. It's bitter and disgusting, so when he shifts the tray closer, a plate with a golden brown grilled cheese in the center, I don't hesitate. My stomach is hollow, and I won't be good for anything soon if I don't eat.

"You...took me." Tears gather in my eyes as Alec looms next to the bed, watching me take a bite of the sandwich. God, I'm so hungry I could eat three of these. "You and your latest *conquest*."

He laughs and glances back at the open door. "After how you left me? How you ruined everything we had together? I deserve to be paid. You were just going to waste that money anyway. Like you've wasted your whole life." He drops a small stack of paperwork on the tray. "Now sign these. Everywhere that's highlighted in yellow."

I squint at the type. So small. And blurry. "What is this?"

"Does it matter?" The pen lands next to the papers, and I just stare at it until Alec leans down and cups my cheek. I try to jerk back, but he doesn't let me move. "Don't fight me on this, Quint. In another thirty-six hours, I'm going to own you.

Completely. Is one little act of rebellion truly worth making me angry?"

No. Because he'll get what he wants anyway. He always does.

So I sign. Even though the words don't make much sense. By the last page, I think I've figured out what this is. Transfer of ownership paperwork. For my company. When I'm done, I'm so very tired. Curling on my side, I don't know how long it's been. What time it is. All I know is that I'm alone, confused, and terrified of what he'll take from me next.

CHAPTER TWENTY-THREE

Graham

I PART THE DRAPES, binoculars in hand, and peer across the landscape. Three miles away, the single-story ranch house sits behind a chain-link fence, all the curtains drawn.

The RV we picked up just outside of Salt Lake City is a piece of shit. The dealer left air fresheners hanging all over the fucking place. "New Car Smell" might be okay in small doses, but there must have been twenty of the damn things stashed in cabinets and hanging from the light fixtures.

Who did the dealer think he was kidding? No one would ever believe this piece of shit was new.

Ry threw them all away within seconds of paying the guy, and now, the cloying scent is slowly being replaced with that of stale cigarettes and something very, *very* rotten.

West stares at his laptop screen, his fingers tight on the joystick in his hands. The drone makes a wide circle around the house, taking a detailed thermal scan. We need some idea of what we'll face when we breach.

"Two heat signatures on the main floor," he says, maneuvering the drone so it lands in a tree a good five hundred feet away from the house. "Moving around well enough. Package is likely in the basement. Lying down, from the looks of it."

I have to see for myself and twist the laptop to face me. "Alec has a partner? Fuck." Tapping my earbud, I wait for the telltale beep. "Golf to Base. You seeing this? Who the hell is he working with?"

"On it," Wren says. "Give us an hour or so."

My fist slams into the table, rattling a water bottle and the various tools scattered over the Formica. "Dammit. We have to get in there now."

"Negative." Ryker slides his tablet in front of me. "With the power that place is pulling? And the wifi signals we can see from three fucking miles away? Harrow built himself a goddamn fortress with so much security, he'd know we were coming the second we jumped the fence."

Blueprints fill the screen, along with orange and green lines for the tripwires and sensors Ry's identified in the hour we've been here.

I memorize the layout, then sit back and close my eyes. Front door. Living room to the right, hallway to the left. Ten feet. A right turn. Basement door at the end of the hall. Down the stairs. Two rooms. Q's in the room on the left.

"We need eyes inside," West says. "Probie, you're up. Take that old beater that came with this bucket of bolts and play the lost damsel in distress. Ask to use his phone." Gesturing to the surveillance equipment strewn across the table, he adds, "Take audio and video in there with you."

Raelynn snorts. "Damsel in distress? Why do *I* have to be the fucking damsel?"

"Because Inara's going to be covering your ass from that walnut tree at the edge of the neighboring property. Unless *you* can guarantee a kill shot from a mile away, you're the damsel."

She huffs. "Fine. I need ten minutes." Disappearing into the bathroom, she bangs around, opening and closing the cabinets, cursing as I keep my eyes glued to the computer screen. Q isn't moving, and the longer I sit there, more worried I get.

"Fuck. There has to be another way...a faster one..." My stomach twists into one giant knot.

"Graham, listen up." Ryker towers over me, hands on his hips, murderous rage simmering in his eyes. "That piece of human garbage disguised as a man isn't going to see tomorrow's sunrise. Neither is his partner. Let the Probie do some recon. We need to know if he's armed. If he's rational. Who this other shitstain is and whether he's there willingly. We will *not* lose Quinton unless we get sloppy about it."

I'm about to protest—or at least tell him he can't promise we'll be successful—when Raelynn stalks out of the tiny bathroom. The entire camper is nothing but silence and hanging jaws for a full minute until the newest member of Hidden Agenda swears under her breath.

"Don't say a damn word. Any of you," she drawls. "This is a one-time-only view."

Her blond hair is pulled into two pigtails below her ears, shining golden waves trailing towards her chest. Her asshugging jeans are now cutoff shorts, and she dumps the extra material in her go bag. Long, lean legs go on for miles, and if I had a straight bone in my body, I'd probably be drooling.

The tank top barely contains her breasts, and several new—and very strategically placed—rips enhance the look. "If I had anything other than a ball cap, I'd feel better about this get-up. But this'll have to do for now."

"Um...yeah," West manages, snapping his jaw shut and tossing her the keys to the car. "You do realize Harrow's gay, right?"

"That's how he's presentin' now," Raelynn shoots back. "Am I the only one who read his whole fucking file along with the dissertation on ASPD? His first victim was a woman. He's either bisexual or doesn't give a lick about who he sleeps with as long as it gets him what he wants. Either way, you want me to get in there? This'll do the job."

After she gears up with a tiny camera hidden in a pair of sunglasses and several of our newest—and smallest—surveillance devices in her pocket, she smooths a hand over one of the pigtails and plasters on a sweet smile. "Now, wish me luck, boys," she says, her Texas drawl so pronounced, she sounds like a different person. "I'm just so lost, and if I can't find my way back to town, well, I just might cry."

The RV door slams, and Inara lets out a long, low whistle as she slings her rifle case over her shoulder. "Damn. I'm not sure if I should be disturbed or impressed."

We all nod, except Ry, who's smirking like he knew it all along. The value Raelynn would bring to this team. This family.

"Impressed." He peers out the window, watching the wheels of the old beater kick up dust as she drives away. "Definitely impressed."

Raelynn

This piece of shit hatchback hasn't seen a shock absorber in years, and the stench? Something died in here years ago. I roll down all four windows and hope the breeze doesn't wreak havoc on my hair. Getting it to behave at a moment's notice? That was the true miracle. Straight out of one of the pamphlets those televangelists send Momma once a month like clockwork.

I liked those jeans, though. I wonder if McCabe will let me expense a new pair?

The dusty road and early October heat remind me of home.

Or...what used to be home. I'll never go back to Texas again unless someone drags me hogtied and screaming.

Playing the part, I stop the car outside the long well-worn approach to Harrow's house, look around, and pull out my phone, holding it out the window like I'm searching for a signal.

That part isn't an act. We're so far out in the middle of nowhere there isn't a signal for miles. I catch movement out of the corner of my eye. Inara's wearing beige fatigues from head to toe, and I only spot her because I know where to look.

If this Alec asshole is as paranoid as McCabe thinks he is, he's already watching *me*, and everything I do from now until I get back on the road needs to be completely in character. I swipe at my eyes and rest my head on the steering wheel for a count of five, then straighten, square my shoulders, and fix my gaze on Harrow's house.

Two minutes later, I park at the end of his drive, and tuck one arm of the sunglasses between my breasts when I get out of the car. The team should be able to see everything through the camera on the frame without me keeping them on inside.

I wish I had comms though. But it's too risky up close. Even as small as these damn earbuds are.

Harrow answers the door before I'm done knocking, looks me up and down, and Christ on a cracker, practically salivates. "Well, this is a surprise. Don't get many visitors way out here."

"Oh, bless your heart for answerin'," I say, raising the pitch of my voice and falling into that distinctive Texas twang I grew up with. "I've gone and done it now. I've driven all over hell's half acre, and if I can't figure out how to get back to State Route 24 soon, I won't be good for nothin' because I'll be out of gas."

"I can help you, sugar." Harrow steps over the threshold, close enough I can smell his cologne. Ugh. Pretty sure you're not supposed to bathe in the stuff. "You see, all you have to do is turn left at the main road," he points as if I'm too dumb to be able to figure that one out on my own, "then go about ten miles until you see a big ole rock formation with a hole in the center. Kind of like a horseshoe. Make a right, go another five miles, and you're there."

"Oh, you are just the sweetest man." I clasp my hands under my breasts, making them bounce a little, and yep. His gaze drops. "Handsome too. How long until I find a cell signal? My momma's probably been callin' me all day, and she don't like it when she can't reach me."

"Oh, that'll be a while, sugar. At least another hour of drivin'."

I drop my chin, letting him see just how heartbroken I am, and bat my lashes a few times. "I don't suppose you'd be even kinder and let me use your phone? I promise, I'll keep the call nice and short. Just so momma won't worry."

His face hardens for a split second, but then he gets himself under control. "Give me just a minute, sweetness. I was folding laundry when you knocked, and well..." Harrow offers me a sheepish smile, but his eyes are as cold as Jack Frost himself, "a gentleman shouldn't let a lady see his pile of briefs."

If that isn't the biggest crock of horse shit I've ever heard. The sunglasses transmit both image and sound, and I bet the rest of the team is rolling on the floor laughing right about now.

It's close to three minutes before he returns. "Come on in, sugar. Phone's right on the wall in the kitchen."

This is risky as all get out, but we need ears in this house, and West is right. There's no other way to get them.

The main room is sparse, but clean. Couch, coffee table, flat screen TV. No evidence of laundry, but like I believed that for a hot second. Harrow walks ahead of me, his jeans molded to a body that's seen better days. Softer around the middle than his file photos, with his crisp button-down shirt tucked in but bulging at the sides.

A quick glance ahead of him at the kitchen reveals a dirty

pan in the sink, along with a mug, three glasses, and a small stack of plates.

Harrow hands me the receiver on an old, *corded* phone. Holy shit. I didn't think anyone made these anymore.

"Bless your kind heart. Well, I don't even know your name, handsome. I'm Ella Rae. Ella Rae Johnson." Holding out my hand, I offer him the widest smile I can force, and he winks at me.

"James Logan. And it's a pleasure, Ella Rae." His grip is weak as shit, limp even, and he nods at the phone. "It's all yours."

Despite his words, he doesn't go far, and I dial the burner phone number Ryker had me memorize on the flight from Seattle.

"Hello?" Wren says when the call connects.

"Momma? I'm so sorry. I got myself all turned around and lost and I'm not going to get to Salt Lake for hours now."

"Ella Rae, I *told* you to take a map with you, child. You tried to go the whole way with that *phone* of yours, didn't you?"

"Yes, Momma. You were right. But I found a true gentleman out here in the middle of nowhere, and he set me to rights and let me use his phone. I'll be on my way in two shakes."

"Well, your brother had a little run-in with your uncle, and the two of them are havin' a stand-off downstairs, so you best be gettin' along."

So Harrow's accomplice is down in the basement with Quinton. Probably to keep him quiet.

"I will, Momma." Hunching my shoulders like she just chastised me, I dip my hand into my pocket and pull out one of the bugs. I can feel the asshole's eyes on me, so I wiggle my hips just enough to hopefully draw his gaze.

It's the simplest drop ever, sticking the bug to the underside of the telephone, and it's nowhere close enough to the basement to hear anything from Q, but at least we'll be able to eavesdrop on Harrow and his accomplice. Land lines are a hell of a lot harder to tap on short notice than cell phones, so this is the only option. "Love you."

When I hang up, Harrow's leaning against the wall at the entrance of the kitchen, and he raises his eyes from the level of my ass to my tits. "All better now?"

"Oh, yes. She just worries so."

Alec offers me his hand, and I take it, maintaining the facade of ditsy Southern blonde, even as warning bells go off in my head. But all he does is lead me towards the front door. The hallway is on my right, and I stumble, letting my hand slip from his as I fall.

"Are you okay?" he asks, bending over me and getting a damn fine view down my shirt.

Giggling is so far out of my area of expertise, I don't even know if I'm doing it right, but I try, then pat the carpet for my key ring. I purposely tossed them two feet down the hall. "Oh my stars and garters, I am just the clumsiest! Now where are those keys?"

My fingers close around them, and with my free hand, I shove the second bug between the carpet and the baseboard. Fucking amateur hour, but it's as close as I can get without risking exposure. The only bathroom on this floor is in the master bedroom, and I'd bet all of the rather generous salary McCabe offered me that Harrow won't let me in there. Three minutes is plenty of time for Tweedle Dumb to head downstairs, but not enough to hide all evidence of a second person's things.

"Well, Mr. Logan, you have been the absolute best. Just a total sweetheart, and I can't thank you enough for rescuin' little ole me when no one else could." I let him help me to my feet, then lean in and give him a quick peck on the cheek. "I'd best be goin' before I disappoint my momma any more than I already have. But if you're ever in Salt Lake City for a spell, you look me up, you hear?"

"Oh, I will, sugar. You can count on it." He watches me until I get into the dilapidated hatchback, and once the old girl turns over, I head back down his drive, make a left, and then floor it all the way to the RV.

~

Quinton

The basement door opens with a slam, and Alec stalks into the room, slides his arm around Dennis's waist, and stares down at me. Five minutes ago, the two burst in and Alec told me if I made a single sound, Dennis would shoot me in the foot after Alec killed the pretty young thing who just asked to use the phone.

For a split second, I thought maybe Graham had come for me. But then my fuzzy thoughts caught up with reality. Alec knows what Graham looks like. If the 'pretty young thing' had been Graham, Alec would have killed him on sight.

The woman's voice got closer for a minute at the end, and I thought I heard her say "rescue." But I don't trust anything anymore. I'm a coward. Not to mention stupid. And helpless. When I move, the room spins and I feel like I want to throw up.

With every patch and pill, more of *me* vanishes. He forced me into a pair of cheap sweatpants and a thin, gray t-shirt, and I can't smell anything but his cologne. He took my company. Probably has my money now too.

Tears burn my eyes as the two of them leave and lock the door. How did I end up here? Three days ago, I was free. I had the man I love in my bed. My kitten purring at our feet. My own clothes. My own space. Now? I'm nothing. No one.

He made me disappear, and no one's ever going to find me.

CHAPTER TWENTY-FOUR

Graham

"SHUT UP." West holds up his hand, then cranks the volume on the laptop.

"*Time for your meds, Quint. Take them or I'll shove them down your throat.*"

Q begs Alec to leave him alone, and my heart crumbles into jagged pieces. The sun is dipping towards the horizon, but it's not low enough for us to gear up yet.

"I need some air." I can't handle hearing another second of Q's suffering when I have the power to stop it. But before I can make it out the door, the sound of a rotary dial telephone echoes through the speaker, followed by a man's greeting.

"What?" the voice asks.

"Tell me no one's found that hulking piece of shit." Alec's words are so clear, it's like he's in the RV with us.

"He's got a second accomplice?" Ry taps his earbud to connect to Wren. "Get us voice analysis, Base. Now. We have to know who else he's working with."

"Already on it."

The pride and pure love reflected in Ryker's multi-colored eyes gives me hope. Not enough, but if Harrow's worried, he'll make a mistake, and that's where we'll best him. But what is he worried *about*?

The speaker crackles before the first man replies. "We left Davis so far from the road, he'll never be found."

"Good." Alec's voice holds a note of relief. "He took Quint from me once before. He won't do it again."

"Big Brother's a hundred miles from the city in the middle of Flash Flood Alley. And there's a storm rolling in," the voice says. "There's no way he'll be alive by morning."

"Why didn't you just kill him in the first place?" Alec's practically whining now, and if it's the last thing I do—or the next to last thing, right before I end him—I'm going to punch out his perfect teeth.

"We went as far as we could in the time we had, Harrow. Any longer, and we would have been missed. Besides, he needed to suffer for what he did to Billy. We left him in agony, and he'll pray for death every minute until the end."

Alec curses under his breath. "If he doesn't die, I'm sending Dennis back to finish the job personally."

The receiver slamming down on the phone is so loud, we all flinch, and Ryker looks to me. "Did Q ever mention the name Dennis?"

"No. But if Alec found someone else he could control..."

Raelynn clears her throat. "Boys? We've got a bigger problem. If they left Connor a hundred miles from Dallas in Flash Flood Alley...there's no way he'll live through the night."

Pulling out his sat phone, Ryker motions to Raelynn. "You know the area. Where would he be?"

She snorts. "You do realize Texas is fuckin' huge, right? Flash Flood Alley runs halfway across the state. I can help you narrow it down, but, you're still talkin' a larger search area than the whole of Seattle."

"Don't care." Ryker hands her a tablet. "Give me approximate boundaries and I'll handle the rest." Striding to the back of the RV, he punches a number into the sat phone. "Stars and Bars? Need a favor. Not a small one." After thirty seconds, he snorts. "No. I do *not* have a tutu on me. You're going to do this anyway."

THE LAST RAYS of the sun vanish from the horizon and I can't sit still. Ry wants to wait until midnight to breach, and all I can do is stare at the fuzzy images from the drone's camera. Q has barely stirred, while the other two have been living it up—or at least moving around normally.

Now, their heat signatures are practically right on top of one another and have been for more than ten minutes. And they're getting hotter. As thankful as I am that Alec isn't trying to use sex to get what he wants out of Q, the idea that these two shit stains are going at it after locking the man I love in a fucking basement is too much to handle.

Jerking to my feet, I stalk into the RV's small kitchen, intending to get a bottle of water, but I'm so angry, when the cabinet door sticks, I let out a roar and plow my fist through the flimsy wood.

A second later, West grabs the collar of my t-shirt and propels me into the back corner of the vehicle. "Put a fucking lid on it or you're off the mission."

I start to protest, until Ryker comes up behind the SEAL. "He gave me the same goddamn order when we were in Russia. Told me to 'fucking listen' to him. After we got Wren back, when I wedged my favorite stick up my ass a second time, he punched me and laid me out flat."

Staring between the two men, I can almost picture it. Ryker's massive in every way. It's not just his height or his muscles, but his presence. His attitude. The absolute conviction and seriousness that infuses everything he does.

West can pass for a regular guy. When he wants to. A guy who looks like he'd be fun to have a beer with. Or a good addition to your paintball team. And he is. Both of those things. As long as he's not on mission. Right now? I think he could fight every single one of us—and win—without breaking a sweat.

Sitting up straighter, I nod. "Lid on and locked." I'd apologize, but this is my family. There's no need. They understand.

The comms receiver West hooked up so we don't have to wear our earbuds in the RV beeps, and Wren's voice spills from the speaker. "Base to Alpha Team. We got an update from... Stars and Bars."

"He needs a new code name," I say with a chuckle that's only partially forced. Austin Pritchard—Stars and Bars to Ryker—used to be the head of JSOC until he helped us rescue Trevor in Venezuela. His superiors frowned on someone with his rank and position engaging with hostiles on foreign soil. Even worse, we basically aided in overthrowing the entire Venezuelan government.

Just a few weeks ago, he came to Ry for help when his girlfriend was being threatened and from what I gathered, the man finally realized he was a part of our family too.

"Spill it, Base," Inara replies.

"Search and rescue is en route to Flash Flood Alley. And we found the accomplice. Dennis Marklin. Forty-six years old, retired from the Dallas Police Department two months ago."

West frowns. "The hell? Harrow hooked up with a cop?"

"There's more," Wren says. "Sending the intel to your tablets now."

"More is an understatement, Base," I say as I scan through pages and pages of data she and Ripper compiled over the past couple of hours.

"Harrow is a fucking one-man black hole." Inara shakes her

head and pulls a pair of camo pants out of her ruck. She'll be perched in the tree at the edge of Alec's property while the rest of us storm the house in case the asshole tries to run.

She's not wrong. After Q filed the restraining order against him, Alec hooked up with another cop. Billy Blumenthal. Six months later, Billy threw himself off a roof. "So Billy dies, and Alec hooks up with Dennis?"

"He probably realized having a cop in his back pocket was helpful," West mutters. "That ends tonight. *He* ends tonight."

TEN MINUTES BEFORE MIDNIGHT, we slip out the RV door and scatter. West, Ry, Raelynn, and I will each approach from a different side of the house. Minimizes the chance Alec will see us coming. A group of four is easy to spot. A single man—or woman—trained in stealth? A hell of a lot harder.

The wind picks up speed as it rolls across the plains, and it's a damn good thing we're all wearing our night-vision goggles. Otherwise the swirling sands would be almost blinding. As soon as Ryker says "go," we're breaking down the door of that goddamn house and getting Q back.

Earlier, West planted small charges at the electrical junction box along the old dirt road, and in a few seconds, he'll arm the detonator. Blowing the power to the main house won't give us much cover. Not with the generator Alec has behind the structure. But we should get at least fifteen or twenty seconds before backup power comes on.

"A guy like this," Ry says, so quietly only the bone-conduction mics in our ears could possibly pick up the sound, "I wouldn't put it past him to have buried land mines in his yard. So we follow the tire tracks and flagstones. *Only* the tire tracks and flagstones."

"You didn't think to tell me that before I drove up there

earlier?" Raelynn hisses.

"You followed the tire tracks, didn't you?"

Raelynn snorts softly. "Fucker."

"Damn straight. Once we breach, it's two by two. Whiskey and Golf in the front, Lima and me in the back. Q's still in the basement. Harrow and Marklin are in the master bedroom and haven't moved much for two hours. Probably sleeping. Don't underestimate them. Especially Marklin. He's trained. Spent five years on the DPD SWAT Team. Priority one is the target. Priority two is putting an end to Harrow once and for all. Whiskey? On your mark."

West replies, "Roger. Blowing the power in three, two, one..."

Two small pops sound in the distance, and we take off at a run. Ten seconds later, light pours from all the windows as the backup generator comes on.

"One heat signature headed for the basement," Ripper says over comms. *"The second is staying in the hall."*

Fuck. If he's not running, then he's pretty sure he can beat us. Though he probably expects Q's brother or one of Connor's guys. Not an entire team of highly trained and lethal mercenaries.

West slams a small battering ram into the front door, and the hinges whine as they protest the assault. A second hit cracks the wood and we're through. We take up flanking positions as we head for the hall, and another crash comes from the back of the house behind the kitchen.

A burst of gunfire sends us dropping to the floor. Full auto. Likely an AK-47. Bits of wood and plaster rain down as we creep closer to the hall.

"Give it up, asshole!" West shouts, then tucks and rolls ten feet to his right. More shots hit the floor where he'd been seconds ago.

"If you want to live, leave now." The man's voice carries the bravado you only get from a hell of a lot of training.

I don't care how good you are, fuck face. We're better.

A metal canister rolls down the hall, and before I can react, someone slams into me, covering my head. The sound is deafening. My ears ring, and the entire world spins. Despite what I think is a very big, very pissed off former Special Forces team leader lying on top of me, the bright light burns my eyes.

And then the weight lifts. Hands yank me to my feet. Everything in the house has a second or third shadowy echo from the flash bang. I can't hear a damn thing, but the taps to my shoulder are clear.

Use the senses you have and stay to the left.

Gripping my M4 with steady hands, I follow West down the hall. "Now," he mouths, and over the ringing in my ears, I can just make out the windows shattering at the other end of the house.

"Fuck. Alec! There are more of them!" The squawk of a Walkie-Talkie is unmistakable, even with the residual ringing in my ears. At least we know who's shooting at us. But that means Alec's in the basement with Q.

Another squawk, and my world comes skidding to a halt. "Tell them if they want Quint to live, they'll leave. Right now."

Q's pained whimper is the single worst sound I've ever heard, but West grabs my forearm, the pressure of his grip keeping me centered.

"Get the fuck out of here or the kid dies," Dennis shouts.

The high-pitched whine in my ears has finally faded away, and I know where this asshole is. With a quick glance at West, I tell him exactly what I need him to do in three hand signals, and he nods.

The second I raise my weapon, he takes off, darting through the hall and into the master bedroom. Dennis fires in his direction, and I round the corner. Two shots. One center mass, the second through his skull, and he slides to the floor in a heap.

Snatching up the Walkie-Talkie, I press the button. "Give it up, Harrow. You won't win."

West, Ryker, and Raelynn join me in front of the solid metal basement door. It's too heavy to be opened with the battering ram and secured with an electronic keypad.

West relays the make and model to Wren and Ryker grabs the Walkie-Talkie.

"Listen, fucker. If you don't give yourself up, I'm going to flay the skin from your balls before I kill you."

"I don't know who the hell you are," Alec growls, "but I don't need to keep Quint alive. I already own his company."

"Base—"

Wren stops me before I even ask. "Base Two is on it, Golf."

Ripper knows more about online financial systems than pros who've been in the business for decades. If anyone can make sure Alec doesn't have a claim to Q's company, it's Rip.

Ryker chuckles into the mic. "You need him alive to get yourself out of there, Harrow. Otherwise, you'd be gone. So why don't you be a good piece of shit and give up now. *Before* we put an end to you."

Raelynn shoulders past Ryker and starts tapping on the wall. "Idiot," she mutters. "Right here." Pounding her gloved fist five inches to the right of the lock, she steps back and stares at Ryker expectantly. "Well? Punch a goddamned hole, Romeo."

Ry glances at West, who shrugs. "Wouldn't be the first time I've seen a reinforced door in a shitty frame."

The small, metal ram sinks deep into the wallboard, and Ryker opens up a hole six inches tall and at least that wide, then reaches his whole arm in.

A shot hits the door, and with a muffled curse, Ryker yanks his hand back. His sleeve's ripped, a small bit of blood staining the fabric. We all press ourselves against the opposite wall as West takes over the ram, busting a second hole and then pulling out his pistol. "Eyes," he hisses, and I grab the snake camera, feeding it through the new hole to get an idea of what we're dealing with.

"Holy fucking shit." It's like a doomsday prepper's wet dream down there. The left side of the room is walled off, but the right... Ammo crates stacked four feet high, floor-to-ceiling shelves full of canned goods, jugs of water and MREs.

We can't see Alec, but a shadow moves in the far corner of the space. "Hand it over," I say, motioning for the Walkie-Talkie. Ry drops it into my hand and adjusts his grip on his M4. "You're surrounded, *Alec*. Dennis is dead, and we know you ordered the hit on Connor Davis. There's no scenario where you walk out of there a free man. Let Quinton go, and maybe, you'll still be able to walk at all."

On the tiny screen, the shadow moves again, and Alec laughs. "So you found a small weakness in the wall. Big deal. You set one foot on the stairs and you'll find yourself in a thousand tiny pieces painting the walls with your blood."

West drops to one knee, adjusts his grip on the pistol, and blows out a long, slow breath. The SEAL's rage matches mine, and the way that one vein in his temple is throbbing, he's running through a dozen different ways for us all to get down there safely.

"We're doing a Blind Faith," he says, holstering his weapon and taking position like he's about to run the 500-meter dash. "Golf? Cover fire. Lima? Be ready to follow me when I signal. Romeo? Count it down."

"Three, two, one..." Ryker shoves his arm through the hole on the right while I fire three shots through the second hole aimed as high as I can. Can't risk hitting Q.

Bullets pepper the door. Ryker swears under his breath and jerks back, more blood coating his gloved hand, but the door pops open.

"Say goodbye to your *friends*, Quint," Alec says, his tone almost gleeful. But the angle, how his voice echoes off the walls, and even the pitch is different now. West and Ry exchange a glance, and before I can ask what's up, Ryker double-times it back down the hall.

Q cries out in pain, and West leaps forward. Catching the left railing with one hand, he swings his legs and vaults himself over the side. We have no idea what's down there—or if Harrow's even telling the truth about the stairs being wired to blow.

A second later, West fires four shots, his signal, and Raelynn mutters, "Y'all are fucking insane," before following the SEAL's lead.

She's not wrong. This could be suicide. But the man I love is down there, and I'm not letting that asshole take his life away. As soon as I land on the right side of the stairs, I make a silent vow to never complain about our sadistic workout routines again.

Peering across the stairs, I meet West's gaze. He holds up three fingers as a countdown, and I center myself with a deep breath.

We're the best in the world. This has to work. If I lose Q, I don't know how I'll live with myself.

～

Quinton

The pain shooting down my back is all I can focus on. That and breathing. I don't know what's going on. It's too loud. My head hurts, there's a strange, acrid smell that burns my nose, and I'm so dizzy.

How did I get here? I remember crying myself to sleep on the thin mattress. A loud noise woke me up. Then Alec cuffed my hands in front of me and dragged me from the room.

My legs are mostly useless, and I can't get any purchase on

the smooth concrete floor. Alec's arm bands around my torso. Struggling earns me a snarl and something hits my temple hard enough to make me see stars.

Several loud bangs hurt my ears, and the terrible smell gets stronger.

"This is all your fault, Quint," Alec hisses. "And you're going to pay for it when we get out of here." We're moving now, and he jerks me, trying to get a better grip, I think. Pure agony covers my back in a spiderweb of pain.

"Please," I whimper. "You're hurting me."

Another hard whack to my temple, and I cry out. More noises I don't understand, and someone shouts.

"Q? Talk to me!"

That voice. I know that voice. I dream about him. Blue eyes. Dark hair. Strong hands. My brain isn't working right. I can't see his face. Why can't I remember?

I have to stay here. Can't let Alec take me anywhere else. Have to fight. With a hoarse scream, I ball up my fists and slam them into Alec's shoulder. He's too strong, but he stumbles, and I try again.

A crash comes from behind us, and the next sound...it's almost inhuman. Loud. Angry. My entire body jerks, my stomach pitches like I'm falling, and I hit something solid and warm.

"Clear!" The word's so crisp, so sharp. I smell blood. Oh, God. What's going on? "Stay down and shut the fuck up."

"Q? You're safe now. I promise." A gloved hand cups my cheek, and gentle pressure skates under my swollen eye. "Fuck, baby. What did he do to you?"

The voice from my dreams. Bay rum. It's too bright. Too confusing. But I know him. "Graham?" All I can see is a hazy shadow. And blue eyes.

"I'm here, Q. I'm sorry it took me so fucking long, but I'm here now."

Collapsing in his arms, I bury my face against his neck, breathing in his scent. Graham found me. He came for me, and everything will be okay now.

~

Graham

How Ryker ended up *behind* Alec, on his knees pulling a tactical knife out of Alec's shoulder baffles me.

His shout of "Clear!" had Raelynn, West, and me racing forward, and we skidded to a stop almost as one when we saw our leader with his arm around Q's waist as he kicked Alec in the head.

Q's mostly out of it, and I think he might have passed out once I had him in my arms. If my adrenaline weren't at an all-time high, I'd lose my shit and start crying, but I'm still so baffled how Ryker managed to get in.

"Fucker had a back door out of here camouflaged as one of those damn garden hose storage boxes." Ryker drags the unconscious asshole to the center of the room, and West pulls out a pair of bolt cutters to remove the handcuffs binding Q's wrists. "Probie, out the way I came. He might not be lying about those stairs and what comes next? Not something you need to see."

"You tryin' to tell me a *woman* shouldn't watch a man die?" she asks, hands on her hips. "If I'm a part of this team, then treat me like I'm a part of this goddamned team."

Ryker rolls his eyes. "Fine. Stay then." Turning to me, he angles his head at Q. "I can take him if you want to be the one—"

"No." In truth, I'd do anything to put a bullet in Alec's head. Anything but let Q go. And he's too fucking *good* to have the sight of me—or anyone—killing Alec haunting his dreams. So I cradle him to my chest and head for the back door.

Inara meets me as soon as we emerge into the darkness and unclips several of the heavier pouches hanging off my belt and vest so I can carry Q. "I'll double-time it back to the RV and pick you all up by what's left of the junction box. You solid?"

She knows. Just how close I am to losing my shit. I wasn't with the team when they had to rescue Royce, but she's told me a little. And I watched both Trevor and Dani fall apart after their ordeals. "I'll hold it together. For him," I say quietly.

"Make sure you do." She slaps my arm lightly, then takes off at a run.

Q hasn't stirred, and I press a kiss to the top of his head. His face is twisted in pain, and it's obvious from the bruises that Alec beat him up. I'm desperate for West to take a look at him. The SEAL's our field medic, and a damn good one. He's damn good at everything, really.

Three shots echo from the basement, almost simultaneously, and a minute later, Ry and Raelynn flank me. "Found Q's laptop in the bag Harrow had with him," Ry says. "Along with twenty-five grand in cash."

"Confirm the minute you're past the fence line," West says over comms.

I raise a brow at Ryker, but he just snorts. "You expect us to leave evidence?" As soon as we pass through the gate, Ry taps his earbud. "We're clear, Whiskey."

"Fire in the hole," West says calmly. Three seconds later, he bursts out of the basement at a full sprint. He's halfway across the property when the explosion rocks the ground, but he doesn't even break stride.

"Wh-what was that?" Q asks, his words slow as he tightens an arm around my neck.

"Justice," I whisper to him. "That's what we do."

CHAPTER TWENTY-FIVE

Quinton

A DULL HUM SURROUNDS ME—A sound I can't identify—and panic paralyzes my muscles and tightens a band around my chest until I can't breathe.

"Hey. You're safe." Warm hands cover mine, and that voice... I'm dreaming. I have to be.

Forcing one eye open, I steel myself to see Alec standing over me, but it's mostly dark with only dim lights illuminating the floor at my feet.

A plane? I fumble for the seatbelt, desperate to get away. A plane means flight attendants. A pilot. People who might believe me. Help me.

"Q! Look at me, baby."

Gentle fingers cup my cheeks, and when I blink hard, the face that swims in and out of focus isn't Alec's. Dark hair. Rough stubble. There's no heavy stench of Old Spice. Only sweat, coffee, gun oil...and bay rum.

This has to be a dream. A hallucination brought on by the drugs, PTSD, and fear. But he leans closer to bring my hand to his lips, and though everything's blurry, there's no way I'd ever mistake Alec for Graham.

My back spasms painfully as I lunge sideways into his arms, but I don't care. "How?"

"That's a long story that you probably won't remember if I tell you now." The seatbelt snaps open, and Graham pulls me closer so I'm almost in his lap. "I took the patch off as soon as we got you out of there and West gave you IV fluids on the way to the airfield. But it's going to be at least a day before you feel like yourself again."

"I know." I don't remember how we got here. It's all shadows, loud noises, terror...

"Pupils are dilated as fuck. Get some water into him." Who's talking? Why can't I see anything? Where's that light coming from?

"If he's stable enough, we need to get the fuck out of here," a woman says from somewhere behind me. "The plane's waiting, and that explosion wasn't...small."

I suck in a sharp breath and struggle to sit up. "There were people. Who—?"

"My team. My family." Graham nods towards the front of the plane, and I blink several times, trying to make everything clearer. It's hard to see, but one of the guys is massive. His head sticks up a good ten inches from the seat back. "They're on our side. Every one of them would die for you."

I don't understand. Why? I'm nothing to them. Alec had guns. Explosives. He told me how well protected the house was.

"Stop looking at that door like you can find a way out," Alec says when he comes to give me another dose of meds. "In another day, maybe two, your balance will be so fucked up, you'll be back in that chair permanently. The stairs are wired with C4. If you set one foot on them..." He spreads his fingers out in a vague representation of a bomb going off. "Bye bye, Quint."

I'm so tired, all I want to do is sleep in Graham's arms, but I have so many questions. How did they find me? Are—were—

we really in Utah? Oh, God. My brother. Struggling to sit up, I grasp Graham's vest. "Connor—"

"Shhh, baby. Look at me, okay?" Graham's words hold weight, and I focus on his eyes. Such a deep blue and full of understanding. "We found him. Well, some of Austin's guys— Austin's part of the family too—found him. He's in the hospital. Broken arm, cracked ribs, ruptured spleen, some internal bleeding, severe dehydration. But he'll be okay. As soon as he can travel, we'll get him out to Seattle. Or...take you to Dallas. You could go back now...if you wanted."

It's hard to concentrate. Only some of his words register, but Connor's safe, and Graham...his voice is full of longing. I don't want to go back. I want to go *home*. Where Graham lives. Where...fuck. "Clementine. How long, Graham? *How long?*"

I'm practically shouting, but she hasn't been alone since the day I rescued her, and she's so tiny.

"I'd never let anything happen to her, baby." Graham pulls out his phone and swipes through the photos. "When we went to your place...well...look."

I'm still dizzy and my vision isn't what it should be, but the man on screen is huge and dressed all in black. Clementine clings to his chest, her head tucked under his chin.

"She was hiding when we breached, and as soon as she saw Ry, she climbed him like a Christmas tree and started purring away." He chuckles, then swipes to the next photo. "She's at the warehouse now."

"Is...is that a dog?" I hate trying to force my brain to make sense of even the simplest information.

With a chuckle, Graham zooms in so I can see my kitten curled up on a big, fluffy blanket, a German Shepherd wrapped around her like a bodyguard. "That's Ripper's dog, Charlie. Those two bonded almost immediately. We'll stop at Hidden Agenda and pick her up before I take you home."

He keeps saying that. Get me *home*. Take me *home*. *Home* is where Alec found me. Watched me. Where the other guy—I can't even remember his name—stole my laptop.

"Q? What's wrong?" Graham cups my cheek, and I struggle not to hyperventilate. *Home* is the last place I want to go.

He wraps his arms around me, settles me against his chest, and I relax. He came for me. I think he loves me. I know I love him. But I can't tell him until my head's clear. Until he knows I'm...me again.

"Stay." It's the only word I can force past my lips. The only one that matters. "Want to stay. With you."

He shudders and brushes his lips to my ear. "I'm not going anywhere, Q. I promise."

There's something in his tone. A seriousness. A weight. Whatever it is...it's enough. For now, it's enough.

Snatches of reality break through the haze of exhaustion, pain, and the drugs still coursing through my veins. A bumpy landing. Graham's voice—though I can't understand his words. A car. A nice one. Big. Comfortable.

Quiet murmurs from other men and women around us. They scare me, but only until Graham reminds me I'm safe. That I'm with him.

And then, a loud purr vibrates against my chest and tiny paws knead my shoulder. I don't think. Just reach up and cradle Clementine. She *mrrps* in my ear and her rough tongue scrapes my chin.

Beyond the inside of the SUV, it's dark, but in the distance, a large warehouse looms, spotlights illuminating the eaves. The breeze carries a hint of the sea. Seattle. Home.

"Where are we?"

I figure it out just as Graham answers, "Hidden Agenda. Had to stop and pick up this little one and all her stuff."

Outside the SUV, men, women, and one German Shephard stand shoulder to shoulder behind him. He follows my gaze, looks back at them, and smiles. "My team. My family. Well, most of them."

"Th-thank you," I whisper. I don't know if they can hear me. Hell, I don't even know their names. But it's all too much right now, and I just stare down at Clementine, tears in my eyes until Graham squeezes my shoulder.

"Ry's going to drive us back to your place, then take Rip home. So they're coming with us, okay?"

I nod, even though I don't know who Ry and Rip are. It doesn't matter, though, because Graham rounds the SUV and climbs in next to me. My head's starting to clear, and as the SUV starts to roll, I bury my face in Clementine's fur.

"I don't want to go home."

"What?" Graham touches my cheek, dipping his head so he can meet my gaze. "Q?"

"He knows...where I live." The sob escapes before I can stop it, and Clementine starts purring even louder and wedges her head directly under my chin.

"He's dead," the bigger man—the one behind the wheel—says, his voice rough and completely devoid of emotion. "He's never going to bother you again. And the two cops who put your brother in the hospital? No one's going to find them. Ever."

I'm so confused. What does he mean? Before I can ask, Graham rests his hand on my knee. "If you want to go home, it's perfectly safe. Ry found your laptop. I'll need to hook up your security system again, but that won't take me more than twenty minutes."

"Please..."

"Graham?" The man in the passenger seat turns around. "We're going to your apartment. It's the best place for both of you tonight. Trust me."

Whatever this guy's deal is, something passes between them. Even with the cobwebs dimming the corners of my mind, I can see it. It's more than trust. It's admiration. And gratitude.

Graham slips his arm around my shoulder and nods without saying a word. I can relax now. Breathe. It's really over.

~

THE STREET IS TOO BUSY. Even this early in the morning—close to 5:00 a.m., I think—there's traffic and people. But Graham keeps his arm around me as we head into a secured building.

My legs feel like jelly, and more than once, my knees buckle, but he holds me close. The man with the dog comes with us, a duffel bag slung over his shoulder and a large plastic tote in his hands.

Once we're inside, Graham eases me down on the couch. "Relax, baby. I'll get Clementine set up and then we can sleep a while." Graham presses a kiss to the top my head, glances at the other guy, and nods.

I'm so tired, I don't care what silent message they just shared, and I close my eyes until the older man clears his throat. "Jackson Richards," he says as he holds out his hand. "But everyone calls me Rip or Ripper."

"You took care of Clementine..."

"Well, Charlie did most of it." Rip reaches down and scratches the dog's one good ear. "I hope you're sticking around, because otherwise, I'm going to have to get him a cat."

Charlie's tail thumps on the carpet, his tongue lolling out of his mouth like he just won the lottery. Or found a twenty-ounce Porterhouse in his food bowl.

"Y-yes. I'm staying." Why would he think I'd leave?

"Mind if I sit?" Rip gestures to the couch next to me, and I stare at the empty cushion until he sinks down next to me. Charlie sits on the guy's feet and rests his muzzle on my thigh.

"He always knows what people need," Ripper says, love warming his tone as he rubs the dog's head.

"Clementine too..." I'm mumbling, my thoughts still too slow, too fragmented.

Silence fills the air for a moment until Ripper lets out a long, slow breath. "I know what you went through, man." He runs a hand through his hair, the movement jerky. "Wasn't exactly the same, but...the drugs and the lies—the brainwashing? I lived it for six years."

"Shit..." Graham told me. I think. Ripper's the guy they went to rescue.

"You'll never be...over it. Never not remember. But you'll get to a point where it's not your first thought every fucking day."

I can only sit there baffled at the raw honesty he's offering me when I don't know him at all.

"The guys—the team...Inara was there too—pulled me out of a goddamned hole. Saved my life. I doubt I had more than a couple of hours left. But the first couple of days I was free? Graham got me through those. I'd never met him before, but that made it easier to talk to him. And...he gets it. He's not going to judge you, and he's definitely not going to stop loving you."

Loving me?

"You ever need to talk about it with someone who's been there," Ripper says quietly, "you give me a call." He reaches into his jacket pocket and pulls out a brand new cell phone—same model as my old one. "We keep a bunch of these around as spares. Because what we do? You wouldn't believe how many phones we drop, step on, or throw." He almost smiles. "Wren got your info from the carrier, so it should be just like your old one was never destroyed. My number's in there. Along with everyone else's. Just look under Family."

Graham

I trust Ripper with my life. But I have no idea if Q was ready to talk to another person. Not up close, one on one. I didn't want to leave them alone together, and my momentary pause had Rip arching his brows and staring pointedly towards my bedroom. Though he's one of the hardest guys to read—harder even than Ryker—the meaning was clear.

Get the fuck out and give us a minute.

So I set Clementine's bed on the low dresser next to the window, clean out half my top drawer for the clothes we brought from Q's place, find a spot for the litter box in my bathroom, and then stop short before I reach the hallway.

I want to see his things here all the time. Or see *our* things together somewhere. Anywhere.

Before I return to the living room, I pull off my boots and tactical vest and shove them into my go bag. Ryker installed an industrial strength washer and dryer at the warehouse, and it's the only thing that can get the stench of blood, sweat, and gun oil out of fabric.

Ripper sits next to Q with Charlie leaning against both their legs. "I mean it. Any time," Rip says. "Don't pretend it didn't happen. And for fuck's sake, don't hide anything from Graham. He got me through the first couple of days, and he understands. Probably a hell of a lot more than you think."

Q nods, and the tears on his cheeks catch the light.

"Ready to go, Charlie?" Rip asks. As soon as he stands, the dog pops up, tail wagging, and after a beat, takes Ripper's place on the couch and noses Q's hand.

For a second, nothing happens until Q, with Clementine perched on his shoulder, wraps his arms around the dog. This is Charlie's gift. He just knows what people need.

When Q lets go, Charlie licks Clementine's side gently, and

the kitten *coos* at him and starts purring even louder. I can't believe they bonded so well in under twenty-four hours.

Then again...Q and I? We shouldn't be here. At this stage where if he weren't so confused and exhausted, I'd be confessing my love for him.

So many members of my little family—West, Inara, Ryker, Ripper, Dax, Ford, Trevor, even Austin Pritchard—found their forevers. Some took longer than others. Hell, Ford and Trevor needed decades. But seeing them with their partners? It taught me something. It taught me a lot of things.

Your family? You get to choose them. I found most of mine at Hidden Agenda. But the last piece? The one who makes me feel complete? He's sitting right in front of me. Found by chance and bravery and pain. And unless he asks me to...I'm never letting him go.

～

Quinton

Light filters in from a crack in the curtains. I'm not sure what time it is. Only that Graham's sleeping next to me and we're safe.

After Ripper and Charlie left, Graham helped me shower. I could barely stand, but smelling Alec's cologne on me? It was making me sick. Then he tucked me into his bed and offered to sleep on the couch.

I must have managed the *"Are you serious?"* look well enough, because he only left me long enough to check the locks before climbing in next to me.

I reach for his hand under the sheet, and as soon as we touch, he links our fingers and yawns. "Figured you'd sleep all day," he says, then turns to me and pushes up on an elbow. "How do you feel?"

"Like I was beaten up, handcuffed to the floor of a crappy van for fifteen hours, drugged, and forced to sign over my entire company."

Graham's eyes widen. His hands frame my face, and he touches his forehead to mine. "Q? Ripper and Wren are tech geniuses. Rip knows the ins and outs of every bank in the world, and Wren...you're going to be shocked as hell when you meet her. She's this petite little thing with red hair and she never curses. Ever. But she basically lives her entire life on the dark web."

I'm not sure why he's telling me all this. Holding a coherent thought for more than a few minutes is still harder than it should be.

"Baby, you didn't lose anything. Wren intercepted the electronic paperwork and made it disappear. Alec had managed to hack into your bank accounts to empty them, but Ripper got it all back. Plus everything he took from you in Dallas."

It takes a few minutes for his words to sink in, but when they do, my eyes start to water. "All of it?"

"Yes. Silver Star Technologies is still one hundred percent yours. As is Zen Oasis. And the townhouse. Everything."

Shifting onto my side, I stifle my groan. Graham carried me out of that basement. Across the yard. On and off the plane. He's held me every minute he could.

But he hasn't kissed me once. Not really kissed me. Chaste brushes of his lips to my cheek or forehead. That's it.

I know why. He doesn't want to hurt me. But I need this—need him—more than anything.

So I cup the back of his neck, pull him in, and press my lips to his. It's gentle. Not too deep. A connection. A tether to help us find our way out of this darkness.

We're both breathing a little harder when we draw back, and Graham's eyes are full of so much uncertainty, it breaks my heart.

"Darlin', I can't go back to that bench. That's where he found me. He had everything all ready. The van. The drugs. Dennis. It only took two minutes."

"Fucking hell. I should have been there." He rolls onto his back and stares up at the ceiling. "I'm sorry—"

"No, Graham. No." I reach for him, not certain I can sit up on my own yet. Not without a hell of a lot of pain, but he slides his arm behind my back and arranges the pillows so I have some support.

Staring down at my hands, all I can see are the reddish abrasions from the cuffs. "You can't protect me every minute. No one can. Just like I can't make sure you're safe when you go out on a mission. If you'd been in town? Alec just would have waited until I was alone. Until you went to the store or the coffee shop or to the Unicorn."

"I know. Rationally, I *know* that." He scrubs his hands over his face, four days of stubble rasping along his palms. "All I could think—the whole time—was how you'd just started taking your life back when that asshole stole it again."

"*Tried*. He tried to steal it. And you stopped him." Tangling my legs with his, I fold him into my embrace, realizing I can comfort *him* for a change. "Darlin', I haven't even begun to process what happened. I don't know how, but I'm damn sure it's not going to be good when I do."

Graham tightens his arm around my waist and presses a kiss to my collarbone.

"Right now, it feels like a nightmare. In a few days...it's going to be a hell of a lot more real. But so is this." I lean down to brush my lips to his. "Us. Alec took my choices away. He drugged me and tied me up and locked me in a windowless room where I thought I was going to die." My voice cracks and a bit of the reality seeps through the bubble Graham's apartment gives us. "But every time I wanted to give up, to stop fighting and let go, I thought about you. And how much I wanted to be with you again. About how much...I love you."

Graham sits up straighter, and when our gazes collide, we're both a little teary. "Did you—?"

"I love you. That's what I wanted to tell you on that bench."

He surges forward, and this time, the kiss is anything but tame. It's raw, desperate, full of passion, but also something else. Something deeper and more important than anything else in this world.

"I love you, Q. I was going to tell you when I got back. Because I don't ever want to leave on a mission again without you knowing I have the best reason in the world to come home."

We cry a little—or, he cries a little, I sob almost uncontrollably for a good five minutes. And when I finally stop, *that* kiss...it leads to so much more.

EPILOGUE

One month later

Graham

"Are you sure about this, baby?"

Q holds my hand, his fingers tight around mine outside Broadcast Coffee. The shop is only two blocks from our condo downtown, and thanks to West and Cam's housewarming gift of a new espresso machine, we're now both hopeless coffee nerds.

He presses closer to me. "No. But if I can do this, I can handle dinner tonight."

The morning rush is over, though there are at least ten people inside at the tables, working or chatting with friends. Q's terrified of crowds, but after we rescued him from his asshole ex, something changed.

He could barely walk for two days, so we spent most of the time in bed or on the couch watching movies, talking, and playing with Clementine. Once he'd felt steady enough to shuffle slowly with my arm around his waist, he'd asked me to take him outside.

"Are you sure?" I cup his cheek, the bruise under his eye still dark purple in spots, but now tinged with yellow around the edges. "You know I'll love you no matter what, right?"

Q nods and though his smile feels forced, he straightens his shoulders and covers my hand with his. "I can't let him steal another day from me, Graham. I've missed out on so much. Feeling the sun on my face. Seeing the cherry blossoms. I've even missed the rain. Some of this I need to do on my own. You can't magically heal me. Or take every step with me. But today, I just want to be able to tell you I love you outside. In the sun."

I hold the door open, and Q takes two steps across the threshold. Today's a good day—physically—and he didn't even need his cane.

"You want me to order?" I keep my voice low, letting him take the lead if he wants.

"I can do it. But stay with me?" Reaching for my hand, he links our fingers.

"Always." I'm so fucking proud of him. Every day, we've made it a little further, tried something new. Last week, not long after the sun rose, we ventured out to the grocery store on the corner.

We only bought one thing. A pint of mint chip ice cream. By the time we got home, Q was shaking so badly, he took a Xanax, then spent the next few hours in his massage chair with Clementine. But two days later, we tried again. And that time, it was easier.

I still worry every time I go to Hidden Agenda. But now that we live in the same building as Ripper and Cara—the complex Ry bought when Rip moved to Seattle—at least I know he's protected. The building is secure as fuck, biometric scanners on every door, and each tenant thoroughly vetted.

Q's met everyone at Hidden Agenda by now—except Cam and Royce, but they've all come to us in twos or threes. Never all at once. Rarely in a space he's never seen.

Ripper's helped both of us deal with the aftermath of Q's kidnapping, and the other night, when Q was working late on the next version of Zen Oasis, Rip invited me over for a beer.

We sat out on his balcony, Charlie between us, and I told him my story. He was quiet for a long time, and then he admitted his own truth.

"Ry and Dax...they don't know," he says, his voice nothing but a hoarse whisper. "Cara's the only one..."

I want to hug him, but physical contact isn't his style. So I nod, stare out over the city, and assure him this conversation is only for us.

"I worry sometimes," I say, staring down at the bottle in my hand, "that Q wants more than I can give. And fuck. I was never a bottom, but I used to like it when guys would...play around a little..." I don't want to get too graphic and trigger him, but I don't have any gay friends in this town. Not ones I trust like I trust Ripper.

"Have you asked him?" Rip takes a swig of his beer and leans forward to scratch Charlie's neck.

"No. I let him grab my ass once and it was...nice. But I'm too scared to do more."

"Why?"

Staring out over the city, I sigh. Puget Sound is dark and quiet, and the buildings are all lit up for the Seahawks game. The sight calms me, and I take another swig of beer. "Because what if I have a panic attack and hurt him?"

Rip flinches. "I hurt Cara once." The admission costs him. More than I thought he had left to give. "Fought her. All because her hand slipped. Her fingers were too close to..." He shakes his head, and the pain in his eyes...he's been through so much. Too much. "I left bruises on her arms. Every day for a week I had to look at what I'd done. But she never blamed me. Not once. Q won't either."

That night, as I buried myself deep inside Q, I guided his hand to my ass. Told him I trusted him. It wasn't much, just a touch. His fingers skimming my crack. But it didn't hurt. Didn't dredge up any bad memories or make me feel like I was broken.

The pressure of Q's hand on mine brings me back to the present, and I meet his gaze. Shit. We're already at the counter.

"'Morning," the barista says with a bright smile. "What'll it be?"

I can feel Q trembling next to me, but when he finds his voice, it's only slightly strained. "Two sixteen ounce pour-overs, please."

"For here or to go?"

The man I love doesn't hesitate to answer. "Here. We'll drink them here."

When we find a small table in the corner, somewhere we can watch the door for threats, I lean in and press a soft kiss to his lips. "You amaze me every day, Q."

He stares out the window, tracking a cloud drifting across the autumn sky. "Manny said something to me not long after you and I met. He was going out of town for a couple of weeks and he left me with an assignment. To go for a walk. He told me therapy could only get me so far. That I needed to remember what it was like to *live* again."

For a few long moments, he doesn't say another word. But after the barista delivers our drinks, he takes a sip and smiles. "I told him I'd try, but deep down, I knew I was lying. Nothing was going to let me *live* again. I was so wrong."

"What changed your mind?" I ask.

"You." His eyes sparkle, but not with tears. No. This is joy. Happiness. Love. "Before, I was so worried if I failed, I'd never have the courage to try again. But you never pressured me. Never asked me for more than I could give. I love you, darlin'."

When we kiss, it's like everything else falls away. We're not two broken people trying to glue ourselves back together. We're whole. We may be cracked, flawed, damaged in ways that will never fully heal, but so is everyone else in this world.

We fit. And no matter what life throws at us, we'll face it together.

Q saved me as much as I saved him. He gave me the courage to face my darkness and know I could come out the other side into the light. Our scars don't define us. Don't control us. They make us who we are.

~

THANK you for reading Braving His Past. This book was harder than any I've ever written for a couple of very personal reasons, but I'm so happy you could meet Q and get to know Graham as well as I do.

If you're a series fan, then you probably understand just how big of a surprise it was to hear about the big news for Ry and Wren in this book.

I would like you ask you for a favor. Please, do not mention this surprise in any of your reviews. Spoilers in reviews can ruin the entire book for other readers, and this is one **heck** of a spoiler. I hope you'll review, of course, but please think of your fellow readers and keep that bit of information a secret.

~

NEXT UP IN the *Gone Rogue* series, you'll meet Griff in Rogue Officer. And the *Away From Keyboard* series will continue soon with Ronan's story, Protecting His Target. Both of those books are available for preorder NOW!

~

I'D LIKE to thank several folks in my reader group, Patricia's Unstoppable Forces, for their help with aspects of this book. Jenn D. Young named Quinton's cat, Clementine.

Mandy Jones and Sue Voris came up with the name for Quinton's app, Zen Oasis. Trust me when I say this: I am terrible at naming things. TERRIBLE. They saved the day.

I'd also like to add a very personal note.

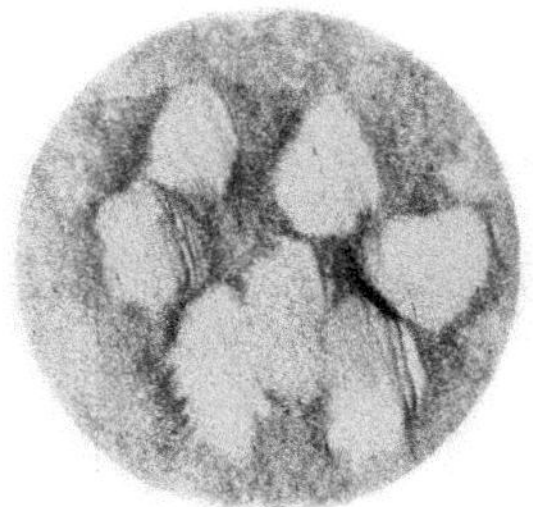

ON MARCH 30, 2021, my husband and I had to say goodbye to our beloved Binky. He was so much more than just a cat. Binky was a big, beautiful, loving, amazing, sensitive soul in a cat's body.

We adopted him when he was six, and he lived to be eighteen. Those twelve years brought me more joy than I could have ever imagined, and his death leaves me with a hole in my heart I will never be able to fill.

To some people, pets are just that. Pets. And that's okay. But to me? To my husband? They're our family. They're our children in every way that counts. We started a website for Binky (and for our other cats and any future pets we bring into our lives). If you'd like to know Binky (and Wingnut and Abbie) better, you can. He'll forever be honored at https://ForBin.ky.

Every book I've ever written has been with Binky at my side. He was my constant writing companion, and even when he tried to step on the keyboard and add his own spin to sentences, I loved him.

Finishing this book without him? It was the hardest thing I've ever done besides letting him go.

So, Binky Buddy? Wherever you are right now? You were the bestest buddy ever. Still are. You made our lives better in every way. I love you. I miss you. And I will never forget you.

ABOUT THE AUTHOR

I've always made up stories. Sometimes I even acted them out. I probably shouldn't admit that my childhood best friend and I used to run around the backyard pretending to fly in our Invisible Jet and rescue Steve Trevor. Oops.

Now that I'm too old to spin around in circles with felt magic bracelets on my wrists, I put "pen to paper" instead. Figuratively, at least. Fingers to keyboard is more accurate.

Outside of my writing, I'm a professional editor, a software geek, a singer (in the shower only), and a runner. I love red wine, scotch (neat, please), and cider. Seattle is my home, and I share an old house with my husband and cats.

I'm on my fourth—fifth?—rewatching of the modern *Doctor Who*, and I think one particular quote from that show sums up my entire life.

"We're all stories, in the end. Make it a good one, eh?" — *The Eleventh Doctor, Doctor Who*

I hope your story is brilliant.

You can reach me all over the web...
patriciadeddy.com
patricia@patriciadeddy.com

facebook.com/patriciadeddyauthor
twitter.com/patriciadeddy
instagram.com/patriciadeddy
bookbub.com/profile/patricia-d-eddy

ALSO BY PATRICIA D. EDDY

Away From Keyboard

Dive into a steamy mix of geekery and military prowess with the men and women of Hidden Agenda and Second Sight.

Breaking His Code

In Her Sights

On His Six

Second Sight

By Lethal Force

Fighting For Valor

Finding Their Forevers (a holiday short story)

Call Sign: Redemption

Braving His Past

Gone Rogue (an Away From Keyboard spinoff series)

Rogue Protector

Rogue Officer

Dark PNR

These novellas will take you into the darker side of the paranormal with vampires, witches, angels, demons, and more.

Forever Kept

Immortal Hunter

Wicked Omens

Storm of Sin

By the Fates

Check out the COMPLETE By the Fates series if you love dark and steamy tales of witches, devils, and an epic battle between good and evil.

By the Fates, Freed

Destined: A By the Fates Story

By the Fates, Fought

By the Fates, Fulfilled

In Blood

If you love hot Italian vampires and and a human who can hold her own against beings far stronger, then the In Blood series is for you.

Secrets in Blood

Revelations in Blood

Holidays and Heroes

Beauty isn't only skin deep and not all scars heal. Come swoon over sexy vets and the men and women who love them.

Mistletoe and Mochas

Love and Libations

Restrained

Do you like to be tied up? Or read about characters who do? Enjoy a fresh COMPLETE BDSM series that will leave you begging for more.

In His Silks

Christmas Silks

All Tied Up For New Year's

In His Collar

www.ingramcontent.com/pod-product-compliance
Lightning Source LLC
Chambersburg PA
CBHW070623170726
48291CB00003B/855